Beware, faint of heart!

*I*t could be that given how wonderful a place Sherbet was, and that four girls all lived on the same street and were all about the same age, you are now expecting a story about girls who are terrific friends, always "there" for one another, eager to help and support one another. Maybe you are expecting to read about their lighthearted adventures, like helping cats down from trees or solving the mystery of the missing hair extensions. I'm sorry to disappoint you, but you may as well know right now there will be no lighthearted adventures. Even worse, the girls on Gumm Street didn't like one another at all.

Luckily, Sherbet provided lots of entertaining things to occupy the girls of Gumm Street, and so they really didn't need one another. It had always been that way, and everyone believed it always *would* be that way.

Well, everyone was wrong.

The
Secret Order
of the
Gumm Street Girls

The
Secret Order
of the
Gumm Street Girls

ELISE PRIMAVERA

HARPERTROPHY®
An Imprint of HarperCollinsPublishers

HarperTrophy® is a registered trademark
of HarperCollins Publishers.

The Secret Order of the Gumm Street Girls
Copyright © 2006 by Elise Primavera
All rights reserved. Printed in the United States of America.
No part of this book may be used or reproduced in any manner
whatsoever without written permission except in the case of brief
quotations embodied in critical articles and reviews. For information
address HarperCollins Children's Books, a division of HarperCollins
Publishers, 1350 Avenue of the Americas, New York, NY 10019.
www.harpercollinschildrens.com

Library of Congress Cataloging-in-Publication Data
Primavera, Elise.
    The Secret Order of the Gumm Street Girls / Elise Primavera.—
1st ed.
        p.   cm.
    Summary: In order to save the town of Sherbet, four girls with
very little in common become involved with some people and
events that seem to bear a resemblance to "The Wizard of Oz."
    ISBN 978-0-06-056948-8 (pbk.)
    [1. Baum, L. Frank (Lyman Frank), 1856–1919. Wizard of Oz.
2. Fantasy.] I. Title.
PZ7.P9354Se 2006   2005037074
[Fic]—dc22   CIP
                                                           AC

❖

First Harper Trophy edition, 2008

FOR MY FATHER, WHO IS GONE

BUT WILL NEVER LEAVE ME

CONTENTS

PREFACE

(which means the story hasn't officially started
but you ought to read this anyway)

**ON PAGES 442–443 OF THIS BOOK, YOU WILL
NOTICE A MAP.**

It shows the town of Sherbet. Sherbet has a board-walk, a candy store called the Colossal Candy Bar, a five-story silver-and-gold ice-cream parlor called the Arctic Ice Cream Palace, a fabulous amusement park, a riding stable with ponies—you name it.

The weather in Sherbet is particularly marvelous, too. It is polite, only snowing in the winter to make things look pretty. It is predictable, raining in the summer every day at exactly 4:00 P.M. for exactly forty-five minutes, followed by a breathtaking rainbow. In short, Sherbet is about a hundred times more wonderful than where you or I live.

Now, go back to the map and look for Gumm Street. It's very important to the story you are about to read.

There were three girls living on Gumm Street who were all about ten or eleven years old. Prudence Gumm lived at #1 Gumm Street. Pru by nature was very cautious, liked to read, and quoted a lot of safety tips. Her favorite was Safety Tip #9: Look before you leap.

Right next door to her at #3 Gumm Street was Franny Muggs. Franny lived in a house that was circular in shape, seven stories high, and resembled a gigantic wedding cake. Franny never looked before she leaped, but she had a lot of good ideas. One of her best ideas was to turn her bedroom into a lookout tower so that she could see everything that was happening in the town of Sherbet.

Across from Prudence and Franny, at #2 Gumm Street, was Cat Lemonjello. Cat's mother was the only daughter of eleven children, and Cat was also the only daughter of eleven children, and for this reason (according to Lemonjello folklore), she was believed to possess ESP.

It could be that given how wonderful a place Sherbet was, and that these three girls all lived on the same street and were all about the same age, you are expecting a story about girls who are terrific friends, always "there" for one another, eager to help and support one another. Maybe you are expecting to read about their lighthearted adventures, like helping cats down from trees or solving the mystery of the missing hair extensions. I'm sorry to disappoint you, but you may as well know right now, there will be no lighthearted adventures. Even worse, the girls on

Gumm Street didn't like one another at all.

And why was that?

Pru thought Franny was reckless, what with her lookout tower and her big ideas.

Franny thought Pru was a big baby, what with her safety tips and her inclination to spend a perfectly good day indoors reading a book.

Pru and Franny had *nothing* in common except that neither one of them liked Cat Lemonjello.

Cat had her own pony, which she rode like she'd been born in the saddle; she could do a one-handed cartwheel; and she could play the piano like Liberace. Pru would have given her eyeteeth to play the piano like Liberace. Franny couldn't ride a pony if you held a gun to her head; she would have been happy to be able to do any kind of cartwheel; and she wasn't so hot at the piano, either.

Can you see why Pru and Franny didn't like Cat? The feeling was mutual, too. Cat thought that Franny was a klutz, and she thought that Pru was just jealous.

Luckily, Sherbet provided lots of entertaining things to occupy the girls of Gumm Street, and so they really didn't need one another. It had always been that way, and everyone believed it always *would* be that way.

Well, everyone was wrong.

The
Secret Order
of the
Gumm Street Girls

*F*ranny *liked the tops of things. She*
liked mountaintops and rooftops, and she
wanted to be at the top of her class and a top-notch
cartwheeler. Why? Because in first grade Franny
became painfully aware of the middle and the possibility that she might be dismally average.

Franny sighed. Now spring break was almost over and, to take her mind off the horrible reality of going back to school, Franny stood at the top of #3 Gumm Street. Up there, she didn't feel average at all. She felt like Sir Edmund Hillary on the summit of Mount Everest or Amelia Earhart buzzing around in her airplane. Up in her tower she was Fearless Franny Muggs, Queen of All She Surveyed.

She squinted through her binoculars. No sign of Pru. No sign of Cat. *Good*, she thought. She swung around in the opposite direction to have a look at #5 Gumm Street. Not a trace was left from the rogue blizzard that had blown in from the west a few weeks before. It had surprised everyone in town—a blizzard in Sherbet? No one even owned a snow shovel.

One midnight right after that, Franny could have sworn she'd seen lights flickering about inside the old wreck of a house at #5 Gumm Street. She had ducked behind the railing of her balcony and strained her eyes through the glasses to see, but the lights had disappeared. Probably zombies, Franny had decided.

If you believe in zombies (and you should), #5 Gumm Street was the perfect place for them. The house had been vacant for as long as Franny could remember, and vines had taken over to such an extent that from a distance the house looked like a giant hair ball. It leaned so badly to one side that it appeared as if it were caught in a perpetually stiff breeze.

There were no signs of zombies today, though. Instead, Franny spied a moving van off in the distance. It came closer and closer and halted right in front of #5!

Two men hopped out. They carried a few boxes and some ratty old furniture into the house. A moment later a Ford Fiesta pulled up. A woman and a birdlike girl with a bed pillow tucked under her arm—who, Franny figured, was probably the woman's daughter—stepped out of the car.

After a few quick trips, the moving men pulled themselves up into the truck and drove away. The woman and girl went inside through the double front doors that hung precariously from their hinges.

Not five minutes had passed when another moving van arrived. The woman came out of the house, and there was a lot of discussion. The moving men kept pointing and shaking their heads yes, and the woman kept shaking her head no. It seemed like she didn't want whatever it was, and Franny was afraid the moving men were just going to leave—which would be awful, because she was dying to know what was in the truck.

But then the girl came outside and said something to the woman, and she seemed to give in.

With much grunting and groaning, the moving men lifted an enormous, gleaming grand piano from out of the truck and gentled it through the front doors.

Franny went inside at this point. Her tower room was about the size of a large horse stall. There was a small freezer for her Popsicles, a microwave for her hot chocolate, and a desk with a globe on it. Thumbtacked to the small closet door was a calendar with a picture of Mount Everest and a quotation from Amelia Earhart: "Adventure is worthwhile in itself."

New people moving into the zombie house— nothing as exciting as this had ever happened on Gumm Street! *I'll bet there's not even any heat or running water inside that house,* she thought with a thrill. *Maybe in the winter they'll have to melt snow to drink, like Sir Edmund Hillary and his faithful Sherpa, Tenzing Norgay, when they climbed Mount Everest!* It was time to meet the new neighbors face-to-face. Franny hung her binoculars from a hook and clattered down the spiral staircase that wound around and around the outside of her wedding-cake house.

Within moments Franny was on the threshold of #5 Gumm Street. She could hardly wait. She'd always wanted to see what this house was like on the inside. From behind the door came the sound of someone playing the piano. Franny remembered her own piano lesson days. The endless practicing, the interminable scales, topped off at the end of each week by . . . The Lesson. It's true that Mr. Staccato, her piano teacher, was very patient and sympathetic, telling Franny that she wasn't tone-deaf, just "musically challenged." But she got worse instead of better, and once she played so poorly she actually thought Mr. Staccato was going to cry. She stopped taking lessons after that. But what she was listening to now . . . well, it made *her* sound like Beethoven.

Franny knocked.

The music—if you want to call it that—continued, but the door creakily opened, and the woman Franny had seen earlier appeared.

7

"Hello," Franny said. "My name is Franny Muggs, and I'd like to be the first one to welcome you to Gumm Street!"

"Thanks, hon," replied the woman. "I'm Pearl Diamond, and that's my daughter, Ivy." She hooked her thumb over her shoulder in the general direction of the piano behind her.

Only one word came to mind as soon as Franny saw Pearl Diamond—*sparkly*. She had gleaming blond hair arranged in a complicated way, and on her T-shirt she had rhinestones in the shape of a French poodle. She had sparkly bracelets, sparkly blue eyes, and sparkly white teeth.

"Tell me, hon, you know any piano-type people around here?" Pearl said.

"I'm musically challenged," Franny replied. "At least, that's what Mr.—"

"Staccato," said a man with an English accent from behind Franny.

Franny turned around and there was her former piano teacher, Mr. Staccato himself. He was an older gentleman neatly dressed as always in a three-piece suit. With him were two fat little white dogs, who stood

solemnly on either side of him looking suspiciously up into the face of this new neighbor.

"Miss Muggs," he said with a nod to Franny.
"And Mrs. Diamond, I presume. And that must be
Miss Diamond"—he politely cleared his
throat—"playing the piano."

"Pearl Diamond—you can call me
Pearl." Pearl extended her hand, and Mr.
Staccato took it by the fingers and made a
slight bow.

"Welcome to Gumm Street," he said.

Pearl thanked him, and her hands fluttered self-consciously to her hairdo. "It's
the darnedest thing. Someone just delivered a piano, and we have no idea
who!"

At this point the music stopped.
Franny heard footsteps and saw
the birdlike girl walk over to
the door.

Pearl put her arm protectively around the girl's thin shoulders.

"This is my daughter, Ivy," Pearl said. "Ivy, this is Franny and Mr. Stiletto—"

"Staccato," Franny corrected her.

"Mr. *Staccato*," Pearl said with an embarrassed little laugh, tucking a stray curl back in her hairdo where it belonged.

"Um, hi." Ivy's eyes darted quickly from Franny to Mr. Staccato to the dogs and finally to her mother, whom she looked at questioningly.

"It must be some mistake—the piano, I mean!" Pearl said, her eyes wide like a game show contestant waiting to see what was behind door number three.

Mr. Staccato leaned forwards, and for a second Franny thought he was going to whisper something in Pearl's ear, like who sent the piano, for instance— which would have been really weird, because how could he know? Then again, he knew Pearl and Ivy's last name, which was weird all by itself. Instead, though, he said in a hushed voice, "My condolences to you both regarding your Aunt Viola."

"Who's Aunt Viola?" Franny said, but everyone ignored her.

"Thank you, but the last time I saw Aunt V, I was Ivy's age." Pearl pulled Ivy a little closer to her.

"We've been on the move the last seven years—kinda had a run of bad luck—but that's all behind us now, right, baby?" Pearl gave Ivy's shoulders a little squeeze, and Ivy smiled weakly, as if she were not quite so optimistic.

"Most interesting," Mr. Staccato mused to himself.

Franny thought that whoever this Aunt Viola lady was, Mr. Staccato sure seemed relieved she wasn't around anymore, because Franny could have sworn he had exactly the same expression on his face as when she had told him she was going to stop taking lessons. She glanced at his two dogs, Fred and Ginger, and they seemed to relax as well. They pulled their tails under, seated themselves, and looked off into the distance, bored.

"Actually, I only met your aunt once, myself," Mr. Staccato said. His face momentarily darkened.

"Then why are you so interested in her?" Franny interrupted, but again the adults acted like they didn't hear her.

"But about the piano," Pearl said, shrugging. "We don't even know how to play this thing!"

"What a coincidence." Mr. Staccato said, and making another little bow, he handed her a card.

"Well, I'll be!" Pearl exclaimed. "If that doesn't beat all."

"That just really beats all!" Franny said cheerfully, trying again to be part of what was going on, whatever it was.

"Doesn't that just beat all, sugar?" Pearl laughed and showed the card to Ivy.

Ivy read out loud, "Mr. Staccato, number seven Gumm Street, Sherbet, piano lessons." She raised her eyes from the card and for the first time looked straight at Mr. Staccato. "You could teach me to play the piano?"

"You never know. . . ." He held Ivy's gaze for a moment while the dogs' ears twitched forwards and back. "You may even have a unique talent for it."

Fred and Ginger jumped to attention. "Good day, ladies." With that, he and his dogs turned on their heels and went briskly down the walk.

"What do you think, baby? Would you like to take piano lessons?"

Franny couldn't believe it when Ivy nodded her head. *Better her than me,* Franny thought.

Noticing Franny once again, Pearl said, "Why don't you girls get to know each other?" Her bracelets jingled as she put on a sequined headband and freshened up her lipstick. "I'm just going to talk to Mr. Staccato again for a moment. Show Franny my Miss Venus Constellation of Stars crown, baby," she called out over her shoulder as she hurried down the steps.

Without a word, Ivy turned and went into the house. Franny followed.

While Ivy rummaged through a few boxes, Franny took the opportunity to steal a look around. It was wonderfully creepy, she thought. The first floor sloped off to the right just like in the fun house at the Sherbet amusement park. In one corner, on the up-hill side, was the piano. Its wheels were locked tightly in place and clung to the ancient floor for dear life, so that the piano wouldn't roll and throw the house any more off-kilter. Crooked stairs with some of the banister missing twisted up to the second floor. On the wall halfway up the stairs was a painting of a lady with a bright pink chiffon scarf around her neck and a beehive hairdo. She wore large earrings in the shape of cherries, or strawberries—it was hard to tell in the gloomy light of the house, but clearly they were meant to be some kind of fruit.

"Who's that?" Franny asked Ivy.

Popping her head out of the box for a moment, Ivy said, "Oh, I don't know. Maybe it's Aunt V—Aunt Viola—she's . . . um . . . dead, but she left us this house."

"Oh?" said Franny, climbing the stairs to get a bet-ter look. A portrait of Aunt Viola, mysterious and dead, no less, *was* interesting. Maybe Aunt Viola was one of the zombies Franny was sure lived in the house.

But as she got closer, Franny suddenly noticed something: a white envelope wedged in the corner between the painting and the frame. The name *Pearl* was scrawled across it in fancy handwriting.

"Look what I found!" the two girls said at the same time.

Ivy walked over and handed Franny the rhinestone Miss Venus crown.

Franny handed Ivy the white envelope.

"Wow," said Franny. She put the beauty pageant crown on her head and looked around for a mirror. "It's heavy!"

Ivy didn't say anything. She stood biting her lip, frowning at the envelope. She'd never known one not to contain bad news.

"Aren't you going to open it?" Franny asked. She decided that Ivy Diamond was just about the skinniest kid she'd ever seen, not to mention one of the quietest. She had nice friendly eyes, but her ears poked out through scraggly dirty blond hair, and her narrow face was an unhealthy shade of tapioca pudding.

"It's for my mom," Ivy said, and quickly shoved it into her back pocket.

A second later Pearl came bustling back into the house. "Baby, get ready for some piano lessons!" she said to Ivy. Then she ushered Franny to the door, saying, "You're gonna have to leave now, honey. Ivy's got a lot of practicin' to do, doncha, baby?"

Ivy stood on the porch and watched Franny make her way down the street.

Franny left this first meeting greatly impressed. None of the other mothers were as sparkly as Pearl, and she'd never known a real beauty pageant winner. Franny liked Ivy, too, even if she didn't have much to say. She thought Ivy was pretty brave to live in a house that had a picture of a dead person on the wall (no way would Pru ever do that), and Ivy didn't seem at all stuck-up like Cat.

"Hey, Ivy?" Franny waved and called to her from the street. "Can you do a cartwheel?"

Ivy shook her head no and waved back.

"Good!" said Franny happily. "Neither can I!"

_L_ife was really great for Ivy up until she was four years old. She'd had a nice house and a dad back then. Pearl had just won the Miss Venus Constellation of Stars Pageant, as well as a champagne-colored Cadillac. It was her "crowning glory," Pearl said, and now she was going to hang up her tiara and take it easy.

That night Pearl wiggled out of her gold lamé gown and sat down to remove her makeup while Ivy played at the counter right beside her. Pearl looked into the large mirror, dipped her fingers in a jar of cold cream, and slathered it on her face.

"Dang it!" she muttered, getting some of it in her eyes. "Now where are those tissues?" Ivy giggled at the reflection of her mother's white face.

And that's when it happened.

Suddenly her mother's reflection was gone. A sickening green oily swirl appeared, and from that emerged a woman wearing a hat that looked like a lamp shade. A long veil made it difficult to distinguish any features on her face. The woman in the mirror grinned, and a mouthful of pointy teeth glittered beneath the black lace.

It is widely known that a person with no reflection in a mirror is a vampire, but a reflection in a mirror with no person?

"Here they are!" Pearl pulled the box toward her, knocking a bottle of moisturizer to the floor. "Oops!" She bent down and blindly felt around for the bottle, while Ivy leaned forwards to get a better look, just in time to see the woman spin her pinky

17

fingers in a circle. Green gems sparkled from rings on her black-gloved hand.

Ivy screamed as spidery cracks formed across the surface of the mirror—and for a second, she thought she saw her father's face reflected in the shattered glass . . . but then the mirror broke and he was gone. Breaking a mirror is very bad luck—seven years' worth, as a matter of fact—and that's the precise moment when the Jinx showed up.

The bad luck started immediately. Earlier that evening Ivy's father had gone out for Listerine, mayonnaise, and Pop-Tarts, and he never came home. The next day Ivy got the worst case of chicken pox ever recorded. Pearl gained eighteen pounds in two weeks, could no longer fit into her gold lamé gown, and suddenly developed a mysterious allergy to mascara, dashing her hopes of an easy life as an MC on the beauty pageant circuit. The suddenly fatherless family lost everything—their house, their furniture, even their champagne-colored Cadillac.

Everywhere Ivy and Pearl went, the Jinx followed. A day at the beach meant narrow escapes from sharks and Ivy and Pearl going home with third-degree sunburns. Picnics would feature colonies of ants, swarms of bees, armies of black bears, packs of wild dogs, salmonella poisoning from the egg salad, and a trip to the emergency room. Vacations, holidays, even shopping trips were fraught with flat tires, empty gas tanks, missing wallets and keys, and never-ending episodes of unexplained itchy rashes.

They moved around a lot, hoping that a new location would bring better luck, but it never did. Still, Pearl and Ivy had survived the Jinx—barely—and in just a little over two months, the seven years would be over and, according to tradition, so would the Jinx. Life already seemed to be improving. Aunt Viola, who was Pearl's only living relative, died—

which of course was bad, but it turned out to be good, too, because she left Pearl and Ivy some money as well as her house on Gumm Street.

But then there was the letter.

Almost seven years of bad luck had taught Ivy that no news is good news, and so she was relieved when Pearl read it, crumpled it up, and threw it in the trash.

"What did it say, Mom?" Ivy asked.

"Your Aunt V was a little off her rocker, darlin'." Pearl brushed some hair off Ivy's forehead. "She lived a long life, honey, but in her golden years she was starting to talk to her Dirt Devil and mail her bills in her washing machine. She ended up in the Sherbet Final Rest Home, and that's where she died."

Ivy bit her lip, and Pearl went on. "Let's not say anything about this letter, okay, baby? We're gonna make a fresh start. Things are gonna be different, sugar, you'll see."

Ivy nodded, but as soon as Pearl left the room, she fished the letter out of the trash to see for herself.

This is what it said:

Dear Pearl,
    You have probably heard by now that I've lost my marbles. Well, I may be old, but I'm not nuts!

Anyway, here's the thing. I'm not really dead; I'm in Boca. Just a little matter of some back taxes I'd rather avoid. See ya soon, kiddo!
Your loving aunt,
Viola
P.S. If you hear anything about a pair of silver shoes—low-heeled sparkly numbers with cute little bows on them—they're mine! I might just be dropping by one of these days to get them, and mum's the word. . . .

Wow! Mom is right, Aunt V really was cracked, Ivy thought. She laughed and tossed the letter back into the trash.

But the next morning when she came downstairs and saw Aunt V's portrait, the line "I'm not really dead" popped uncomfortably into her head. How could you be dead one minute and not dead the next? The thought gave her the willies. Then again, the living were here one minute and gone the next. Ivy thought about her father. He had deserted them and in his place, nothing . . . nothing but the Jinx, that is.

"Your daddy'll be back, baby, just you wait and see!" Pearl said all the time. But Ivy wasn't so sure. In fact, Ivy wasn't so sure about a lot of things, most of all coming to live at #5 Gumm Street, in a house left to them by a dead—not-dead aunt.

Or maybe I'm just nervous about my first piano lesson, Ivy reasoned as she left the house and walked down the street. Ivy was expected at #7 Gumm Street, Mr. Staccato's, at 11:00 A.M. The Jinx had not made her especially hopeful about new experiences. But as she climbed the stairs of Mr. Staccato's front porch, her apprehension began to diminish slightly, for at least she had made it this far without being caught in a torrential downpour, getting run over by a car, or having a bird do something on her head.

Ivy approached the front door and immediately noticed the handwritten note Scotch-taped at about knee height:

She hoped Mr. Staccato was a better piano teacher than speller. She knocked three times and opened the door.

There on the other side were the same two dogs she'd seen with Mr. Staccato. Turning abruptly, they walked in a deliberate way toward the center of the house. Once or twice they looked over their shoulders and motioned with their heads for her to follow.

They led Ivy to a room that was like nothing she had ever seen before. There were many framed pictures on the wall—posters, really—which looked like they had been taken from old theaters. Some had titles written across the tops in bold lettering from movies Ivy had heard of, like *King Kong*, and some were of actors she had heard of, like Judy Garland. But all of them were from movies and plays way before her time.

The room was like a little museum. Enclosed in a glass cabinet were odd bits of glamorous clothing—a set of white cotton gloves here, an embroidered satin vest there. There were also shelves filled with old books with gold-embossed lettering on the spines. Although there was a feeling of oldness about everything, there was not a speck of dust or mustiness about the place. On the contrary, the gold frames around the posters twinkled from the light cast by the crystal lamps scattered about the room.

Ivy was brought back to attention by the impatient sneeze of one of her guides. The dog led her to the next room, where there were two comfortable corduroy couches on a deep red Oriental rug. Both dogs jumped onto one of the corduroy couches, which faced a pair of cream-colored doors. By alternately looking at Ivy and then at the empty spot between them, they indicated that Ivy should sit.

Ivy sat. Not knowing what to do next, she turned to the dog on her right, who smiled reassuringly at her.

From behind the doors, Ivy could hear someone— probably a student—playing something that sounded like a show tune from Broadway. The player was pretty good, Ivy decided. She took a deep breath. "Relax," she said to herself, and looked at the doors and then her watch. It was 10:59. A minute later the music ended and the doors opened, flooding the waiting room with light.

Ivy automatically stood and squinted, waiting for her eyes to adjust.

Out marched a girl just about Ivy's age. She had chin-length white-blond hair that had been cut in a wispy style. She was thin but wiry, and as she passed, Ivy could see on the back of her lesson books the word *Cat* in three-dimensional writing. The girl seemed not to see Ivy. Instead, she hurried by coolly, as if she were late for another appointment.

The next moment Mr. Staccato appeared in the doorway. The dogs jumped off the couch and ushered the girl out of the waiting area.

"Miss Diamond," Mr. Staccato said, and motioned Ivy inside.

The lesson room was cozy and cheerful. The piano stood against the wall opposite a large bay window.

"Right, then!" said Mr. Staccato. His English accent reminded her of a butler in a movie, and she half expected him to start serving tea any minute.

Ivy sat down on the bench in front of the piano.

Mr. Staccato leaned casually against the side of the piano and studied her. "Your mother tells me that you would like to learn to play."

"Yes, please," said Ivy, who was on her best behavior.

"And why is that?" he asked. This was said not in a challenging manner, but rather because he seemed genuinely curious, and so Ivy found herself answering in a completely honest way.

"I'm trying to find out what I'm good at."

"Ah!" Mr. Staccato's eyes twinkled. "You are trying to find your unique talent!"

Ivy nodded. "Yes, my unique talent . . . that's it."

"It's a very good thing to know," Mr. Staccato said. "Everybody has one."

"Really?" Ivy said hopefully.

"In fact, some people have several unique talents." Mr. Staccato paused and straightened a pile of already straight sheet music.

"They must be really lucky." Ivy already knew she would not be among that group.

"One would think, but along with talent comes a great deal of responsibility, my dear." Mr. Staccato wagged his long, thin finger like a metronome. "That is, if you look at it from the other way around. Isn't that right, Fred, old chap?" One of the dogs, who had just wandered into the room, agreed with a nod of his head and then wandered out again.

"I guess I don't know," said Ivy. "I haven't been so hot at anything yet. . . ." The Jinx had seen to that.

"Well, my dear, I have some very good news for you," Mr. Staccato said cheerfully.

"You do?" Ivy wasn't used to very good news, or even *sort of* good news, for that matter.

"I was one hundred and fifteen before I found out what my unique talent was," Mr. Staccato said. "My point being that you have plenty of time."

One hundred and fifteen?! Ivy was shocked. "But you

don't look one hundred and fifteen!"

"You see?" Mr. Staccato folded his arms and raised an eyebrow. "Many things are not what they appear to be. In fact, often they are the complete opposite!"

Ivy thought about this for a moment. "So you mean, if you think you're having a lot of bad luck, it could really be good in some way?"

"Precisely!" said Mr. Staccato.

Ivy wasn't so sure, but it did make her feel a little better. "And after you turned one hundred and fifteen, what did you find out your talent was?"

"Recognizing unique talent, actually," he said, and then added, "Middle C, this is where it all starts."

"Or sometimes where it all ends, right?"

"Yes, Miss Diamond." Mr. Staccato laughed softly. "Sometimes where it all ends." He pointed to a key on the piano, and sensing that there would be no further discussion, Ivy settled down to learn.

The hour flew by, and Ivy was surprised when one of the dogs appeared in the room as if to remind his master the time was up.

"Thank you, Fred," Mr. Staccato told him. Fred nodded and then trotted off as if he were extremely busy.

"Mr. Staccato . . . um, sir?" Ivy said. "The dogs?"

"Fred and Ginger." Mr. Staccato walked over to a supply cabinet in the corner.

"Yes, um . . . sir, they seem so . . . like . . . human."

Mr. Staccato pulled out some books of scales and walked back to the piano. "They've always been this way. I hardly even notice anymore." He raised one eyebrow and, leaning toward Ivy, said in a low voice, "They came with the house."

"They did?" said Ivy.

"They belonged to the old chap who lived here before me."

"He didn't *want* them?" Ivy whispered. The dogs were not in the room, but Ivy knew that even normal dogs had extraordinary hearing. These two had an extraordinary command of English as well, and she didn't want to be the one to spill the beans about their not being wanted.

"It's a long story" was all Mr. Staccato would say. He handed Ivy the lesson books. "I suggest you practice for an hour every day, Miss Diamond." He opened the cream-colored doors. "You haven't much time to learn a piece for the recital."

"Recital?" asked Ivy.

"Yes," replied Mr. Staccato. One of the dogs jumped off the corduroy couch holding a printed invitation in his mouth, which Ivy assumed she was meant to take.

"Thank you, Fred," said Ivy. Or was it Ginger? She wasn't sure.

Sitting on the couch in the waiting room now was another girl. She had large, round eyeglasses and a long, straight ponytail that she twirled around and around one finger. She was engrossed in a book. Ivy ventured a smile, but it must have been a really good book, Ivy thought, because the girl never looked up from it.

The dogs escorted Ivy back the way she had come, past the posters and the glass cases, past the books with the gilt lettering in the bookshelves, past the glittering crystal lamps.

That's funny, Ivy thought, pausing in front of an unusual-looking cupboard next to the fireplace. It had a closed window right in the middle of it, just large enough for a person to climb through, but she couldn't see what was on the other side because the glass was opaque. There was something written above it....

A wet nose nudged her leg. She was being urged on toward the front door, which opened before her.

Walking down Gumm Street, Ivy suddenly stopped to listen. "Go away!" she shouted at ... *what*?

For the last seven years, she'd been hearing it. A sniffing sound, a scratching or skittering noise—it always came from behind her and was never very loud, just loud enough to be annoying. When she looked, there was never anything there, but Ivy was sure it was the Jinx.

"Go *AWAY*!" she shouted again, shaking her fist. She realized she still had the invitation in her hand. It read:

Musical Recital
at
Mr. Staccato's
and You are invited!

When? JUNE 15TH 2:00 P.M.
SHARP!

Where? NUMBER 7 GUMM STREET

SHERBET

Please RSVP BY JUNE 1
FRED (or GINGER.)

Reading it, Ivy thought, *Wait a minute, the recital is on the same day as the expiration of the Jinx!* She counted on her fingers to make sure that she was correct, then folded the invitation and slipped it inside her music books. Her mood lightened. The day of the recital would be the beginning of a whole new life.

Ivy looked both ways and then hurried home. A black cat darted across her path, and a green snake hissed from the weeds, but that was all.

Ivy just hoped that she would make it to the recital in one piece.

PRU

*P*ru *pushed her large, round eyeglasses*
up her nose, smoothed her long ponytail, and
shoved the recital invitation into her lesson book as
she left Mr. Staccato's house. *Another recital,* Pru
thought, *another chance for Cat to be the big star!*
Pru sighed. Maybe Franny had the right idea for once

in her life when she quit taking piano lessons.

Pru was looking forward to getting home. She knew just what she would do once she got there, and smiled in anticipation. But the next moment she frowned. Before she could put on her thick cushy socks and her favorite snuggly sweater and jump under her quilt, where she could finish reading *The Wizard of Oz*, she would have to pass by #2 Gumm Street—Cat's house.

There was absolutely no hope that they wouldn't be outside—the Lemonjello kids were *always* outside, all eleven of them. Pru could already hear them hooting and hollering, and sure enough, as she rounded the corner, there they were, gathered under a branch of that awful treehouse of theirs with their backs to her.

Pru crossed the street.

Don't make eye contact, she instructed herself, and focused instead on her quiet, warm, peaceful, *safe* bedroom window off in the distance. She was almost home. . . .

In thirty feet she would touch down on her driveway. . . .

Al-l-l-l-lmost there . . .

Twenty feet . . .

Fift—

"HEY, PRU! WATCH THIS!" Cat called out.

Pru stopped dead in her tracks. Crouching on a branch ten feet off the ground was the littlest Lemonjello. Just looking at him up there made Pru's legs weak and her palms sweat. With his eyes fixed on the ground below, he stood up, wobbled for a second, and—as Pru's stomach flipped over—leaped off the branch, his arms windmilling in the air. He landed safely on the ground with a satisfying *whump*. The other Lemonjellos shrieked with delight.

"Come on, Pru, it's your turn!" Cat yelled. She knew Pru would never do it, but liked making her squirm.

Pru could think of twenty good reasons in no time flat why she should *not* jump out of that tree (or any other for that matter). She recited only one: "Safety Hazard Number One Hundred Thirty-Three: Trees are the third leading cause of accidents on the playground."

"Chicken! Chicken!" the Lemonjello boys chanted.

Pru flipped her ponytail over her shoulder and started down the street again.

"It's easy!" Cat yelled, and

Pru turned to see Cat herself climbing up the tree this time.

Cat balanced on an even higher branch. She bounced a few times on the limb like it was a diving board and then sprang in the air, her white, wispy hair floating around her face like a starburst. Cat hit the ground, and all her brothers screamed and clapped.

"So _what!_" Pru shouted. Clutching her book tightly to her chest, she started walking toward her house again. *Just because* they're *crazy enough to jump out of a tree doesn't mean I have to*, she thought. Pru looked back angrily at #2 Gumm Street, but something wasn't right: Cat was still lying on the ground, her brothers all around her.

Pru dropped her books and ran over. "Cat! Cat!" She pushed the boys aside. "Let me in!" she cried, kneeling beside Cat, who didn't even look like she was breathing. "Say something, Cat!" Pru pleaded.

"Pru?" Cat said in a barely audible whisper.

"Yes?" Pru said gently.

Cat shot up and did a one-handed cartwheel. "YOU'RE A BIG CHICKEN!"

The boys went wild. "Big chicken! Big chicken!" they jeered, laughing hysterically.

Pru stomped off, her face red. She snatched up her books and ran the rest of the way home. Once inside her room, she pulled on her cushy socks and her snuggly sweater. *I'll never speak to that Cat Lemonjello for as long as I live!* She went to close the window shade. *There's Franny*, thought Pru, *out there on that wretched lookout tower of hers. It's a wonder she hasn't caught her death of pneumonia . . . and all those stairs! Safety Hazard #3: Stairs are the number-one cause of accidents in the home. I'm so glad we don't have stairs in* our *home*, Pru thought smugly. The Gumms lived in a sensible one-story house surrounded with concrete because "spiders, ants, and beetles found in the common garden and outdoor landscaping are the number-one culprits behind most insect bites."

It was surprising how many everyday things could be dangerous. That very morning Pru had overheard her mother telling her father what had happened a couple of weeks ago to some old lady in the Sherbet Final Rest Home. While making a snack, she stuck a fork into the toaster and electrocuted herself to death . . . *just . . . making . . . TOAST!*

Why can't people be more careful? Pru wondered. Settling on the bed, she thought about what had happened that afternoon. "I'm not a chicken," she told herself, and tucked the quilt up under her chin. She was starting to get nervous all over again and grabbed a tissue because there was a good chance she might cry. "I'm just very sensitive."

Pru dabbed an eye and blew her nose. She couldn't believe at one time she had actually been *friends* with such a stuck-up, crummy person as Cat.

Which brings us to an interesting phenomenon. Have you ever noticed how the most disagreeable people are often kids you actually once liked—*friends*, in fact? Here's how it happens: You're going along—you and your friend—having a wonderful time. You have that funny thing you say, and your friend always laughs. You tell each other everything, even the embarrassing things, like how you used to suck your thumb up until you were eight years old. Then one day your friend doesn't laugh as loud when you say the funny thing. So you try to think up a new funny thing, but nothing you think up is funny to your friend anymore. It's no big deal, though, because after all this person *is* your friend.

But then one day at school you are late to the assembly, and you ask your friend for frontsies so you don't have to sit next to the kid who used to eat paste in kindergarten, and your friend says she can't because she already gave someone else frontsies and that's the rule, but she can give you backsies, and you say okay, but you don't like backsies, and if it were *you* and your friend asked for frontsies, you know you would give her frontsies. So now you're starting to not like your friend so much, and your friend wears the green outfit with the kick pleat, and even though it's cute, you don't tell her because she's getting stuck-up. But then she doesn't tell you what she got on her report about Eli Whitney inventing the cotton gin. So you don't tell her about the turtle your brother found in your driveway.

And finally one day you realize that your friend is no longer your friend. And you can't believe you were ever friends with such a crummy person in the first place.

That is how it was with Cat and Pru. They had been very close friends going all the way back to their days of strained carrots and sippy cups, but then things soured.

Pru sniffled and remembered. *It's just like the Halloween in third grade when Cat came dressed as a witch and said I was copying, when I wasn't even in a stupid witch costume at all—I was Florence Nightingale—but she's so ignorant, she doesn't know the difference. Or like in fourth grade when she was spreading rumors that I had stupid-looking shoes—laced shoes* aren't *stupid; they're very sensible.*
Pru was positive of that because her mother

had written an entire series of articles on the subject.

Wanting to escape Cat and this latest humiliation, Pru reached for her book. The recital invitation fell out. Pru sighed. There was no way she would be able to concentrate enough to read until she had decided on a piece to play for the recital. And then she thought of something better, *way* better. A plan—a plan to get even with Cat: Project Star of the Recital!

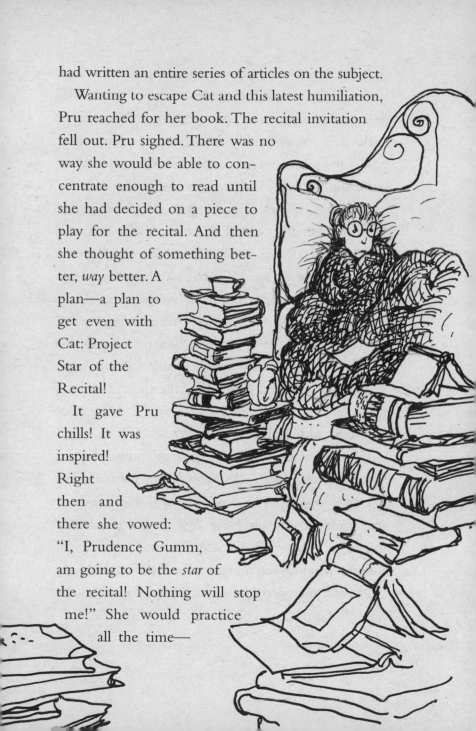

It gave Pru chills! It was inspired! Right then and there she vowed: "I, Prudence Gumm, am going to be the *star* of the recital! Nothing will stop me!" She would practice all the time—

early in the morning, after school, and before she went to bed at night. *Cat's sure going to be sorry. Maybe she'll even cry.* The thought of Cat crying made Pru smile.

But her smile quickly faded, and Pru shook her head. *I've been so worked up, I completely forgot to pull the shade,* she thought. Pru watched Franny silhouetted against the darkness high atop her lookout tower. This immediately called to mind Safety Hazard #803: Mountaintops, rooftops, and *lookout towers* are the number-one cause of vertigo, pulmonary edema from altitude sickness, and head trauma from falls.

Franny and her big ideas—which were mostly hare-brained, Pru thought—like having Sir Edmund Hillary Day at school, or her anti-zombie spray, which was supposed to fend off the undead but was really just an old Windex bottle full of garlic juice that stank to high heaven.

Pru pressed her face closer to the window. Franny's binoculars were pointed straight at #5 Gumm. *What was she looking at?* Pru shivered; she couldn't believe that someone actually now *lived* in that dilapidated horror of a house. Pru shook her head again, made sure the window was locked (it was), pulled down the shade, and snuggled under the safety of her quilt for a nice long read.

A CAT

*I*t *was still dark outside when Cat* rolled over and looked at her alarm clock. It glowed back at her: 4:05 A.M.

Cat turned onto her back and stared at the ceiling. She had been uneasy, and the feeling was growing worse. *This bad feeling is probably Pru thinking*

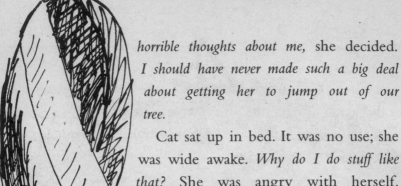

horrible thoughts about me, she decided. *I should have never made such a big deal about getting her to jump out of our tree.*

Cat sat up in bed. It was no use; she was wide awake. *Why do I do stuff like that?* She was angry with herself. Provoking Pru had to be the cause for that nagging bad feeling. Cat threw the covers back and

got out of bed. It was even too early to go out for a ride on her pony.

She put on her clogs and, grabbing her blanket and flashlight, opened the trapdoor in the middle of the floor. She sat down, swung her legs over the lip of the opening, secured the blanket around her waist, and pushed off.

Down she slid, around and around, and a second

later she was zooming through the swinging door of
the great room and catapulting off the slide, where
she plonked onto the mattresses that had been strate-
gically placed there for this very purpose.

Cat's parents, Lynette and Lenny Lemonjello, had
bought the property at #2 Gumm Street just before
the birth of their first child. Nobody else in Sherbet
wanted the lot because it was only big enough for a
good-sized toolshed—that is, if you got rid of the

tree. Yes, the tree. The tree was magnificent. It was
stupendous! Unfortunately, every square inch of the
entire property was occupied by the tree.

There were plenty of naysayers who thought the young couple was making a *big* mistake.

"You'll never chop that tree down," they said.

"Too big." They shook their heads.

"Fall down on people." They nodded.

"Will make a right mess," said some.

"Will leave a big hole," said others.

"What are you gonna do?" they all wanted to know.

"Do?" the Lemonjellos inquired.

"Where you gonna live . . . *in the tree?*"

"Why, yes," replied the Lemonjellos.

And that's exactly what they did. They hollowed a space out of the trunk for their car, and the tree hardly seemed to mind; it was a minor inconvenience compared to being chopped down. The Lemonjellos then set about building their house where the trunk split off into branches. As their family grew, they just added rooms onto different branches, and these eventually became connected by a series of bridges, stairs, and slides. All the slides converged into the great room, and this is where Cat had landed.

She picked herself up and carefully made her way over to her mother's study. It was pitch black, so it was a good thing she had the flashlight. Cat headed straight for her mother's desk, where she found a yel-

low legal pad, a pen, three pennies, and a small paper-
back book. She brought all these items to the rug and
sat down cross-legged, the blanket around her.

Cat pointed the flashlight at the cover of the book:
The Groovy I Ching, translated by Lynette Lemonjello.

Cat couldn't believe that people actually bought

loony books like this, but they did. The Lemonjellos had even been able to afford to buy a health food store from the royalties.

She opened the book and began to read.

> *This is a translation of a groovy book, written by a bunch of really enlightened, spiritual Chinese dudes thousands of years ago.* (Oh, sure, Cat thought.) *It was used to understand why heavy stuff goes down, but also—and this is the really cool part—it can help divine the future!*

Hmmm. She had seen her mother use the book in times of crisis, but Cat hadn't ever actually tried to do it herself. She tugged the blanket a little tighter around her and tried to think about what exactly she should ask the *I Ching*. Cat flipped through a few pages until she read this:

> *Step 1. Asking a Question. (This is really important—like major—toward gaining insight to the future!) Do not ask yes or no questions (this really ticks off the I Ching spirits). Instead, ask for advice or the meaning of something.*

Okay, thought Cat, *if I'm going to do this, I may as well do it right.*

She wrote on the pad: "What is the meaning behind these uneasy feelings that I have been having lately?" Cat closed the book. She held the three coins in her hand and, shutting her eyes, tried to meditate as she'd seen her mother do. A minute seemed like an hour, and before long she couldn't stand it and anxiously began to shake the coins in her hand. She let them tumble out onto the carpet and then, like the book instructed, examined the positions in which they'd landed: tails, tails, heads.

She consulted the diagram from the book to see the corresponding line to draw for this combination: a long line. She drew that.

She thought about her question again, shook the coins in her hand, and threw them out on the floor: heads, heads, tails. The book said this was a broken line, so she drew that.

Six times in all Cat threw the coins, until she had six lines drawn on her pad, one stacked above the other. *I hope I'm doing this right*, she whispered to herself. The flashlight shook slightly in her hand.

It was cold in the room, and Cat pulled her blanket over her head while she studied the chart at the back of the book. She looked for the set of lines that matched the ones she'd drawn and then read its corresponding number: 36. Now all that was left to do was to look up the number and she would get the answer to her question. She anxiously flipped through the book past all the other numbers with their meanings, and there it was: "36: DARKNESS IS COMING AT YOU, DUDE."

Cat's stomach lurched. She blew her warm breath on her hands, which were like ice now, and began to read:

Darkness is coming at you, dude.
Sorry to tell you this, but . . .
Grab your crystals.
Chew some garlic.
Darkness comes.
Of course, it's karmic.

That doesn't sound good at all, Cat thought. *Then again, Mom is kind of nuts.* Cat's mother told fortunes, read tea leaves, looked at people's auras, and—on

Tuesdays and Thursdays—balanced their chakras for free at the health food store. *Maybe I'm not doing this I Ching thing right,* Cat thought, and got up to carefully put the book back on the desk.

Suddenly she had the overwhelming feeling that all she wanted to do was to get out of there. She quickly straightened up the study to erase any telltale signs of her visit and left. She was very tired now. It was still only 5:30; maybe she could get a half hour of sleep before the household came alive.

However, in bed all she could think about was: "DARKNESS IS COMING AT YOU, DUDE."

What in the world could that mean?

few hours later, while Cat was still
stewing over her *I Ching* riddle, Ivy stood
at her bedroom window. She was picking off the last
of the rhinestones her mother had insisted on gluing
to her T-shirt ("to jazz it up a little, hon"). But now
there were dark glue spots, and Ivy had just decided

to change her shirt when Franny appeared on the balcony of her tower that was above Ivy's window. Noticing Ivy, Franny waved and shouted something.

"What?" Ivy shouted back.

"I'll walk with you to school!" Franny pointed below. "Meet me downstairs!"

Ivy ran down the stairs, out the door, and over to the Muggs' front lawn as Franny came clattering down the winding stairway.

"Look at that." Franny pointed up ahead at two figures walking down opposite sides of Gumm Street. "That's Pru Gumm. And that's Cat Lemonjello."

"Those are the two girls I saw at Mr. Staccato's," Ivy said.

Franny and Ivy started down the hill.

"Let me guess," Franny said. "Cat acted like you weren't alive, and Pru had her nose stuck in a book."

"How'd you know?" Ivy thought about how Cat had hurried right by her at Mr. Staccato's as if she were invisible.

"Because Cat doesn't know *anybody* else is alive on this earth except Cat. At least, she doesn't know *I'm* alive." Franny made this last remark to herself. "And Pru *always* has her nose stuck in a book—that is, when she's not making up dopey safety tips."

Ahead Pru marched, her back erect, arms clutching a load of books, nose tilted slightly upward. Completely ignoring her, Cat bounced along on the other side of the street with the sun glinting off her blond hair. The two girls were separated by only a few yards of blacktop, but it may as well have been the Grand Canyon—in winter. Ivy could feel the chill from almost a block away.

"So you and Cat and Pru aren't friends?" Ivy asked.

"Okay." Franny stopped. "If you're going to live on Gumm Street, there are some things you've got to know."

Ivy nodded, eager to learn whatever she needed to fit in.

"Cat doesn't like Pru, Pru doesn't like Cat, neither one of them likes me, and I don't like them!" Franny took out a Jelly Squirtz and popped it in her mouth. "Oh, and you can't be friends with all three of us."

"But why don't you like each other?" Ivy wanted to know.

Franny's face darkened like a thundercloud. She hooked her thumbs into the straps of her backpack and started down the street once more. "Cat and Pru think they're really great because they're in Tuna-on-Rye."

Ivy looked puzzled.

"Everybody wants to be in Tuna-on-Rye." Franny quickened her pace.

"Why?" Ivy asked.

"Because it's all the brainy kids, and absolutely every one of them can do a cartwheel," Franny said glumly. "It's always been that way—ever since Hieronymus Gumm started the school."

Franny was right. Hieronymus Gumm, founder of Sherbet Academy (and the man responsible for naming the street the four girls lived on), believed that all children were gifted in some way and had a God-given right to develop their interests—even if it was only knowing how to pick out the best couch upon which to lounge and watch TV. Of course, he agreed that everyone should be given a good dose of reading, writing, and arithmetic, but he also wanted courses such as Scuba Diving and How to Make Flying Cars, to name a few, included in the curriculum. He knew that not everyone was cut out to be an astronaut or prima ballerina, and for those individuals he insisted there be classes such as Daydreaming, Makeup Tips and Hairdos, Snacks, and The Art of Leisure.

To maximize the chances that each student would

find his talent, Hieronymus devised a system—a test—and placed the students accordingly. He named the four groups after his favorite sandwiches to avoid any kind of notion that one group was better than another. Sad to say, this is where his system failed, because, of the four groups—Liverwurst, Egg-Salad, Tuna-on-Rye, and Bacon-Lettuce-and-Tomato—everybody wanted to be in Tuna-on-Rye, and no one wanted to be in Liverwurst.

"What group are you in?" Ivy asked.

"Liverwurst," said Franny.

"Why don't Cat and Pru like each other?" After all, they were both in the good group; it seemed reasonable that they would be friends.

"Cat and Pru don't like each other because Cat thinks she's a really big deal, and Pru thinks *she's* a really big deal, and one's always trying to be a bigger deal than the other."

Ivy understood now. Even though she was never the object of anybody's jealousy.

"I don't like *them*," Franny said matter-of-factly, "because Pru's a big chicken, and Cat's stuck-up."

Ivy didn't want to put Franny on the spot, but she was too curious. "So why don't Pru and Cat—"

"Like me?" Franny finished Ivy's sentence. "Well . . ."

She exhaled deeply and her cheeks puffed out. "Here's the thing . . . I have a lot of good ideas, like anti-zombie spray and Sir Edmund Hillary Day, and Pru doesn't like any of them." Franny stopped and scrunched up her nose. "I don't think Pru likes my lookout tower, either."

"And why doesn't Cat . . . um, like you?" Ivy asked.

"Cartwheel school." Franny's cheeks flushed with color. "I had this really, really, *really*, great idea: cartwheel school!" Franny repeated. "Cat can do perfect cartwheels—one-handed ones, even. *I* thought for kids who couldn't do them, Cat could kind of show us—I mean, the kids—step-by-step how to do a cartwheel."

"So what happened?" Ivy asked.

"Nothing," Franny answered dully.

"Nothing?"

"She thought it was a lame idea and didn't want to be associated with klutzy kids who can't do cartwheels."

"Oh boy." Ivy knew that she couldn't do a cartwheel either.

Up ahead, Sherbet Academy shimmered in the sun, a pale peach-colored dome that looked very much like—well, like a scoop of sherbet. The

campus was dotted with ancient stately trees and fantastic topiaries. Sculpted shrubs in the shapes of gigantic disembodied pencils magically wrote on tablets, globes rotated on their own, and enormous bushy green numbers were caught in mid-flight on their sides and upside down.

Franny and Ivy approached the building. *Whoosh*, the sliding glass doors glided open, and the girls entered an enormous sunlit atrium. Ivy stopped for a moment to marvel at the high-speed elevators that whizzed up and down the north wall. At the far end a statue of Hieronymus Gumm rose 150 feet in the air. Looking very debonair with an eyebrow raised and a roguish smile on his face, he had one hand placed jauntily on his hip, the other gesturing at a glittering mosaic on the wall made of thousands, perhaps millions of colorful wrappers of what he was famous for—gum!

"Look at that!" Ivy ran to the center of the lobby. "Is it a wishing well?" She peered over the cold stone lip of its curved wall.

"Yes, but a long time ago it was also something else," Franny replied with somewhat less enthusiasm. "It once was used as a jail."

That's right, a jail—for children. Franny told Ivy how it came to be. Hieronymus Gumm was immensely intelligent, curious, and a most whimsical fellow, but he also had some rather controversial ideas about how to discipline unruly students. At the center of his school, he dug a wishing well, over which he hung a gold-plated bucket. At the very bottom of the well he had builders construct an exact replica of the candy cottage from the Grimms' fairy tale where the lost children Hansel and Gretel nearly ended their days. Any little miscreants would be strapped into the golden bucket and cranked down to the bottom of the well by Hieronymus himself, where they were deposited into the cottage's oven through the chimney (it was a wide one, mind you, allowing for fat children who might get stuck) and left for two hours to contemplate their sins. The oven door was—of course—locked, so there was no way to escape. When Hieronymus Gumm went off to meet his maker, this peculiar form of punishment was abolished, but the well and the cottage remained.

The bell rang just as Franny finished her story. She hurried Ivy toward a corner of the enormous hall where a red light flashed below a sign that read NEW STUDENTS.

"Just follow the green blinking arrows into the room at the end of the hall. You're going to take the test—try and get into Liverwurst with me, okay?"

"How do I do that?" Ivy said, still thinking about the jail for children, which seemed rather harsh.

"Just put down the stupidest answers you can think of and you'll end up in my group. I'll meet you here for lunch at noon!" Franny called over her shoulder.

"I won't forget!" Ivy called back to her. But just then the flashing red light changed to green, and a series of blinking green arrows directed her down a carpeted corridor. She followed them into a windowless room with two closed doors on the far wall. A chair, a desk, and a large glowing computer screen sat in the middle.

Ivy sat and a giant HELLO appeared on the screen. WHAT IS YOUR UNIQUE TALENT? EVERYBODY HAS ONE. TO FIND YOURS, JUST ANSWER THE FOLLOWING QUESTIONS!

CHECK IF ANY OF THESE APPLY. CAN YOU . . .

SING?

DANCE?

PLAY THE HARMONICA?

CRY ON CUE?

TIE A SQUARE KNOT?

FRY AN EGG?

DRAW A COCONUT?

STAND ON ONE LEG WITH YOUR EYES CLOSED?

HOLD YOUR BREATH FOR NINETY SECONDS?

MAKE YOURSELF DREAM ANYTHING YOU WANT?

FIND A NEEDLE IN A HAYSTACK?

This was going to be more difficult than Ivy thought. There didn't seem to be a way to answer the questions as stupidly as she could. How was she ever going to get into Liverwurst? The test went on and on, and all Ivy could do was try to answer as honestly as possible. What was her favorite color? Did she like poodles or Chihuahuas, shower gel or bar soap?

Just when she didn't think she could take another minute of trying to decide whether holding her breath or drinking water upside down had ever cured a case of hiccups, a large CONGRATULATIONS! blinked on the screen. THE LIVERWURST DOOR WILL MOMEN-TARILY OPEN. PROCEED THROUGH THE LIVERWURST DOOR!

Ivy heaved a sigh of relief and stood before the door.

Unfortunately, just at that moment, the students over in Makeup Tips and Hairdos all happened to plug in their hair dryers at the same time, causing a short in the wiring. The screen before her went dark, the lights went out, and Ivy could hear kids' voices from behind the doors say, "Oh-h-h-h-h-h-h," the way people do whenever lights suddenly go out. Then the lights flickered back on, and the students clapped the way people do whenever lights that have suddenly gone out come back on.

A door sprang open: Tuna-on-Rye.

It seemed the Jinx would decide her group, not Hieronymus Gumm. Ivy resigned herself and walked through the door.

Perhaps the coincidence of a power failure just a few hours after the *I Ching*'s prediction of "Darkness is coming at you, dude" had unsettled Cat, because as the teacher questioned this new student, something caught Cat's eye.

The new girl stood there pale and wan before the class, answering questions about who she was and where she came from, and as she did, Cat could have sworn the girl's shadow seemed to be lengthening in the most

unnatural way. The teacher rattled on—"How nice to have a brand new shiny Tuna-on-Rye student," and wouldn't she "be a dear and pass out the worksheets on string theory and quantum gravity?" and so on.

Cat watched Ivy's shadow swirl and darken to a pitch black. A tail grew and slithered in and out of the

legs of her unaware classmates. Repulsed and fascinated at the same time, Cat saw a snout form at the shadow's head. Ivy made her way down the row toward Cat, delivering her worksheets. All the time the shadow circled around and around each desk and chair as if to make the student's acquaintance. Closer and closer Ivy came, and Cat held her breath, until at last Ivy stood before her and smiled shyly.

"Worksheet?" Ivy offered.

The shadow curled around Cat's chair like a dog sniffing out new territory. "Get away from me!" Cat kicked out at it, missing Ivy by a hair. Her foot connected with her desk, which crashed to the floor and flipped upside down, making a terrible racket.

Everyone immediately turned around, and Cat realized then that there was nothing there, nothing at all.

"Miss Lemonjello!" said the teacher. "Go to the principal's office right now!" Kicking your desk upside down was frowned upon at Sherbet Academy—even if you *were* in Tuna-on-Rye.

Leaving the classroom, Cat glanced back at Pru—who was smirking—and smirked right back at her like she didn't care. She didn't—at least not about Pru, for once.

Cat pushed her bangs off her damp forehead and

took a deep breath, glad to be away from . . . what? What was it that she had seen? She made her way down the hall and thought about the *I Ching*'s prediction of darkness on its way and the circumstances of this new girl—this Ivy's—arrival. The lights had gone out, and Ivy had appeared along with her slithering, shadowy friend. For the first time in her life, Cat Lemonjello could say she was officially scared. Sitting down on the long, hard bench next to a second grader with a buzz haircut who was picking his nose, Cat never thought she'd find herself so happy to be spending the day in the principal's office.

Franny was right, Ivy thought. Cat *was* stuck-up—not to mention unfriendly. But then Ivy looked down at the front of her shirt, which she had forgotten to change before she left. There were the dark glue spots where she'd picked off the rhinestones earlier. *No wonder Cat didn't want me*

near her, Ivy thought miserably. Watching Cat being sent to the principal's office, Ivy couldn't help thinking that somehow *that* was all her fault, too. It was probably the Jinx. Ivy slumped lower in her seat in an attempt to be as invisible as she could. She looked around to make sure that no one was looking at her, only to see that she was being stared at by Pru. She shrank even lower.

Ivy shouldn't have worried about Pru's stare, though. What she didn't realize was that anyone who wasn't a friend of Cat Lemonjello's was a friend of Pru's. That was automatic. Pru lost no time and approached Ivy after the morning classes broke for lunch.

"I like your shoes," Pru said.

"Thank you. I like yours, too," replied Ivy, who didn't really like Pru's shoes, which were lace-ups and had a distinct orthopedic flair.

Pru brightened. She didn't get many compliments on her footwear. Getting directly to the heart of the matter, she said, "You can have lunch with us if you like." The five girls behind Pru nodded their heads in agreement.

"Sure, great!" said Ivy with genuine enthusiasm. She had never made friends at any of the schools she went to, so this was a happy new experience for her.

And it was why Ivy forgot all about Franny, who was waiting for her in the lobby that very minute.

Ivy followed Pru and her gang to the cafeteria, and after having her tray filled with the usual lunch stuff, sat down, ready to enjoy being part of a real group. And then she remembered Franny.

"Um . . . um," Ivy stammered. "Um . . ." she repeated. Then it came to her: "I have to do something."

"Something? What something?" Pru didn't like secrets. They made her uncomfortable. The five other girls all looked at Ivy with expressions on their faces that said, "Have you gone mad?"

Ivy said the first thing that popped into her head. "I have to see the nurse."

"The nurse?" said Pru, moving her chair a few feet back. Safety Tip #373: Always stand at least six feet away from an infected person. "Why?"

Why? *Why?* Ivy thought hard. *Athlete's foot? No. Boils? No. Acid reflux? No.*

"I need to take a pill," she said, stalling.

"A pill for what?" Pru said, moving her tray closer.

"For . . ." Ivy racked her brain. *Head? Hand? Elbow? Internal—think internal . . . Heart? Too serious. Spleen? Close . . .* "My liver, yes, I need to take a pill for my liver!"

All the girls around Pru gasped. "No!" "Oh my!" "A liver pill!" "How awful!"

"A liver pill?" said Pru. "What on earth is that? What do you have? Is it catching?"

"Oh no, nothing like that," reassured Ivy. She hadn't had this much attention since she'd gotten stuck in quicksand at the first grade picnic during the nature walk. "My liver is just . . . weak."

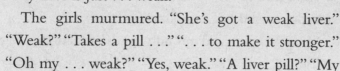

The girls murmured. "She's got a weak liver." "Weak?" "Takes a pill . . ." ". . . to make it stronger." "Oh my . . . weak?" "Yes, weak." "A liver pill?" "My aunt had that."

"Yes," continued Ivy, "and they say this wonderful pill will improve it! So, I have to go take it now. . . ."

Ivy backed out of the room. "So, I'll be right back and everything."

"Okay," said Pru, who wasn't so sure now that she wanted to eat her lunch across from someone with a weak liver, but felt she had to pursue Ivy given how much Cat disliked her. "Do you know where it is?"

"Where what is?" said Ivy.

"The nurse's office."

"Yes," said Ivy, who had no idea where it was.

Pru and her friends watched Ivy turn and walk out of the lunchroom.

But Ivy wasn't going to the nurse, was she? Ivy was headed to the lobby to meet up with Franny. Ivy entered the grand hall, and there at the foot of Hieronymus Gumm sat Franny, in a trancelike state, eating a bag of cookies.

Ivy waved. "Franny!" she called.

Franny looked up, waved back, and began rummaging through her backpack, from which she produced a second bag of cookies.

"Lunch!" she said proudly, and handed the bag to Ivy.

Ivy seated herself next to Franny. She accepted the present and laughed. She could eat this entire bag, and there was no one to tell her not to!

"So, where did they place you?" Franny asked. "I was hoping you would be in my class."

"You're not going to believe this. . . ." Ivy couldn't help talking with her mouth full, she was so hungry. "Tuna-on-Rye," she said between chews.

Now, while Ivy's placement was a very good thing for Pru (because she had the chance to add Ivy to her group and outnumber Cat's group), it was a very bad thing for Franny. She had always been miserable because Cat and Pru were in Tuna-on-Rye and she wasn't, but to find out that she was truly the *only* girl on Gumm Street who was in stupid Liverwurst was a terrible blow, and she didn't take it well at all.

"Tuna-on-Rye?" squeaked Franny, who had suddenly gone white.

"Yeah," said Ivy popping another cookie into her mouth. "But I don't belong there. When I walked into the class, Cat—"

Franny shoved all her cookies into her backpack and stood up. "I have to go."

"Wait," said Ivy. "Why?"

"I'll see you later." And just like that, Franny was gone.

Ivy sat there, stunned by Franny's sudden departure. She ate another cookie and pondered the meaning of it. As she sat there pondering and eating and eating and pondering, she didn't notice Pru and her friends making their way straight toward her.

"I thought you were going to the nurse," said Pru.

Ivy jumped up. "I—I did."

"Already?" Pru asked in disbelief.

"Well, yeah, it was just a shot, and the nurse gave it to me right away."

"I thought it was a pill." Pru remembered distinctly it was a pill—she would have *remembered* a shot. "Anyway, why are you eating those cookies? I thought you were

coming back to the lunchroom."

Ivy was utterly out of ideas. "Because I'm hungry?"

"Well then, I guess you won't be very hungry for lunch. C'mon, girls," Pru said. She didn't want to be rude, but this new girl was too odd. *The next thing you know, she'll be up in that horrid tower with Franny.*

The group turned as one and walked away. "What'd she say?" "Did she get the shot?" "It's not a shot, it's a pill!" "Okay, okay, it's a pill. . . ." Their voices trailed off.

Ivy sat there trying to take in everything that had happened. She'd managed to alienate Cat, Franny, and Pru all in one morning. Maybe *that* was her unique talent—to make sure she alienated everyone she ever met. The one thing it seemed she hadn't alienated was the Jinx. Ivy had a glimpse into the future of what life in this school would be like. *Well,* she thought, trying to be more positive, *it can't get any worse, can it?*

But it could. And would.

IVY'S EMPLOYMENT

*I*ndeed, six weeks later Ivy decided that her life *had* gotten worse—courtesy of the Jinx. She didn't know how, but she hadn't been killed yet—somehow at the last minute she'd been mysteriously pushed out of the way of a cement mixer, had miraculously outrun a pack of rabid chipmunks, and

74

avoided the banana peels that seemed literally to drop out of the sky.

Maybe I have a guardian angel, Ivy thought, and laughed grimly, picturing a once pink-cheeked cherub gone all gaunt and hollow eyed from over-work. It was no laughing matter, though. Ivy was failing in Tuna-on-Rye, Franny still wouldn't talk to her, Pru wouldn't even make eye contact, and Cat maintained at least a hundred-foot distance whenever possible.

And then, with only three weeks left in the school year, Ivy's teacher informed her that she "needn't come back tomorrow."

"Why not?" asked Ivy.

"Because you don't belong here anymore," the teacher said absently. She had never understood how Ivy ended up in her class in the first place, and was glad not to have to keep giving her Cs and Ds when all her other students got As. It brought the class average down.

"Well . . . where do I belong, then?" Ivy's lip trembled as she began to grasp the awful meaning of what the teacher was saying.

"I have no idea, dear," the teacher said, and hurried over to break up two students who were shouting about whether the exact value of pi could ever be calculated.

Ivy walked out of the room in a daze. *It was all the Jinx's fault!* She entered the grand hall, where the statue of Hieronymus Gumm stood tall and proud. She sat at his foot the way she had many weeks ago with Franny, and watched the elevators go up and down, and down and up, feeling as though she was no part of anything, and she wished that she were anybody else but herself. Ivy wished she were smart. She wished she didn't have stringy hair and ears that stuck out. Maybe then other kids would like her . . . maybe then she would have . . .

Ivy stood and walked slowly to the center of the atrium. She leaned over the stone brim of the wishing well. Its ancient frayed rope dangled uselessly, the weight of the gold bucket having snapped it many years before. Cold air from below blew up into her face, and Ivy shivered.

Still, it *was* a wishing well.

Ivy dug through her pockets and found a penny. She placed the coin between both hands as if in prayer and closed her eyes. "Friends," she whispered, and threw the penny. It hovered glinting in the air for a second before falling down into the gloom.

Looking up, Ivy watched all the students happily rushing to where they belonged, and she realized that she had absolutely nowhere to be. She couldn't even go home, Ivy thought sadly as she left the school. Her mother was trying so hard, and Ivy couldn't bear the thought of disappointing her. She felt more wretched and alone than ever.

As Ivy walked quickly past her house, it occurred to her that since she'd come to Sherbet, the only place she'd felt all right was at Mr. Staccato's. When she was there, she imagined the Jinx sulked outside, waiting for her, uncomfortable and out of place. And just the other day, Mr. Staccato had told her that he thought she was "very tenacious" when she had shown up for her lesson despite the several nasty stings she had received after being attacked on the playground by a swarm of bees.

Tenacious. That sounded like a good thing. She had looked the word up in the dictionary at school the next day and read: "Persistent; continuing even when faced with problems or difficulties." No one had ever told her she was tenacious before, and Ivy found herself thinking about this a lot. Sure, she might have a Jinx, but she was tenacious! Yes, Ivy loved her lessons with Mr. Staccato, even though they were difficult and she still could hardly play the piano at all.

To understand how Ivy felt about Mr. Staccato, think about that teacher who you perhaps didn't like at first because he or she was really hard, and never mentioned how terribly clever you were or even that you had good deportment. You didn't like that teacher, did you? But some kids did. In fact, some kids worked very hard for that teacher and didn't laugh at the unkind nickname that someone in the back of the room had come up with. And then one day you got a comment on your paper—that teacher was the only teacher who wrote comments—and it said you did a good job and it told you things about yourself that you'd never heard before, and you received a B+, which normally you would have had a hissy fit over, but that teacher hardly ever gave As, so a B+ really meant something. And you found that you actually looked forward to seeing that teacher now, and you wanted to read more comments from him or her, and maybe you'd even get an A someday. And then one day that teacher was out sick and you got a substitute teacher and the whole day was dull and boring and ruined, and much to your surprise you found yourself looking forward to the next day when you could see that teacher who had now become your favorite teacher. If you've ever had a teacher like that, then you will know what Mr. Staccato was like, and how Ivy felt about him.

Ivy climbed the steps to the porch of #7 Gumm Street. Her next lesson wasn't until the following week, but Ivy thought that maybe she could just sit in the waiting room and do her homework.

She gave the required three knocks and opened the door as usual, but neither dog was there to greet her. She began to have second thoughts about her impromptu visit, but she could not go home, not right away. So she tiptoed through the front entryway and into what she had come to think of as "the museum room." It was strange being in there alone. Ivy had always wanted to stop and look, but Fred and

Ginger always hurried her along. Ivy knew that snooping wasn't really the thing to do under such circumstances, but she quickly convinced herself that she was just "browsing." Besides, she couldn't stop herself if she wanted; there was so much to look at.

There was the curious cupboard with the opaque window in the middle that had caught her attention the very first day, and Ivy went to have a closer look. The cabinet door had a silver knob, and even though she was a little afraid, Ivy gave it a slight tug. It wouldn't open. She pulled harder, but it didn't budge.

It must be locked, she thought. Ivy knelt down and with her finger traced along some letters written in a silver decorative arc along the top of the door: WHAT IS MY UNIQUE TALENT?

Odd thing for a cupboard to say, Ivy thought, but then remembered that Mr. Staccato had used that same expression. "Unique talent," he had told her. "Everybody has one."

She turned her attention to some of the other things. Gleaming behind a glass case were milky white gloves, as well as a top hat and a black cane with a little card placed beside them saying, "*Top Hat*, circa 1935." There were all kinds of items in other cases: a cigar that had been partially smoked and a poster advertising a movie *The Cocoanuts*, which called it an "All Talking-Singing Musical Comedy Hit!"

There were framed photos arranged on a table. Ivy picked up one of Mr. Staccato. He was sitting in the booth of what looked like a fancy nightclub. Dressed in a tuxedo, he had his arm around the shoulders of a beautiful blond lady. They smiled merrily into the camera. The photo was in black and white, and like

everything else in the museum room, it looked like it was from many years ago, except . . . Mr. Staccato looked exactly the same age in the photo as he did now.

Ivy placed the picture back on the table. *Maybe I had better leave*, she was thinking guiltily when she spied something in a case in the far corner of the room. So extraordinary was this last oddity that it took her breath away, for behind the glass, winking and shimmering back at her, were seven ruby-red shoes. The card read:

> **Ruby-Red Slippers:** *The Wizard of Oz*, **circa 1939. There were many pairs of slippers made by Wardrobe. These are the last in existence from this classic MGM film.**

"Wow," whispered Ivy. How did Mr. Staccato get so many of them? The sequins on the slippers sparkled just like real rubies. One shoe in particular glittered so in the light from the little crystal lamps that Ivy was mesmerized; she jumped when she heard a gasp behind her.

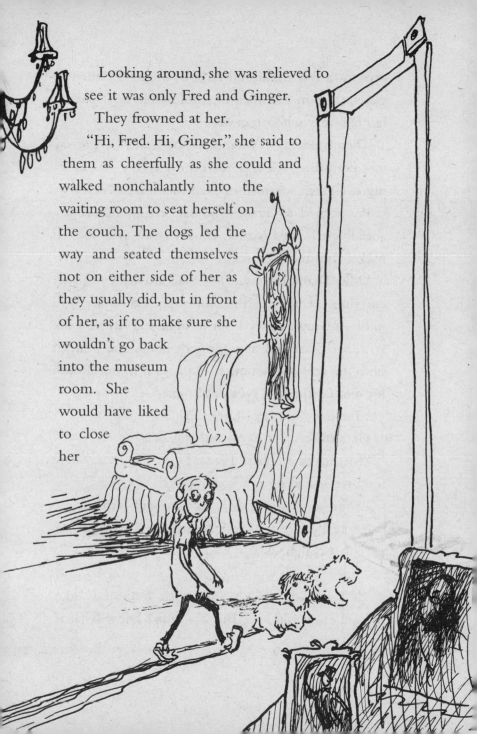

Looking around, she was relieved to
see it was only Fred and Ginger.
They frowned at her.
"Hi, Fred. Hi, Ginger," she said to
them as cheerfully as she could and
walked nonchalantly into the
waiting room to seat herself on
the couch. The dogs led the
way and seated themselves
not on either side of her as
they usually did, but in front
of her, as if to make sure she
wouldn't go back
into the museum
room. She
would have liked
to close
her

eyes for a few minutes, but both dogs continued to glare at her in the most uncomfortable way, making her feel very self-conscious.

Then suddenly Ivy thought she heard Ginger say in a perturbed voice, "Did you ever?" Ivy was looking at Ginger, when from Fred she heard, "Never!"

Ivy turned to Fred, who sat staring innocently ahead. She looked hard at Ginger again, who looked back at Ivy and sneezed.

"Miss Diamond!" said Mr. Staccato with surprise, entering the room. "I'm not supposed to see you until—" Ginger dashed out of sight and rushed back with Mr. Staccato's appointment book. She jumped onto the arm of the couch and held it in her mouth for him to inspect. "Not until next . . ."

"Tuesday," said Ivy. "Um . . . sir."

He looked up at her over his glasses.

"Mr. Staccato . . . sir," Ivy said, "can't I just stay here for a while and do my homework?"

"Your homework?" Mr. Staccato said, startled.

"Actually, um . . . Mr. Staccato, what I would like is—" Ivy coughed.

"Yes?"

"I was going to ask you, what I mean is, like, hmmm . . . could I—" But Ivy didn't know what to say. What she really needed was a friend, a father, a good place to live, and mainly not to have a Jinx, but how could she ask for these things from her piano teacher? The longer Ivy sat there, the larger an awful feeling in her heart swelled until it filled her throat and was about to pour from her eyes as tears. But Ivy did not cry. Instead, she settled on the next best thing.

"Could I have . . . a job?" Ivy asked.

"Did you ever?" said Fred.

"Never!" sniffed Ginger.

"That'll do, dogs," Mr. Staccato warned.

"I can do things," Ivy said, gaining confidence. Mr. Staccato hadn't said no, after all! "I can pick up your groceries and bring in your newspaper, and I . . ." She tried to think of something else useful that she could do. Ivy looked at Fred and Ginger, who were still frowning. "I can wash out the dog bowls!"

At this they grinned, wagged their tails, and looked expectantly at Mr. Staccato.

"I suppose I could use some help," he said hesitantly. "I am getting on." He quickly added, "It will have to be a business arrangement, though. I'll give you your lessons free in exchange."

Ivy nodded her head up and down. "Okay."

"And how often did you have in mind?" Mr.

Staccato asked. "Say, three days a week?"

"Oh, I'll just come, maybe . . . every day?" Ivy replied. "If that's all right with you and all."

Mr. Staccato raised his eyebrows and looked at Ivy over his glasses again.

"And I'll come right after school—three o'clock on the dot!" she added.

"You must be punctual."

"Punctual," she agreed.

"And conscientious."

"I can be conscientious, too, I promise. I'll be really, really tenacious, Mr. Staccato, sir."

"Then let's shake," he said.

They shook hands. "Now I must get ready for my next student!" Mr. Staccato said, and went into his music room.

"Mr. Staccato?" Ivy asked.

He was just about to close the door.

"Are you really one hundred and fifteen years old?"

"Actually, I'm one hundred twenty-two," he said. "Curious, isn't it?" And then he closed the door.

Ivy found the kitchen, washed out Fred's and Ginger's bowls, tied up her teacher's old newspapers for recycling, and took out the garbage. With a soft rag, she carefully dusted the furniture and straightened the pictures under the watchful eyes of Fred and Ginger while Mr. Staccato taught his four-o'clock student. Long after the five-o'clock student had gone and Mr. Staccato had turned on the lights, Ivy continued, plumping the cushions and rearranging the silverware drawer. At last Mr. Staccato said, "That'll do, Miss Diamond," and Ivy had no recourse but to leave.

Ivy hadn't thought about her problems once since she'd been at Mr. Staccato's. As soon as she stepped outside into the circle of buttery lamplight from his front porch, however, Ivy could see they were all there waiting for her.

The Jinx still lurked in some dark hiding place, the teacher at school was once more saying, "You don't belong here anymore," and even the wind seemed to be whispering to her in her own voice, wishing *Friends*. . . .

Ivy looked back longingly at Mr. Staccato's, the only place she felt safe. As she did, her shadow, cast in that circle of light, changed alarmingly before her eyes into a hypnotic oily swirl, angry and dark. She held her breath and backed away, not daring to wait and see what final grotesque form it would take. Ivy ran for all she was worth.

She raced down Gumm Street toward her vine-choked house. The upstairs windows were blackened like eye sockets in a skull, but one light glowed downstairs, which meant that her mother was home. If only Ivy could get there! But coming right toward her was Franny.

"Ivy!" Franny yelled, and grabbed her by the arm. Ivy tried to pull away.

"Ivy!" shouted Franny again. "You heard the news!" She pulled Ivy by her hand toward the wedding-cake house.

"What news?" Ivy said, gasping for air as Franny dragged her up the stairs and into her tower room.

"You're in *my* class now!" said Franny, who could hardly contain her joy. She and Ivy could be in Liverwurst together! Who cared about Pru and Cat when Ivy was in her class?

"Hey, are you all right?" Franny asked. She closed the door of the tower room behind them.

"I'm all right," Ivy said, and looked out Franny's window. She cupped her hands alongside her face to block out the light of the tower room. Out in the darkness, the moon peeped through some clouds that scudded across an ultramarine sky. But there were no shadows or strange shapes. There was nothing there except the twinkling lights of Sherbet below.

Ivy thought about her wish earlier at Hieronymus Gumm's well. "I'm all right, now," Ivy repeated, and turned to make sure Franny was really there—because as you know, Ivy wasn't used to having her wishes coming true.

CAT'S CONJURATION

Cat had risen early and gone out horseback riding, hoping it would clear her head. Unhappy at being taken out of his cozy stall without his breakfast, her pony's ears pointed back in the direction from which he had come as he poked along the sandy road toward the beach. Cat irritably dug her heels into his sides to get him to move a little faster. She was not in a very good mood, either.

Lately she'd been overwhelmed with ESP insights. She knew exactly when the pizza deliveryman would arrive. She had taken to answering the phone before it rang. She knew that River, Chakra, Jagger, and Dylan's baseball team would win, while Lennon, OM, Bowie, Skye, Storm, and Ziggy's soccer team would lose. But what she really wanted to know remained annoyingly elusive. What had she seen in class the day the new girl, Ivy, arrived?

Cat had seen the thing many times since then as well. Even more disturbing, she seemed to be the only one who could see the dark feral shape following Ivy around, and hear its sharp toenails clicking against the smooth hard floor of the school. Why was this?

"Stupid ESP," Cat muttered, and absently brushed the pony's mane over to the right.

A waning crescent moon lazed in the west. Cat thought it was cool to see the moon in the morning after the sun was up. It seemed like a good time to do ESP—that is, if she could figure out how.

Cat shut her eyes and tried to concentrate—it was a strange sensation riding this way, kind of fun, and

Cat giggled. Getting serious again, she wished she knew something magical to chant. She'd seen her mother close her eyes and in a spooky voice say, "Have you a message for me?"

"Have you a message for me?" Cat whispered. A few minutes passed and nothing happened. "Have you a message for me?" she repeated, feeling a little silly. But all was quiet except for the waves breaking on the shore in the distance.

"It's useless." Cat sighed.

Cat opened her eyes and shortened her reins. *I'd better pay attention to riding,* she thought, and it was then, when Cat looked around, that she realized she was no longer on the sandy road.

She stopped and twisted in the saddle to look behind her, then remembered an old trail that forked off the main road. Her pony must have taken a turn while she'd been concentrating on her ESP. It was hushed and much dimmer here because the trees had grown close together. Early-morning fog settled sleepily along the ground, and moisture clung to the leaves and dripped off tangled vines. She turned the pony around and headed back the way she had come. The pony thought he was going home and began to pull and jig anxiously.

"Stop it," Cat said sharply. She tightened the reins and gripped him more securely with her legs. The hair on the sides of the pony's neck where the reins rubbed had started to turn dark with sweat, and he jumped at the sound of twigs snapping beneath his hooves. She was wishing they would hurry up and get back to the sandy road, when suddenly there was a loud *SHOOSH!*

The pony shied, and Cat lost her balance. She grabbed for the mane and tried to pull herself back into the saddle, but she had lost her stirrup and her leg had slipped halfway up the pony's side. With her

arms around his neck she tried to right herself and almost did, when there was another loud *SHOOSH!*

The pony bucked and bolted. Cat was thrown out of the saddle.

As she fell, she looked up through the dense trees. Between the branches she could see the sky filled with an enormous green hot-air balloon, which floated down in slow motion.

Cat landed hard. "Crap!" she shouted. The pony galloped away down the trail, the stirrups banging at his sides, urging him on even faster. This would definitely get back to Pru when the pony showed up at the stable without a rider. Pru would tell everyone— *"Cat Lemonjello isn't as great a rider as she thinks she is!"*

"Crap!" Cat yelled again, and punched the ground with her fists.

"You should have your mouth washed out with soap!" The very loud, very deep voice sounded like it was right next to her.

Cat was too annoyed to be startled or afraid. She looked all around and there was no one there.

"Is that your balloon, mister?" Cat said, because if it was, she wanted him to know that thanks to him she'd just fallen off her pony.

"I *said*"—the voice came from behind her this

time—"you should have your mouth washed out with soap!"

"Oh yeah?" Cat still could see no one. She stood up angrily, slapping dirt and leaves from her pants. "Where are you?"

"I am everywhere," answered the voice, "but to the eyes of common mortals, I am invisible."

"Oh, for crying out loud!" Cat stomped off down the trail toward the road. She wasn't in the mood for games.

"I could turn you into a mulberry bush! Or a piece of taffy, if I wanted," the voice said less ominously from above her.

Cat stopped. For the first time, she noticed a clearing up ahead. Rising above the treetops was the green balloon she had seen floating down.

Still aggravated, Cat made her way toward it. "Go ahead, I dare you!"

"Stop right where you are, if you know what's good for you...." the deep voice threatened, but not quite as convincingly as before.

"I've always wanted to be a piece of taffy," Cat said, swiping away some vines. Standing there in the basket of the balloon, wincing, was probably the most ordinary-looking little old bald wrinkled man she'd had ever seen in her life. Cat forgot about being mad

and started to laugh. "*You're* going to turn me into taffy?" She snorted.

"I can't turn you into taffy or anything else for that matter," he said defensively. "The point is, what do you want?"

"What do *I* want?" Cat said with exasperation. "I don't want anything—except my pony back."

"Well, then, why on earth did you conjure me?" the old man said impatiently.

"Conjure you?" Cat said. She took a step back. Looking at the old man now, Cat suddenly had the most overwhelming feeling that she had seen him somewhere before . . . but where? "You mean like I made you up . . . in my . . . mind?"

"For someone with ESP, you sure don't know much." The

96

old man shook his head in disgust. "You brought me here because of that thingamajig following Ivy Diamond around, remember?"

"Exactly," Cat said. "So?"

The old man yawned. "It's nothing more than your run-of-the-mill Jinx." He then licked his finger and held it out as if he were checking the wind direction.

"Jinx?" Cat said backing away.

"Ah–h–h–h, don't worry about *him*." The old man waved his hand, dismissing the entire subject.

"Who?"

"The Jinx." He snorted and shaded his eyes and looked up into the sky.

"Phew!" said Cat, relieved. "That's good!"

"Kid, you've got w-a-a-a-a-y bigger problems than that Jinx!"

"I do?" Cat said.

The wind kicked up, blowing the balloon sideways. "Whoa, Nellie!" the old man exclaimed as he lost his balance for a moment. "You've got some b-i-i-i-i-g weather coming in from the west." He held onto the ropes of the balloon, looked skyward again, and sniffed the air. "Old Hurricane Cha-Cha—when she hits, watch out! She's one nasty little gal."

"Hurricane Cha-Cha? " Cat asked nervously. "We

don't *have* hurricanes in Sherbet."

"Well, you will, and that's not all! Then . . . you got your backwards tidal wave headed this way."

"Backwards tidal wave?" Cat wondered if it was possible to conjure a lunatic. "How can that be?"

"Forwards tidal waves curl forwards and crash down on ya." As he spoke, the old man pulled up one of the sandbags that were keeping the balloon grounded. "Backwards tidal waves curl backwards and lift ya up, up, and aw-a-a-a-y!"

"I'm sorry, but I don't believe in backwards tidal waves," Cat said, getting angry all over again—he still hadn't told her anything!

"Yeah, well, suit yourself!" the old man grunted as he busied himself with sandbags. "But many things are backwards that you thought were forwards, kid; you'll learn that soon enough." He fired up the jets. *SHOOSH!* "Yep, no doubt about it, backwards tidal wave. I feel it comin'. Feel it in my bones—if I had bones, that is." He poked the air with a finger. "You be careful, kid!"

"Wait!" Cat yelled. "Who are you?"

"Oh, now where's the fun if I told you all that?" The old man grinned mischievously, and the balloon began to rise.

"But you didn't tell me *anything!*" Cat screamed. "What about my message?"

He shouted back, "Hieronymus Gumm"—*SHOOSH!*—"behind!"

"What?" Cat screamed. The jets from the balloon made it difficult for Cat to hear. She ran through the woods after the balloon.

The old man was laughing. "Wishing"—*SHOOSH!*—"wel-l-l-l-l-l!" he called back, his laughter fading away.

The balloon drifted up into the sky. Cat slowed to a jog and finally stopped. As she watched the old man sail away, she felt her eyes growing heavier and heavier until she could barely keep them open. *SHOOSH . . . BOOM! SHOOSH . . . BOOM!*

Cat opened her eyes.

She was sitting on her pony at the end of the sandy road, staring at the beach. A stiff wind churned the water, which looked angry and cold. The tide was coming in. *SHOOSH . . .* a wave crashed on the shore. *BOOM!* And then another, and then another. Over the ocean a hot-air balloon with the initials O.Z. flew toward the horizon and then dipped behind a cloud with a green flash of lightning before disappearing completely from sight.

MR. STACCATO'S STORY

*I*t was a little over a week before the recital, and Ivy was at Mr. Staccato's practicing her piece. Most kids don't like to practice—we know, for example, that Franny abhorred it—but to Ivy, practicing was a relief because for that one hour it seemed like there was no Jinx. Thank heavens his expiration date would arrive in a little over a week!

The lesson ended. Ivy put away her music and went to the museum room to get her feather duster. Ivy ran the duster over the old books and remembered how upset Fred and Ginger had been the first day she'd gone there to clean it. They had even fetched Mr. Staccato out of his lesson—something never done except in the case of dire emergencies. He had come out and said, "Don't fret, dogs, Miss Diamond will be very careful, won't you, Miss Diamond?"

And she *was* very careful, but whenever Ivy was in that room she couldn't take her eyes off the ruby-red slippers shimmering inside the glass case. One time she thought she saw a shoe move ever so slightly. Another time it seemed to have a silver halo of light around it. But when she looked closer, the halo was gone, leaving Ivy standing there gazing and wondering if it was just her imagination.

Ivy dusted her way over to the table with the yellowing photos on it. She picked up the picture of Mr. Staccato and the beautiful blond woman, ignoring the disapproving comments from Fred and Ginger—"Did you ever?" said one. "Never!" said the other.

It was Friday, and Mr. Staccato's lessons were over early. Ivy had been waiting for just this kind of opportunity, because she had something on her mind. After the last student had left, Ivy carried the photo into the music room, sat on the piano bench, and said, "Mr. Staccato, sir, um, can I ask you a question?"

"Yes, Miss Diamond, what is it?" He was putting away several books of scales.

Ivy held the photo up. "When was this taken?"

Mr. Staccato looked at the picture and then quickly looked away. "1938," he said. Fred and Ginger hurried over to their master and glared at Ivy.

"But that was . . ." Ivy thought for a few seconds. "That was over sixty years ago . . . and—"

"I don't look any older." Mr. Staccato walked out of the music room, beckoning Ivy to follow. Entering the museum room, he stood before the ruby-red shoes glittering in their case. "And you would like to know why that is."

"I just . . . um . . . I don't know, I was just wonder-ing . . . that's all."

"In almost a week, it will have been seven years ago that I first came to Sherbet." Mr. Staccato sighed and walked slowly over to a leather chair. Easing him-self into it, he motioned for Ivy to have a seat across from him. He leaned toward the strange locked cup-board with the window in the middle of it. Mr. Staccato muttered something, and Ivy almost said, "What?" because she thought he might be talking to her. Immediately the door popped open, and Ivy couldn't help wondering if it was the words he had said that unlocked the door. He took out a little glass and poured himself some sherry from a crystal de-canter. Next he took out a tin of cookies and gave one each to Fred and Ginger. Reaching inside the cupboard a third time, he handed Ivy a cup along with the cookie tin.

Ivy looked at her cup. She had no idea how he had done it, but it was full of hot tea, complete with milk and sugar. Ivy nodded a thank-you and tried to steal a look into the cupboard as he was closing it to see what else could be inside, but he was too fast. She set-tled into her chair and took a bite from a cookie.

Ginger jumped up on Mr. Staccato's lap, and he

scratched behind her ears as he began to speak. "In order to know about the photo, you must know about the ruby-red slippers!" He closed his eyes for a moment. "I came to America many years ago to seek my fortune, and I was able to get a job in vaudeville right away."

"What's vaudeville?" Ivy wanted to know.

"Before there were movies or television, there was the stage—vaudeville. There were all kinds of performers—comedians, singers, dancers, ventriloquists, jugglers, anything you could think of. My job, of course, was to play the piano for them all."

"Did you like it?" Ivy asked.

"I did at first. It was wonderfully jolly, staying up late and sleeping in the morning, traveling the country. It was while I was employed

in vaudeville that I met Mrs. Staccato." Mr. Staccato pulled absently at a stray thread on the arm of his chair.

"I didn't know there was a Mrs. Staccato," Ivy said softly.

Mr. Staccato continued, "She was a dancer. We fell in love and married. Then movies became all the rage, and people were no longer interested in seeing vaudeville. Mrs. Staccato and I were tired of traveling anyway, so we headed to Hollywood, where we figured we would easily find work."

"And did you?" asked Ivy.

"Yes, straight away, and things were marvelous." Mr. Staccato leaned on one elbow and smiled at his recollections. "It was all tuxedos and ball gowns, movie stars and fabulous dinner parties where everyone was frightfully glamorous. And from every movie I worked on, I took some item of memorabilia, which is what you see here." Mr. Staccato waved his hand at the cases.

"So the picture was taken at one of these parties?" Ivy said.

"Yes. It was the late thirties, and I was working on a film called *The Wizard of Oz*. The party was to celebrate the opening of the film."

"I've seen that movie!" Ivy said. The dogs looked up briefly, wagged their tails, and then went back to their cookies.

"I had my eye on those ruby-red slippers, as a gift for Mrs. Staccato, and when the movie was completed, I was able to buy three pairs from Wardrobe."

"Three and a half pairs," Ivy corrected, knowing that there were actually seven shoes.

"Three pairs," Mr. Staccato repeated, "of ruby-red slippers. I also bought one shoe that was . . . different. At the time I didn't think anything of it, and just put it with the others and forgot about it."

"Did Mrs. Staccato like the shoes?" Ivy asked.

Mr. Staccato sadly shook his head.

"She didn't like them?" said Ivy. "*I* would have liked them!"

Mr. Staccato looked down, "Shortly after I gave them to her, Mrs. Staccato passed away."

Fred and Ginger sniffled.

"That's awful," whispered Ivy.

"The flu," said Mr. Staccato, handing Fred his handkerchief. "I was very sad for a very long time. Life had lost its meaning, and nothing mattered any longer to me."

Ginger howled.

"That'll do, Ginger," Mr. Staccato said reprovingly. "I just chucked it all—the movies, the glamour, the money, my job. A week after she . . . passed on, I packed a few articles of clothing plus my collection of what you see here, and I got in my car and just drove and drove, losing all track of time. And then one afternoon, off in the distance, I saw a most unusual thing. It was a rainbow, but formed of colors I had never seen before in a rainbow—emerald greens and touches of silver. It was most strange. 'Well,' I thought, 'That's it, Staccato, you've finally gone round the bend!'" Mr. Staccato was speaking more quickly now. Ivy listened, a half-eaten cookie in her hand.

"I headed in that direction, and by and by I found myself driving over the bridge that leads into Sherbet. I will never forget crossing the Sherbet Avenue Bridge. I actually could *feel* the clouds of despair that I had been living with for so long float away in moments."

"But, Mr. Staccato?" Ivy interrupted. "When did you leave Hollywood?"

"1940," he answered.

"But you said you came to Sherbet seven years ago." Ivy said.

Mr. Staccato looked at Ivy calmly but did not speak.

"If you came here seven years ago and you left Hollywood in 1940, where were you for"—Ivy counted on her fingers—"for fifty-nine years?"

"My dear," Mr. Staccato said, raising one eyebrow, "I have absolutely *no* idea."

He remained silent for a few moments, deep in thought. The room was dappled with late-afternoon sunshine, but Ivy felt a chill and wished she had more than her thin T-shirt. Mr. Staccato continued his story.

"I checked into the Sherbet Plaza Hotel, and for the first time since my loss, I slept soundly. I awoke refreshed and decided to take a walk and find out just what kind of marvelous place I had wandered into. I walked for many hours, and finally ended up on this very street. And there I saw this house, a lovely cottage which reminded me of my childhood home in England. It had a For Sale sign on the lawn, and as I stood there admiring it, a little wrinkled elderly chap came to the door, as if he'd been expecting me. I will never forget his words. 'Thank goodness you've come!' is what he said. He invited me in, and as he showed me around, I noticed that he seemed very unwell. When I mentioned this, he made light of it, and said that the dogs took very good care of him!"

"I remember you said that they came with the house," Ivy said.

"Along with a few *other* items," Mr. Staccato replied mysteriously.

Fred and Ginger both nodded to confirm this and then turned back toward their master.

"The old man insisted I stay for a while. He said that he had recently become interested in collecting, just like myself, and wouldn't I like to see his first acquisition? In spite of my rising alarm, for he was extremely short of breath, I humored him. To my complete shock, he showed me a shoe that was the mate of the odd one I had bought in Hollywood."

Mr. Staccato stiffly got out of his chair and went over to the case that held the slippers.

"But it looks just like the others," said Ivy. "I don't understand why—"

"I have *disguised* it to look like the others, my dear!" Mr. Staccato replied, and Ivy thought he looked troubled.

"But why—" Ivy began.

Mr. Staccato held up his hand to hush her. He paced the room slowly now as he spoke, his eyes returning over and over to the case with the ruby-red slippers.

"I was very surprised to see that shoe. When I asked him how he had found it, he replied most mysteriously that on the contrary, *it* had found *him*! He said that he merely had it for safekeeping until the *real* owner arrived. When I asked who that might be, he answered slyly, 'You will know her, dear boy, when you see her.' He chuckled and said he had a feeling I had 'a unique talent' for it.

"By then my desire to own this house was overwhelming. I offered him a check right then and there. He was delighted, and said that I could move in the next morning. He had been wanting to go for the longest time but couldn't until he found just the right owner. Then he said I should keep my money because where he was going he wouldn't be needing it! I insisted, though, and placed the check in his hand.

"The hour was very late by then, and I offered to help him to his bed. He waved me off, saying he was fine, and that there was more I needed to know."

"More you needed to know about what?" Ivy asked.

"About the shoes!" The case sparkled, illuminating the twilit room for a brief instant. Mr. Staccato went back to his chair and sat again, lacing his fingers across his chest.

"He spun fantastical stories, and was rambling about the powers the shoes possessed. Most of what he said I dismissed as the delusions of old age. At this point my host became subdued, as if the effort of telling the story had drained him of his remaining dregs of energy. Finally, he made me promise to return at dawn. But, he said, if there was a storm, I should come right away with *my* shoe and get the other shoe. He was adamant that not just anyone could fill these shoes, and under no circumstances was I to give the pair to *anybody* except the true owner! I asked how on earth I would know the true owner, and he replied, 'Consider both sides, my boy. Both forwards and backwards! Then and only then will you know the true owner of the shoes!' I promised, although the request was odd, and left.

"Back in my room, it seemed like a dream. I was sure the next day he would decide to keep the house after all. But I was tired and soon went to sleep. It would not be for long, though; perhaps an hour later I awoke to the thrashing of rain against my window, and thunder and lightning of a magnitude that I had not heard before nor since. The wind was howling, and my first thought was of the old man. I quickly dressed and ran back. Halfway down Gumm Street, I stopped and stood unbelieving in the drenching rain. Above the house a figure floated up into the clouds and disappeared into the night. I ran as fast as I could to the old man's house. His two dogs were there—I had not caught their names and ended up having to name them—but . . . he was gone."

"Do you mean . . . dead?" Ivy asked, her eyes wide.

Fred and Ginger looked up at Mr. Staccato with the same question in their eyes.

"He was just . . . gone. Not there. I never heard another thing from him, the check was never cashed . . . he had simply vanished."

Ivy sat mulling this over. "The old man . . . he's not dead," Ivy said, quite certain.

"How do you know?" asked Mr. Staccato.

"He's magic," Ivy declared. "Magical people don't die; everybody knows that." As she spoke, Ivy realized that maybe Mr. Staccato might be magical. Look at how old he was! "I think you're magical, too," Ivy went on. "You might even live forever!"

Mr. Staccato said softly, "I'm not going to live forever, my dear."

Fred and Ginger, horrified, shook their heads back and forth no.

Ivy didn't want to hear any of it, either. "Mr.

Staccato, you'll *always* be here."

"Oh, good heavens, I wouldn't want to go doing *that* now, would I?" he said.

"Why not?" said Ivy.

"My dear, whatever would I do for all eternity? Seems rather tiresome, don't you think? And besides, nothing lasts forever—not me, not you, not Gumm Street or Sherbet . . . not even the North Star. And if the North Star can't last, how do you think poor old Mr. Staccato can?"

Ivy sat there staring at the pattern on the carpeting feeling very deflated and sad. Yes, sometimes people *did* go away forever. An ordinary person could go out to buy Listerine, mayonnaise, and Pop-Tarts, and not return. But Mr. Staccato was different. He was magic.

"So there it is, my dear." Mr. Staccato leaned back in his chair. "And I'm very tired now, and it's getting late. . . ."

"Yes sir," Ivy said, getting up. She thanked him for the tea, and Fred and Ginger showed her to the door.

10

Sunday, June 15, 2:30 A.M.

Cat kicked the covers off and lay in the darkness, thinking.

Friday had been the last day of school. Cat smiled.

A string of lazy summer days stretched out before her—no more tests, no more memorizing boring stuff, no more weird Ivy, no more Pru. And, hopefully, no more conjuring little old bald men in green balloons.

She put her legs up over her head and tried to balance her pillow on her feet.

There was only one day between Cat and her freedom, and that was today, the day of Mr. Staccato's recital. Pru would be there, there was no escaping that, and the more Cat thought about it, the more restless she became. She flipped the pillow in the air, caught it between her knees, and placed it back on her feet. *I've always been Mr. Staccato's best student*, she thought, and bounced the pillow up in the air again. *Mr. Staccato never actually says it*, she mused, *but everybody knows it*.

Tired of the game, she let the pillow fall. *I wonder what Pru is playing today?* Cat closed her eyes and thought as hard as she could. Little sparkles appeared before her tightly shut eyes and then a vision of Pru. She was at the piano, but she wasn't playing. It was like she was made out of stone, and then she stood and hardly anyone clapped! Pru looked humiliated!

Cool, thought Cat and grabbed a flashlight and a new copy of her mother's *Groovy I Ching*. She had taken to consulting it so frequently that she had purchased her own copy, thus avoiding midnight excursions into her mother's office. Cat slid open the small drawer by her bed that held the three pennies she used these days.

"What effect will Mr. Staccato's recital have on my life for the summer?" she asked.

The answer was disturbing: CRITICAL MASS.

It explained:

Bummer!
Heavy stuff is coming down.
Grab your backpack and leave town.
No yoga pose or meditation
will help you in this situation!

Heavy stuff? What did *that* mean? *I'm just a kid*, Cat thought; *I can't leave town! Where am I supposed to go? What's going to happen?* Ordinarily Cat would have laughed off the *Groovy I Ching*'s advice as just a lot of her mother's New Age mumbo jumbo, but she couldn't laugh off the anxiety she'd been feeling since that Ivy girl came to town. *She's probably going to be there today as well. . . .*

Cat brushed the coins into the drawer next to her bed, threw the *I Ching* in there, shut the drawer, and lay back down under the covers.

It's going to be a great summer, Cat told herself, drawing her knees up to her chest. *I hope.*

SUNDAY, JUNE 15, 10:00 A.M.

When Pru awoke the morning of the recital, she could hardly believe the day had actually arrived. The date had been an abstract number floating coolly off in the distance. She had been waiting and waiting, and now today was the day! Pru was raring to go! Pru was ready for the big time! Pru was . . . terrified right out of her mind.

What I need is some water, Pru decided. Safety Tip #1039: Always drink eight 8-ounce glasses of water a day to prevent eczema, sinus pressure, gout, kidney stones, dizziness, fatigue, halitosis, and gas. She reached for the glass on her night table and took a gulp.

Oh my God . . . She swallowed several times. Was her throat sore? She clutched her hand to her neck and swallowed again, this time as hard as she could. Yes! Her throat was sore and her stomach kind of hurt and her head ached . . . she was definitely coming down with something. Pru drank half the glass and then pulled her comforter up to her chin. The thing to do was to keep warm and drink plenty of fluids; getting up now would be very, very bad.

It was a shame, too, after all her practice, because if she stayed home she couldn't go through with Project Star of the Recital, the thing that would prove once and for all, in public, that she was better than Cat.

Wait, Pru thought, *I've* got *to do this!* She put her legs over the side of bed and examined her tongue in the mirror.

Was it coated? No. Red and blotchy? No. She opened her mouth wide. Signs of white patches on her throat? The roof of her mouth? No . . . and no. Maybe she wasn't sick after all, but she *was* kind of cold. *I will get up and get dressed now and have something warm to drink—warm is good—but maybe first I'll get a cool compress. . . .*

SUNDAY, JUNE 15, 1:45 P.M.

Make something good happen today. Make something good happen today. Make something good happen today, Ivy repeated over and over to herself the day of the recital. She stood very still in her room listening for scratching sounds, sniffing sounds, skittering sounds, but there were none. Ivy heaved a sigh of relief. She felt lighter and freer than she had in . . . well, seven years, to be exact.

Today was a new day—it was the first day of the rest of her life without the Jinx! Even though it was already clear that she was no Cat or Pru when it came to the piano, Ivy's hope was that she would play really well now! *Make something good happen today,* she thought again.

Out the window, it was sunny with the promise of a beautiful summer to look forward to. Franny and Ivy planned to go to the recital together, where Ivy's mother would meet them. Pearl had just left. There was a sale on rhinestone scrunchies that she had been looking forward to all week.

Franny arrived at #5 Gumm just as Ivy was trying to figure out what to wear. She didn't have too many choices. There was the T-shirt with the glue spots; a pair of jeans embroidered with two big-eyed sad kittens on the back pockets; a sweatshirt with "You Go, Girl!" written out in sequins; a couple of patriotic spangled sweaters; some skirts and shirts in assorted candy colors that made her eyeteeth ache; and a little holiday number with a Christmas tree on it that had seen better days.

"I know," said Franny, taking off her sweater and the "Carpe Diem!" T-shirt underneath, "wear this!"

"I don't know." Ivy hesitated.

"It's new," Franny cajoled, still holding out the shirt.

"Oh, all right," said Ivy. She put it on. The shirt hung almost down to her knees like a tunic.

Happy now, Franny sat in the old hammock that served as Ivy's bed and began swinging back and forth.

Ivy combed her hair over her face. "I hate my hair," she said.

"Everybody hates their hair," said Franny. "Want me to cut it?"

"Do you know how?"

"Sure," said Franny. "How hard can it be?"

"I don't know, Franny." Ivy wasn't sure this was such a good idea, but Franny had already run off to collect some haircutting things.

Now, Ivy had very long hair that was very thin, and if you know anything about haircutting then you will know that thin hair is the most difficult and unforgiving kind of hair to cut. As soon as Franny cut one side short, she found that she had to cut the other side shorter.

"Franny . . . !" Ivy put her hand to her head and screamed. "How much are you cutting off? I thought you knew how to cut hair!"

"I thought I did, too," said Franny, her brows knitted in concentration. "But I can fix it, I know I can—just give me a minute."

Franny cut and cut and snipped and combed.

"Hurry up, Franny!" Ivy said impatiently. "It's getting late!"

Franny snipped away. "I think I've almost got it. There. Done."

Ivy ran to the mirror to see her reflection. "Look at me!" she wailed.

Franny stood behind her. Even she had to admit

she had made a complete mess of Ivy's hair. "Do you have a hat?"

"NO!" yelled Ivy.

"How about a scarf? A headband? Big barrette?"

Ivy brushed as much hair off herself as she could. "Forget it!" she cried. "It's beyond help. Let's just go!"

Ivy and Franny raced down the stairs of #5 Gumm Street. The wind blew cold through what little bit was left of Ivy's hair, and she felt an unpleasant prickle on her exposed scalp. *The day* has *to improve*, she thought. After all, the Jinx was gone now—wasn't it?

THE RECITAL

Cat took a little bow. She had played well, as she always did—and even with a bare minimum of practice, too! She had picked just the right music: a bouncy little tune, the kind that made you tap your foot and feel happy. The audience was applauding and her brothers River, Chakra, and

Dylan were whistling, while Lennon, OM, Skye, Storm, and Ziggy stomped their feet. Jagger, sitting at the end of the row, laughed, and Bowie jumped up and shouted, "Way to go, Cat!"

Cat went back to her seat and watched Pru step up to the piano. Pru was as white as the sheet music she was placing on the stand with visibly shaking hands, and Cat couldn't help but feel a warm glow at seeing the smug look that Pru usually had on her face replaced with outright terror.

Pru herself felt as wooden as the bench she was sitting on. What was she *doing* here on a Sunday dressed up in organdy, velvet, and patent leather, in front of all these people? She had been planning for this day for so long, and now the only place she

wanted to be was under a fuzzy blanket reading a book.

Pru started to play.

Cat put her hand over her mouth to hide the smile that was forming, because Pru was playing very hesitantly, even hitting some wrong notes. As Pru continued, however, something changed. The longer Pru played, the more sure she became. The audience was captivated, and it became more and more evident that Pru was achieving something that Cat had not.

Cat scanned the audience for Mr. Staccato and saw him a few rows back, his head tilted to one side as he watched. He leaned forwards, one hand supporting his chin, his attention more focused than Cat remembered him *ever* being when she played. Cat even found *herself* being drawn in and touched by Pru's performance, much as she hated to admit it. No doubt about it, Pru was doing well, and Cat didn't like it one bit.

While Pru was enchanting everyone, Ivy and Franny were running down Gumm Street as fast as they could.

Ivy reached Mr. Staccato's porch first, never breaking stride, her feet barely touching the steps as she took two at a time. She flew in through the open front door, raced through the museum room, and stopped at the entrance to the waiting room to listen. She could hear the sound of piano music and walked softly across the carpet of the waiting room so as not to disturb the recital taking place behind the cream-colored doors. Ivy turned the handle on the doors quietly and slowly tiptoed in as unobtrusively as possible.

There were very few things in this world Franny hated more than being left behind—Amelia Earhart would never be left behind! Neither would Sir Edmund Hillary! Thinking of nothing beyond catching up to Ivy, Franny thundered up the porch steps. She stumbled through the front door, tried to right herself on her way through the museum room, and almost succeeded by the time she hit the waiting room.

But then she skidded to a halt, and the rug flew out from under her feet. She crashed into the cream-colored doors, which burst open with such force that

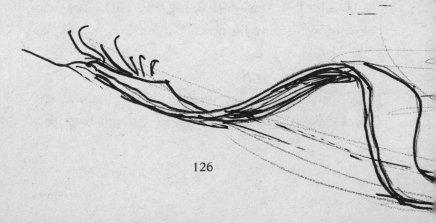

every man, woman, child, and dog turned around.

Pru had stopped playing, and the room was perfectly silent— except for the word "klutz" that came from where Cat and her brothers were sitting.

Ivy caught a glimpse of Mr. Staccato, his face surprised and frowning at the same time. She could feel her own face burning red as she helped Franny up.

"Did you ever?"

"Never!"

"Excuse us," Ivy said in a small voice.

"Sorry," said Franny. They squeezed past the back row to two seats in an obscure corner of the room.

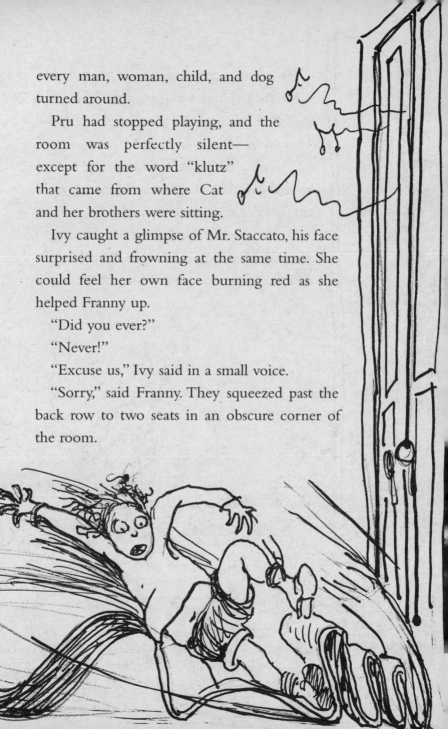

The audience turned back to Pru, but what they found was Pru with one hand raised and the other frozen in place on the keys.

She scanned the music frantically to find where she'd left off, but the black scrawl of the notes danced confusingly before her eyes. She might as well have been trying to read Chinese for all the sense it made.

The audience waited for fifteen awful

seconds before Pru finally looked at them and said, "Oh, forget it."

From rows three and four (those reserved for the Lemonjello clan) came the sound of snickering, followed by some sniggering, which turned into guffaws, that evolved toward gales of laughter all initiated by Cat Lemonjello.

Mr. Staccato would have none of it. He hurried to the front of the room, immediately silencing the Lemonjellos.

"Thank you so very much, Miss Gumm. I'm sure we all agree, that was beautifully performed!" he said.

Pru collected her music and left the piano, giving Mr. Staccato a furtive look to see if he was really serious.

"We'll have to work a little on the ending, but that is why we have these recitals!"

Pru managed a weak smile and walked stiffly back to her seat. There was a smattering of halfhearted applause, and Pru wondered if it was possible to actually drop dead from embarrassment. She hoped so, since it seemed much easier to be carted out of the room on a stretcher and whisked away in an ambulance than to have to face everybody after the recital was over.

Franny elbowed Ivy and whispered, "Are you next?"

"I don't know," Ivy mouthed back, and nervously tugged at her shirt.

When the clapping died down Mr. Staccato began to speak again. "We have one last student to hear from. Miss Diamond, will you please come up and play your piece for us now?"

No one dared laugh as Ivy walked to the front of the room. Cat held her breath, almost afraid to look. But today there was no dark feral shape, no creepy toenail clicking, nothing but a kid in a dorky "Carpe Diem!" T-shirt that hung down to her knees, with a haircut from outer space.

It would have been a dramatic moment for the audience if this skinny, pitiful-looking kid with the ears and the hair that stuck out sat down and played like Beethoven. But Ivy, never a great player to begin with, was completely unnerved by Franny's entrance and Pru's subsequent debacle, not to mention her haircut. She hit one wrong note after another. The minutes crept by. *Will this never end?* Ivy thought miserably and winced as she made yet another mistake. The audience sat cringing, and the second that Ivy finished, after polite applause, she made a mad dash for the other room.

"That wasn't so bad," Franny said.

Ivy made a face, and Franny tried again. "Well, the shirt looked, like, really good up there." Ivy just shrugged, and Franny was thinking of a diplomatic way to tell Ivy that she was probably musically challenged when Pru stormed over.

"Thanks a *lot*, Franny!" she shouted, her face blotchy and red from crying. "It's all your *fault!*"

"*My* fault?" Franny pointed to herself in disbelief.

"And you, too!" Pru yelled at Ivy. "I hope you're

both *happy!*" Pru's face crumpled in despair. Her hands balled up into little fists. Project Star of the Recital had been ruined.

Before Franny and Ivy could defend themselves, Ivy's mother arrived.

"Good God Almighty!" Pearl cried. She dropped her shopping bag and several scrunchies scattered on the floor. It took a great deal to rile Pearl. She could handle her daughter's lack of musical talent; she could bear living in a house that was literally falling down around her cubic zirconium-bedecked earlobes. It was okay that they had no money, she could deal with hard times. . . . But a bad haircut? "That hair!" Tapping her sandaled toe, Pearl got more and more worked up. "Sometimes you don't have *grits* for sense, girl, you know that? Not *grits!*"

Ivy looked down.

"Y-you've *both* totally ru-ru-ruined my *l-i-i-i-i-fe!*" Pru wailed, her shoulders heaving with sobs. Conversation in the next room stopped as people craned their necks to see what all the fuss was about. "It's all your *fault!*"

Using Pru's exact words, Franny blurted out, "It's all my fault, sir . . . ma'am—I mean, Mrs. Diamond, ma'am. I cut Ivy's hair."

132

"*You?* Give me strength!" Pearl said looking toward the heavens.

"I'm sorry," said Franny, her eyes welling up with tears.

"Oh, sure, you're *sorry*," Pru carried on. "You're not s-s-s-s-sorry!"

"I'm goin' home now," Pearl declared, "and I want *you* to git your fanny on home, too, Ivy."

Ivy and Franny headed toward the front door. But there was more. As they passed the first row, they heard Mr. Staccato say to Cat, "I'm very disappointed in you, Miss Lemonjello." The next thing he said they couldn't hear, but they could see the color drain from Cat's face.

Cat would do most anything for Mr. Staccato. She would turn over a new leaf and practice till her fingers bled. She would promise and cross her heart and hope to die that she would never again do what she had done today. But there was one thing she would not do—even if not doing it meant she could no longer be a student of Mr. Staccato's. Cat stood up stiffly and stomped past Ivy and Franny, hissing, "This is all your fault!" And if looks could kill, the girls would all surely have been dead, for Cat Lemonjello would sooner stick needles in her eyes than apologize to Pru Gumm.

"Franny Muggs, I will *never* speak to you ever again!" Pru screamed, and ran from the room. "Or you either, Ivy Diamond!"

"Fine, don't!" shouted Franny.

"Did you ever?" said Fred to Ginger.

"Never!" said Ginger to Fred.

That Sunday afternoon, Franny, Pru, Cat, and Ivy felt like they were walking out of one another's lives forever. Yes, they still lived on the same street, but they were further apart than they'd *ever* been. The girls swore to themselves that they would *never* talk to the others again. *Who needs her?* each of them thought. But things are rarely as they seem—in fact, sometimes they are the complete opposite. This was the end, they were certain. But actually, it was just the beginning.

IVY'S UNIQUE TALENT

12

vy knew she was supposed to go right home after the recital and that she would be in even more trouble with her mother for not doing what she was told, but Mr. Staccato had asked her to stay. There was something very important that he needed to speak with her about. That could only mean one thing: Ivy was in trouble with Mr. Staccato, too.

Everyone had left, and Ivy waited forlornly before the case with the ruby-red slippers. *I should just go away*, Ivy thought. She wished she could put the slippers on and click her heels three times. "There's no place like home," Ivy whispered to herself. *Where is that? Where is home?* she wondered. *Surely not #5 Gumm Street.*

"Egads, that was the worst recital we've ever had!" Mr. Staccato was saying to Fred and Ginger as he entered the room. He collapsed into a chair by the fireplace and wearily closed his eyes for a moment.

It's all my fault, Ivy thought. She had hoped when she first came to Sherbet that the Jinx would expire and that she and Pearl would be starting a whole new life. But the seven years were up, and her luck hadn't changed at all. Then Ivy did something in front of Mr. Staccato that she thought she'd never, ever,

ever do. She started to cry.

"Oh dear," said Mr. Staccato. He got out of his chair, went to Ivy, and gave her his handkerchief.

Ginger and Fred looked at Ivy and began to cry as well.

"Don't be mad at me, Mr. Staccato," wept Ivy. "I can't help it—I've got a Jinx!"

"Oh my," said Mr. Staccato, trying not to laugh.

"It's true!" said Ivy. "Nothing ever goes right, and no one likes me, and it's awful all the time and . . . and . . . my h-h-hair-r-r-r-r!" she wailed.

"I'm not angry with you," Mr. Staccato said. "There, there." He led her to the other chair by the fireplace. He sat across from Ivy and rested his forearms on his legs so that his face was level with hers. "My dear, I would like to give you a bit of advice. I've lived a long, long time as you know, and if I've learned anything, it is that there is an astonishing characteristic about hair. . . ."

CARPE DIEM!

Ivy looked at him and sniffed.

"It grows back," he said. "I also happen to know it is absolutely not true that no one likes you. Fred likes you, don't you, old chap?"

Fred nodded his head vigorously.

"And Ginger likes you. . . ." At which Ginger jumped up onto Ivy's lap and gave her a lick on the chin. "And *I* like you! Furthermore, you have a good friend in Miss Muggs, and a mother who loves you."

Ivy wasn't so sure about that one. She could still hear her mother saying, "Sometimes you don't have *grits* for sense, girl, you know that?" Ivy started crying all over again.

"I know how you feel." Mr. Staccato said gently. "But when I feel that way, I think about what a very wise old man once told me."

Ivy took a deep breath to calm herself.

"He said to take the situation and look at it backwards—sometimes things look different when seen the other way round. For example, instead of thinking of your Jinx as *unlucky*, why not try to think of it as *lucky*."

"Lucky?" Ivy said quietly.

"I will tell you something else," Mr. Staccato continued. "You have a unique talent."

"Really?" Ivy brightened a little. "For what? Music?"

"No, my dear, I'm afraid music is not your unique talent." Mr. Staccato sat back in his chair, crossed his legs, and regarded her.

Ivy thought about how terribly she had played this afternoon, but she knew she could have played better if not for the Jinx! "I'm sorry I played so badly. I know I can do better, Mr. Staccato. It's the Jinx's fault. If it weren't for him—"

"Miss Diamond, if it weren't for the Jinx—as you call it—you would not *have* your unique talent!"

"How can you say anything good about the Jinx? I have had nothing but bad things happen to me for the last seven years! Even my own father doesn't want to be with me!" Her chin trembled uncontrollably and, as much as she tried to prevent them, big tears splashed onto her cheeks, because thinking about her father leaving made her feel worse than any of the things that had happened since the Jinx came. She had always tried to push it out of her mind—until now.

"My dear, your talent is your *strength*."

"Strength?" Ivy hiccupped. "I'm the biggest weakling around. I can't carry *anything* heavy!"

"I mean strength as in the ability to continue on in the face of extreme misfortune," Mr. Staccato explained. "You have courage, my dear—you are tenacious."

Ivy slumped back down in her chair. None of these things even sounded like talents to her. Being able to sing, or paint pictures, or play the piano—*that* was a talent! Mr. Staccato was just trying to make her feel better, and it wasn't working.

Ivy could feel him watching her, but she wouldn't look back and so didn't see the lines of concern around his eyes, which were deep and careworn. He leaned his face against his hand and spoke.

"Did you ever wonder who sent that piano to your house when you moved to Sherbet?"

Ivy *had* wondered and even had entertained the notion that maybe her father wasn't really gone for good and that *he* had sent it.

"*I* sent the piano," Mr. Staccato said.

"You?" Ivy said. "But why?"

"I needed to get to know you and your mother." Mr. Staccato moved his head from his hand and leaned it against the back of the chair. His voice sounded tired. "I needed to be sure. . . ."

"Of what?" Ivy was genuinely puzzled.

Mr. Staccato rearranged himself so that he was sitting up straighter. "There is something I need to tell you."

The mood in the room had suddenly changed. Fred and Ginger sat down next to their master, and Ginger whimpered softly.

"My time is growing short," Mr. Staccato said softly.

"No!" Ivy cried, and really looked at Mr. Staccato for the first time. She had been so wrapped up in her own problems that she hadn't noticed how unwell he looked.

Mr. Staccato stood up from his chair with more effort than Ivy ever remembered. His tall frame now bent, he walked slowly over to the ruby-red slippers twinkling inside their glass case. He was quiet for a few moments and seemed to be deep in thought.

"Mr. Staccato?" Ivy said softly. "Are you okay?"

He turned toward Ivy. "There is something I want you to have after I'm gone."

"What?" Ivy said.

"This," he said, lightly tapping the knuckles of one hand against the case.

"The . . . r-ruby-red s-slippers?" Ivy stammered, almost too stunned to speak.

"The shoes," Mr. Staccato replied.

It's a funny thing isn't it, being given a personal object—not like your cousin's hand-me-down chemistry set, or your sister's kneesocks—more like your grandmother's pearl ring, or your Uncle Joe's old Waterman pen that you had your eye on ever since you were a little kid. Did you find that once you had been given the object and it was separated from its original owner, it changed, and that much to your surprise, you no longer wanted to write with the pen or wear the ring? Instead, you found a favorite box and placed the object there, because every now and then you liked to take out the pen and remember Uncle Joe, and how when you lost the entire baseball game because you struck out when the bases were loaded at the top of the ninth inning, and everyone, even your parents, was mad at you, and you wouldn't eat or come out of your room, Uncle Joe came over that night and brought a hamburger wrapped in wax paper up to you. Or you took out the ring and held it in your hand and thought about Grandma and how, when you ruined the school play because you forgot all your lines and the entire class and your whole family thought you were a total loser, you got on your bike and rode over to her house because you knew, no matter what, she thought you were wonderful. And now Ivy thought of owning the shoes and it just didn't seem right, because it would mean that Mr. Staccato wouldn't be here anymore, talking to her, like he was now.

"But I don't want the ruby-red slippers." Ivy's head was spinning and she struggled to speak. "I mean I *do* and thank you, but they belong to you, and they should stay here with you . . . forever."

Mr. Staccato held up a hand, interrupting her. "Do you remember the day you came for your first piano lesson?"

Ivy nodded.

"Do you remember what I said about having many talents?"

"You mean that thing about responsibility?" Ivy remembered it well because she still didn't understand what he meant.

"Along with talent comes responsibility," Mr. Staccato said solemnly, and his silver hair seemed to almost glow like a halo around his head in the dim light. "Well, Miss Diamond, you are ready . . . ready to take on the responsibility of your talent."

"What do you mean?" Ivy asked.

"My dear . . . *you* are the real owner of the shoes!"

"Me?" said Ivy. "But how do you know?"

"I have considered all sides, both forwards and backwards!" Mr. Staccato sat back in his chair, and Fred jumped up into his lap and looked at his master with concern. "But I'm afraid that there is not much time. . . ." He rubbed his hand across his eyes, and Ivy could see it was shaking slightly. "Someone will come—she will try and take the shoes—just the way your Aunt Viola did seven years ago!"

"Aunt V?" Ivy said, surprised.

"Yes. But one cannot *take* the shoes; they must be *given!*"

"But why did Aunt V want the shoes?" Ivy remembered Aunt V's crazy letter. *She must have had a thing about shoes,* Ivy thought.

"For all the wrong reasons." Mr. Staccato paused for a moment and shook his finger at Ivy. "*Never* give the shoes to *anyone* . . . and *never* forget your unique talent."

"My strength?" Ivy said.

"Your strength," said Mr. Staccato. "Only a person with the strength and tenacity that *you* have demonstrated over the last seven years can fill those shoes someday—and you will need every bit of it for the trials that are ahead of you!"

"I have *more* trials ahead of me?" Ivy didn't know if she could take any more trials. Just then the phone rang.

Mr. Staccato looked at her over his glasses. "There is more that you must know, Miss Diamond." He answered the phone. "She's right here," he said, and handed it to Ivy.

"What part of 'git your fanny on home' did you *not* understand, missy?" Pearl was saying.

"Um . . . no part, I guess," Ivy tried to explain. "But Mom, Mr. Staccato just gave me the shoes and—"

"I don't care if Mr. Staccato just gave you the Hope Diamond—git . . . your . . . fanny . . . on . . . home!" Pearl shouted.

Her mother had never been this angry at her before—in fact, she hadn't seen her mother this mad at *anyone* since Sugar Marie Culpepper took the crown from her in the Miss Peach Melba Contest.

"I'm countin', girl, and you had better be comin' through that front door by the time I git to a hundred. . . . *One* . . ."

"I'll be right home!" Ivy said, and hung up. "I'm sorry, Mr. Staccato, but I was supposed to be home an hour ago—and my mother is *really* angry." Ivy hurried toward the front door. "Thanks for the shoes and

all!" she called. Outside, dark
clouds were marching in from the
west, and the wind whipped her
hair around.

"There is more that you must
know!" Mr. Staccato rose from
his chair, pitching Fred back
onto the carpet. The curtains
from the windows billowed into
the room in a ghostly, un-
wholesome way. "My
dear, wait!" he said, and
held out a hand to her.

But Ivy never heard.
She raced toward home.
The wind gusted, blow-
ing the leaves through
the air. She
had never seen such
weather in Sherbet! Now it
was going to storm, and Pearl would
be worried on top of being angry with Ivy.
The first few drops of rain were beginning

to fall. Ivy knew it was about to pour, but she felt a pang of regret for dashing off so quickly. She turned and ran backwards. "And thanks for telling me my unique talent!" she shouted. "I'll see you tomorrow!"

She looked over her shoulder a few hundred feet from her house and saw his figure still standing in the doorway, his flannel trousers flapping in the wind against his thin legs. He raised an arm, calling her back, which Ivy mistook to be a wave.

"Tomorrow!" she yelled again, and waved to him. She ran to #5 Gumm Street, and Mr. Staccato watched her until she had disappeared from his sight.

THE STORM FROM THE WEST

Oh, what a miserable evening it was over at #3 Gumm Street that night! Franny's Mount Everest books lay in a pile. For once their stories of doom and disaster paled in comparison to her own life. She couldn't even bring herself to look at her Amelia Earhart poster and had covered it with a piece of paper. The tower room, usually filled with the sound of popping corn, was instead loud with the patter of rain against the windows. Her Popsicles went untouched in the freezer, and even her Jelly Squirtz had lost their appeal.

I don't deserve to eat, Franny thought. She had gone to bed and lain there in the dark for hours feeling sorry for herself, thinking over and over, *everybody hates me*. She had never seen Pru so upset, and Cat was mad at her, and that meant that now all Cat's brothers were mad at her. Even Ivy's mother was mad at her, and Ivy was probably mad at her, too.

Franny got out of bed, pulled her slicker on over her pajamas, and took her binoculars outside. It was raining hard. She pulled the hood over her head and stood, her hands resting lightly on the railing, while the rain soaked her bare feet and ankles and the hem of her pajama pants. The only other time she had seen such bad weather in Sherbet was the blizzard right before spring break.

Franny listened. She could hear the ocean crashing on the shore. Far below a mournful bell tolled three times, muffled by the wet darkness of the night. It was very cloudy and she figured that she wouldn't be able to see much, but she held the binoculars up to her eyes and looked through them anyway. There was no Big Dipper, no Little Dipper, no North Star, either. She lowered the glasses toward the horizon. Not even the moon. Just a lot of clouds, and rain, and Mr. Staccato.

Mr. Staccato? She rubbed her eyes and looked again through the binoculars, her body rigid with concentration because she couldn't believe what she was seeing.

Floating high above his house, Mr. Staccato was ascending into the night sky.

Franny's heart began beating wildly in her chest, at which point Mr. Staccato looked right at her and called out eight words that made absolutely no sense. And then, much like a balloon, slowly and silently, he drifted, up, up, up into the stormy sky and disappeared.

You can only imagine Franny's complete horror and confusion. She brushed the hood of the slicker off her head and continued to look through the binoculars, straining her eyes to see into the rain and the darkness, but there was nothing, nothing at all.

Franny ran inside, and in the time it took for her to retrieve a bag of marbles and a flashlight, the rainstorm grew worse. When she came back outside, the

sky was boil-
ing with black
angry clouds and
the rain lashed her legs.
The first marble hit
its mark, but it
took several more
to rouse her next-
door neighbor.

Finally, groggy
from being awoken,
Ivy opened her win-
dow and peered up
at Franny.

"Something's
happened!" Franny
shouted down.

"What?" Ivy said.

The wind suddenly switched
around to the west, and with the most
tremendous *who-o-o-o-o-sh!* ripped Aunt V's
old weather vane from the roof and spun it off
to heaven only knew where. Ivy quickly shut the
window.

Franny was blinking her flashlight like crazy and

shouting something unintelligible. Ivy grabbed the blanket off her hammock. Franny was in trouble, and Ivy was going to help. Down the stairs and out of #5 Gumm Street Ivy ran.

The trees were thrashing wildly about in the wind, and the air was full with the crack of tree limbs breaking off and skipping across the street. Dodging the branches, Ivy ran next door and up the seven flights of stairs. Her lungs felt as though they were about to explode from the effort as she burst into the tower room.

"Franny, what's wrong?" Ivy gulped for air.

Franny was standing in the middle of her room, her eyes wide, her face white except for two dots of color high on each cheek.

"He's dead," said Franny.

"Who?"

"Mr. Staccato," said Franny. Her hands clutched the sides of her pajamas.

"What are you talking about?" said Ivy. "We saw him this afternoon!"

"I just saw him floating above his house," Franny wailed. "He looked right at me, Ivy, and said the craziest thing." She threw herself on the bed and looked at Ivy with pleading eyes. "I tell you he's dead—it was his spirit rising!"

"What did he say, Franny?" Ivy sat on Franny's bed and grabbed her arm.

"It made no sense," Franny cried. "You'll think I'm nuts!"

"What was it?" Ivy said impatiently, shaking Franny.

The tower room vibrated with the force of the wind as rain battered against the windows.

"He said—" Franny looked at Ivy. "This is so weird. He said . . . 'You make a better door than a window.'"

"You make a better door than a window?" Ivy repeated and stood up. "You're right—you *are* nuts! He's not dead," Ivy continued. "You were totally dreaming, Franny!" Ivy said, but she felt hot all over and her heart was thudding in her ears. It was exactly like Mr. Staccato's story of the old man who used to live in #7. . . . But Ivy pushed the thought out of her head—Franny had just had a nightmare, that was all.

Franny sat on the bed afraid to utter another word, but she knew what she had seen. Mr. Staccato was dead, she was sure of it.

"Ivy—" she started.

"No!" said Ivy, grabbing her blanket. "I'm going

back to my house. . . . What's that?"

Tap-tap-tap. Tap-tap-tap.

Both girls turned and looked at the door that led out to the balcony. They looked at each other.

TAP-TAP-TAP! Louder knocks sounded at the door, but they could see no one there. Franny got up and crept over to the door. "Stand back," she whispered to Ivy, and took hold of the flashlight the way you would a baseball bat.

She flung open the door, but there was nothing there . . . except the sound of *sniff . . . sniff, sniff.* Franny looked down and standing at her feet were two wet, bedraggled, crying dogs.

"Fred!" Franny couldn't believe her eyes.

"Ginger!" shouted Ivy.

The two dogs were a sorry sight to see. Tails between their legs, they squelched listlessly into the tower room and then dissolved in tears.

Ivy knelt down and said, "Ginger, where is Mr. Staccato?"

Ginger stopped crying for a moment, looked heavenward, and then started up all over again.

"He's not," Ivy insisted.

Fred and Ginger nodded sadly.

"But he can't be," Ivy said, her own eyes filling with tears.

The dogs only looked at her and hiccupped a few times.

"Are you sure?" Ivy said to them.

There was a flash of lightning, followed by a clap of thunder, and the rain started to come down even harder.

Ivy couldn't accept it. She had just seen Mr. Staccato. He had given her the ruby-red slippers. No, she couldn't think like this, he wasn't gone. It couldn't be true!

"I have to go see for myself!" Ivy cried, jumping up and snatching her blanket. "I'm going to Mr. Staccato's right now!"

"Ivy, you can't go now," said Franny. She grabbed the hem of Ivy's blanket and pulled her back down. "It's too awful out!"

As if to prove her point, a gust of wind slammed against the tower, pummeling the windows. Ivy huddled on the floor again with Franny, Fred, and Ginger. Ivy thought about her mother, who would wake from the storm and, finding her daughter missing, would be frantic.

"I'd better get home," Ivy said, "but tomorrow first thing, I'm going to Mr. Staccato's."

She wrapped herself in the soggy blanket and motioned for the dogs to follow. "Fred, Ginger, you're coming home with me!" They ran back down the stairs to her house.

She and the dogs made it home just in the nick of time, because not two minutes later, Pearl woke up and went to check on Ivy. The four of them spent a truly miserable night beneath the kitchen table, which was the only dry place in the house.

At around seven in the morning, the storm seemed to finally blow itself out. They crawled from under

the table and splashed through puddles to the porch
to see what was left of Sherbet.

What they saw was not what they expected.
There were still some suspicious clouds lingering,
and Pearl held a hand outside to feel for rain, but
instead of broken branches and torn-up yards,
Sherbet was as it had always been—mani-
cured lawns, sunny skies, chirping birds.

"Praise God!" said Pearl, who was relieved but also very rattled. She took
two aspirin and went back to
bed. But before she left she warned
Ivy, "This might not be over. Could
be we're just in the eye o' the
storm."

Cha Cha

*O*nce her mother was asleep again, Ivy dressed and headed out the door with Fred and Ginger. Franny was already waiting for her.

They were soon outside #7 Gumm Street. Above them a funnel of white clouds swirled around and around a patch of blue sky. "I'm going in," said Ivy. "I think you should wait here."

"No way," said Franny, "I'm going in with you."
Fred and Ginger nodded.

"All right," said Ivy, "but if anything happens we
have to run, okay?"

Fred and Ginger started to whine as the four tip
toed up the front steps. Ivy silently opened the door,
then peeked inside and quietly called, "Mr. Staccato?"

Everything was very still. They could feel that
something was missing. As the girls and the dogs
crept into the museum room, it became clear that
Mr. Staccato was no longer there.

Ivy stood before the glass case that held the ruby-
red slippers. They glittered, and Ivy bent down a
little to gaze at them. She recalled what Mr. Staccato
had said. "Along with talent comes responsibility. . . .
You are ready . . . ready to take on the responsibility
of your talent. . . . *You* are the real owner of the
shoes!"

"Come on, Ivy, let's go. I'm getting the creeps,"
Franny said anxiously.

Instead, Ivy unhooked the latch and opened the
case. She reached inside to touch one of the shoes.

There was a sparkle of light, and she pulled her
hand away because it kind of tingled. But it hadn't

hurt, so she reached
in and touched the
shoe again. This time nothing
happened. She picked up the
shoe and then another and clutched
them to her.

All at once there was a low rumbling
sound. The light faded fast.

"What is that?" Ivy said.

Franny dashed over to Mr. Staccato's
French windows and pulled back the
drape. Rolling out of the west was an

enormous black cloud. Two faint beams of light within the cloud seemed to be racing straight toward them.

"Oh . . . my . . . gosh," Franny said.

The girls scooped up Fred and Ginger and dove for cover between the two chairs by the fireplace. *Beep! Beep! Beep!* blared a distant, angry car horn. An instant later the cloud obliterated every bit of light and it began to rain as hard as it had only an hour or so before, followed by great crashes of thunder and flashes of lightning. The lamps and pictures on the walls rattled, Mr. Staccato's sheet music flew off the piano and blew into the museum room like so much confetti, and the piano lid slammed down with such force that the strings sang a ghastly chord.

As quickly as it had come, the storm was gone, and there was complete silence. And then the sound of footsteps.

"Mr. Staccato?" Ivy called. She was *right*! He *hadn't* died!

Franny ran out of the museum room. "Come on, Ivy, *hurry*," Franny said, bobbing up and down by the front door the way little kids do when they have to go to the bathroom. "Let's hide!" Franny ran out the door and hid behind the boxwood bushes next to the porch.

Mr. Staccato?" Ivy called again.

But it wasn't Mr. Staccato. Coming into the room was a woman dressed completely in black. A woman who might not understand why Ivy was holding two slippers from Mr. Staccato's collection!

With no time to return the shoes, Ivy shoved them inside her pants, concealing them under Franny's oversized T-shirt and her sweatshirt. Fred and Ginger squeezed close and sat on Ivy's feet.

"May I help you?" the woman said, entering the museum room.

She was wearing a glamorous outfit that consisted of a long, brocaded, bathrobelike garment over tight black calypso pants and a form-fitting black bodice. Long black gloves covered her arms.

"No, thank you, ma'am," Ivy said.

"Dear!" the woman said, and Ivy tried to control a rising panic. She had seen this woman before. Seven years ago, in fact, in the reflection of the makeup mirror. It was the woman wearing the hat like a lamp shade with its long veil covering her face.

The woman made a beeline for Ivy and pinched her cheek. "Please refrain from addressing me as 'ma'am.' It sounds so . . . *matronly*."

Fred and Ginger growled.

Ivy winced, and the woman let go.

"Who are you?" Ivy demanded.

The woman passed by the mirror on the wall and stopped to examine herself.

"Do you think this outfit makes me look fat?" the woman said, turning around.

"Oh, not at all!" Ivy shook her head back and forth.

The woman proceeded to the couch and collapsed dramatically on it. She hung her head and dabbed theatrically at her eyes through the veil with a tissue.

"My poor dear brother has passed away!" she cried.

"Brother?" said Ivy.

"Yes . . . Mr. Staccato." She dabbed some more at her eyes. "I'm his sister, Cha Cha!" She made a little flourish with her hands and snapped her fingers.

"He's really . . . dead?" Ivy said softly.

"As a doornail," she answered.

"You're Cha Cha?" said Ivy. "Staccato? Cha Cha Staccato?"

"*Ms,*" emphasized the woman. "Not Miss, not Mrs., but *Mzzzz* Staccato, got it, kid? I mean, that is how a woman of the world such as myself should be addressed."

Now, Ivy was not a great student, but she was a very smart girl and she did a bit of quick arithmetic.

"So how old are you?" she said suspiciously.

Cha Cha stood and sashayed over to the mantel. Leaning against it, she said, "Don't you know, dear, that it's very *rude* to ask a lady her age?"

Ivy said nothing.

Cha Cha cleared her throat. "But I have nothing to hide. I'm fift—I mean, thirty-nine." She took her hand off her hip for a second and fluttered her outstretched fingers up and down. Several large emerald rings on her gloved fingers glittered. "Heh!" Satisfied, she replaced the hand on her hip.

"Well, then, you're *not* Mr. Staccato's sister!" Ivy said, knowing that Cha Cha could be no less than one hundred and ten in order to be telling the truth.

"Ha ha ha!" Cha Cha threw her head back with laughter. "You *are* a sketch! Did I say 'sister'? I meant 'niece.' I'm his *niece*!" She paused and snapped her fingers again like little castanets.

Ivy was horrified.

So were Fred
and Ginger.

"Did you ever?"
said one.

"Never!" said
the other.

"We're going to have *so* much fun together!" Cha Cha said. "By the way, who *does* your hair—it's *marvelous!*"

Ivy backed out of the room. "Um, my mother is expecting me home, ma'am, um . . . miss—sorry, Mzzzz Staccato."

"You mean Pearl Diamond?" Cha Cha's eyes twinkled beneath the veil as she, too, started moving toward the door.

"Ah, yeah, I've got to be going now, thanks." Ivy turned and ran for the door, with Fred and Ginger close behind.

Ivy slipped out just before Cha Cha blocked the door with her fishnet-stockinged, patent-leather-shod foot. The little dogs were too quick for her, too, and leaped over her leg and out the door.

"Rats!" Cha Cha said, but then corrected herself. "Tell Pearl I just can't *wait* to meet her!" she sang out.

Down the steps and around the corner Ivy, Fred, and Ginger skidded. Franny followed right behind. "Let's get out of here!" Ivy said. But before they did, Franny pointed. In Mr. Staccato's garage was something that had not been there before, the unmistakable rear end of a car that Ivy was all too familiar with: a champagne-colored Cadillac.

A CURIOUS DISGUISE FOR A RUBY RED SLIPPER 15

The two ran as fast as they could all the way down Gumm Street.

Ivy could see her mother standing on the front lawn, arms folded, waiting.

"You'd better disappear," Ivy told Franny. "Take Fred and Ginger."

Franny did just that.

Ivy walked up to meet her mother and braced her-self. She knew she was in trouble for leaving the house right in the middle of "the eye o' the storm."

"Ivy!" her mother shouted. She threw her arms around her daughter, and Ivy squirmed, afraid her mother might feel the shoes under her sweatshirt. "I'm so sorry, baby," she said. "Poor Mr. Staccato, so sad." Pearl released Ivy and held her at arm's length. "I know he was a special friend to you, but he was very old, darlin.' "

This is better than being yelled at, Ivy thought.

"I just heard," said Pearl as they walked inside.

Up till now Ivy had not had the chance to think about Mr. Staccato really being gone, and she couldn't believe it. She had seen him only yesterday. He had spoken with so much kindness that Ivy could feel tears well up again.

Now he was gone—and under the same strange circumstances as the old man who had lived in #7 Gumm Street! There had been a terrible storm and Mr. Staccato had vanished, just like the old man. And that cryptic message he had left with Franny—surely he was trying to tell them something . . . but what?

Pearl was still chattering, ". . . and then the phone

rang and it was that darlin' niece of his."

"Niece?" Ivy flushed and her heart began to pound.

"Yes, his niece, Miss Cha Cha? She's an independent woman, just like us, honey. She told me all about her poor dear uncle passin'." Pearl looked heavenward. "May he rest in peace." Pearl straightened her sequined headband. "But here's the best part," she said, growing more animated. "Cha Cha—I mean Mzzzz Staccato, that's what she likes to be called— she's in the beauty biz, just like I used to be!"

Ivy felt ill.

Pearl took Ivy's hand in hers and said softly, "Maybe Mzzzz Cha Cha can help us, Ivy. We're gonna get back on our feet, baby." She kissed Ivy on the forehead and looked down.

"What's that?" Pearl said, staring.

"What?"

"On the palm of your hand, honey."

Ivy had no idea what her mother was talking about and looked. There, in the center of her right palm, about the size of a quarter, was a round gray eye. Ivy rubbed her hands together and said, "I was just fooling around." She laughed nervously and thought back to how the shoe in the case had sparked when she had touched it and how her hand had felt tingly. She pulled her sweatshirt over her palm. "It's just one of those fake tattoo thingys."

Pearl smiled. "I've got to run. Mzzzz Staccato wants me to come over toot sweet—that's French, darlin', Mzzzz Cha Cha says it all the time—she's such a woman of the world!" Pearl shimmied into her rhinestone cardigan and kissed Ivy on the cheek. "I just can't wait to meet her!" Pearl squealed, and ran out the door.

No sooner had the door shut but the phone rang. Ivy picked it up.

"Dear!" said a voice, and Ivy knew immediately who it was. "I believe you have something of mine?"

"What?" said Ivy.

"I'll be over at your house this afternoon to pick up the shoes."

"Shoes?"

"And a word of warning, dear," Cha Cha continued. "I have Judge Gumm on speed dial, and I'm *sure* he would be very *interested* in your little morning visit here at #7 Gumm Street."

"Um . . . okay," Ivy said.

"Okay, *wha-a-a-t*?" Cha Cha prompted.

Silence.

"*Mz-z-z-z*?" she hinted.

"Mzzzz Staccato?" replied Ivy.

"Thatta girl!" Cha Cha said enthusiastically. "You know, dear, we can do this the easy way, or we can do it the more . . . *unpleasant* way." Cha Cha paused. "TAKE YOUR PICK!" she screamed, and the line went dead.

Ivy dropped the phone and ran up to her room. She ripped off her sweatshirt, and the shoes tumbled out onto the window seat. Ivy looked next door and saw Franny waving her arms at her like a crazy person.

Ivy opened the window. "Help, Franny!" she shouted.

Two minutes later Franny tore into Ivy's room, Fred and Ginger in tow.

"You're not going to believe this! Cha Cha called!" Ivy cried. "She knows I've got the shoes!"

The two dogs gasped and Franny's jaw dropped. "Deny everything," Franny declared. Fred and Ginger nodded adamantly.

"It's too late for that," Ivy said. "She's going to tell Judge Gumm if I don't give them back!"

171

"Oh no-o-o," Franny groaned, and sat down in the hammock. Ginger sprang into her lap and whimpered.

"And look at this." Ivy held her palm up, and Franny and Fred and Ginger squinted their eyes to see.

"It's a shiny mark. It kind of looks like an eye or something. Where'd you get it?" Franny asked.

"I think when I first touched them." Ivy nodded in the direction of the shoes.

"Geez!" Franny said, suddenly noticing something. "Ivy, you should take better care of that T-shirt I gave you!"

'What do you mean?" asked Ivy.

"You've got red stuff all over it." Franny got out of the hammock to show Ivy.

There was something on the front of the "Carpe Diem!" T-shirt where Ivy had shoved the shoes between the waistband of her jeans and the shirt.

Ivy held the shirt out from her body. "It must be . . ."

"The shoes!" both girls said. Each picked one up.

"The red must be coming off of them!" Franny rubbed hard at hers with a tissue she had in her pocket. "Well, it's not this one," she said.

Ivy scratched her fingernail against the heel of her shoe. Red came away on her finger. "Look at this," she said, handing the shoe to Franny.

"That's so weird." Franny held it up to the light. "It looks like silver underneath."

"Wait a minute." Ivy ran out of the room and came back in with her mother's nail polish remover and some cotton balls. "Let's use this!"

Franny and Ivy rubbed carefully on either side of the slipper.

Beneath the red paint, the shoe was gleaming silver. Franny placed it on the cushion of the window seat and stood back.

Ivy picked it up again. "Remember the first day we met and you found that letter?"

"Yeah, the one on the picture of your dead aunt?" How could Franny forget?

"It was from Aunt V." Ivy polished the cool, smooth silver of the shoe against her shirt and held it up. It shed a remarkable dazzling light. "She wrote that she wasn't dead and that if we found a pair of silver shoes with bows on them, that they were hers."

"This sure has a bow," Franny observed. "But there's only one shoe."

"Mr. Staccato told me that Aunt V tried to take the

slippers from him seven years ago!" Ivy ran her hands through her hair, making it stand on end. "Franny, Mr. Staccato gave *me* the ruby-red slippers."

"Wow!" said Franny. "Really?"

"And it's all just like he said—he told me that someone would come and try and get them away from me, just like Aunt V did with him, but that I wasn't supposed to give them to *anybody*. I won't give them to that Cha Cha! But what if she calls Judge Gumm?" Ivy cried. "I could be arrested!"

Franny took the silver shoe from Ivy and picked up the ruby one. "I don't know why anybody would want *either* shoe. They don't look very comfortable."

"Franny," Ivy said desperately. "What if we ask Pru for help?"

"Forget it," said Franny. "I can't."

"Why not?" Ivy protested. "Maybe Pru could talk to her father?"

"Yeah, except for one small detail." Franny put her hands on her hips. "Pru's not talking to me for the rest of her life, remember? And I'm not talking to her."

"I know," Ivy said, twisting the T-shirt in her fingers. "But Cha Cha will be here any minute. *Please*, Franny!"

Franny shivered. But she had to admit that seeing Ivy hauled off to the slammer for stealing, and Cha Cha getting the shoes which didn't even belong to her in the first place, was *way* worse than groveling to Pru. "Okay!" Franny said, and flew downstairs to the phone and dialed.

Pru picked up on the first ring.

"I know you really, really, really, really, really, really hate me right now. . . ." Franny sputtered.

"You got that right," Pru said sharply. Angry and humiliated, Pru had retreated to the sanctuary of her room and surrounded herself in a healing cocoon of books and cereal.

Franny continued, "And I'm really, really, really, really, really, *really* sorry . . . but here's the thing . . . can you come right over to Ivy's?"

"I'm not speaking to you," Pru said.

"Ivy and I have a problem."

"I'm not speaking to Ivy, either," said Pru icily.

"It's urgent," persisted Franny.

"Tell somebody who cares."

"It's an emergency, Pru!" Franny's voice rose to a hysterical pitch.

"So what?"

Franny and Pru could probably have gone on like

this all day, but then Franny finally said the magic
words: "We need your help."

If there was one thing that Pru loved more than
her books or cereal or being the best, it was someone
needing her help. *They need* my *help*, thought Pru. *Of
course they do!*

But at the front door of #5 Gumm Street, Pru
started to have second thoughts. "I'm not going up
those stairs!" Pru poked her head inside. "They're de-
crepit!"

"Keep it down." Franny put her finger to her lips.
"You'll hurt Ivy's feelings."

Insensitive, thoughtless people—like Cat Lemonjello for example—go around hurting other's feelings, but not me! Pru thought. She gritted her teeth and picked her way carefully up the stairs. Dangers were everywhere: uneven steps, rickety hand railings, cobwebs hiding poisonous spiders, killer molds, mice with hanta virus. . . .

Afraid to sit on, lean against, or touch anything, Pru stood in the doorway to Ivy's bedroom, arms folded tightly against her chest.

"Mr. Staccato is dead," Franny said bluntly.

"No!" gasped Pru. "How do you know?"

"I saw his spirit rising over his house last night," Franny said.

"Now I get it!" Pru threw her hands up in the air. "This is just another big fat joke on me!" She turned to leave.

Franny jumped up and went after her. "Pru, it's *not*. We need your help because there's a new person living at #7, and she's threatening to call your father and tell him that Ivy stole something of hers out of Mr. Staccato's house."

Pru stopped halfway down the stairs. "*Did* she take something?"

"Well . . ." Franny hesitated. "Sort of."

"What did she *sort of* take?"

Ivy appeared at the top of the stairs and held up the red shoe. "This."

Pru slowly walked back up the stairs, her eyes on the shoe the entire time. "The ruby-red slippers," she said, amazed to see one out of its case.

"Precisely!" said Franny and went to sit on the lime-green shag rug in the bedroom. Forgetting all about fleas, dust mites, and stray antibiotic-resistant bacteria that might be living in the rug, Pru sat down too, followed by Ivy, who placed the red shoe in the center.

Pru stared at the shoe and didn't say a word.

Ivy and Franny told Pru how Ivy had taken the

shoes from #7 Gumm Street, and about the woman with the lamp shade hat called Cha Cha Staccato. Ivy brought over the silver shoe from the window seat and placed it on the rug next to the red shoe.

Pru picked up the silver shoe. "What happened here?"

"The red kind of came off, see?" Ivy held up the bottom part of her shirt for Pru to see. "So we kind of . . . rubbed off the rest?" her voice trailed off. She was a little afraid of Pru.

Pru put the silver shoe down, got up, and walked out of the room.

"Are you going to talk to your dad?" Franny cried.

"No!" said Pru firmly. "Don't leave this room and don't touch those shoes, do you understand? I'll be right back!"

Bang! The door shut downstairs and she was gone.

"She's going to tell," said Ivy. "I just know it."

Ivy and Franny waited in the dreary room. Outside the sun was shining, and it was another glorious day in Sherbet, but gloom hung in the air of #5 Gumm.

Bang! The door slammed again and they could hear footsteps coming up the stairs.

Pru entered the room as cautiously as before, but this time she was holding a book. She sat on the carpet once again with Ivy and Franny.

"I've been reading this book," Pru said in a whisper.

"Why are you whispering?" Franny said, annoyed.

"*Sh-h-h-h-h-h!* Franny, this is *serious*; just listen." Pru put the book down on the rug and began to thumb through it. "There's something in here, something . . . about . . . the shoes."

Ivy and Franny leaned over to look.

"Here it is!" said Pru pointing to a page. "Okay, okay, listen to this.

> *"Dorothy looked, and gave a little cry of fright. There, indeed, just under the corner of the great beam the house rested on, two feet*

—"that belonged to the Wicked Witch of the West," Pru interjected breathlessly—

> *"were sticking out, shod in silver shoes with pointed toes."*

Pru shut the book, and the girls could see the title on its cover: *The Wonderful Wizard of Oz*.

"*Silver* shoes?" Franny asked. "I always thought they were red."

"Silver shoes," Pru repeated, and pointed at the one shoe. Neither Franny nor Ivy knew what to say.

Pru flipped through the book a little further, and then read again.

*"For the Silver
Shoes had fallen
off in her flight
through the air, and
were lost forever in the
desert."*

"Until now," Pru said softly.

Franny and Ivy glanced at each
other. They were both thinking the
same thought—*No way!*—but neither
dared speak. They knew they were on
thin ice with Pru.

Pru broke the silence. "How did Mr.
Staccato get these shoes in the first
place, I wonder?"

Ivy repeated what Mr. Staccato had told her that afternoon in the museum room. When she was done, Fred and Ginger barked an affirmative and wagged their tails.

Pru leaned back and observed Fred and Ginger as if she were seeing them for the first time. Then she opened a page of her book to an illustration of Dorothy's famous terrier and held it up next to the dogs.

"These two are *definitely* related to Toto," Pru said with an air of authority.

Franny and Ivy looked at it, and then at the dogs, who nodded.

"Mr. Staccato said the *other* owner didn't want them," Ivy whispered to Franny and Pru.

Pru hugged her knees to her chest while Franny and Ivy looked back at her blankly. "You have to give that shoe back, Ivy."

Ivy put both shoes in her lap. "I'm not giving either of the shoes back," she said tearfully, and cradled them between her knees in the oversized T-shirt. "Mr. Staccato said *I* was the true owner, and he said that I was never to give the shoes to anyone else."

Pru frowned. "You *have* to, Ivy. Who knows what kind of weird powers that silver shoe has."

"I have an idea!" Franny said. "We should call Cat. You know how she says she has ESP or whatever; maybe she can help."

"I thought you didn't *believe* she had ESP," Pru said to Franny.

"I don't." Franny folded her arms. "But in case she does . . . I mean, what do we have to lose?"

"We have to hurry." Ivy rocked back and forth. "Cha Cha could be here any minute."

Pru got up. "If you call Cat, I'm leaving." She reached back to tighten the band around her long, streaming ponytail. "And I'll tell my father." She knew it was a cheap shot, but she couldn't resist.

Franny stood as well and put her hands on her hips. "Mr. Staccato is dead, and Ivy is in trouble. Can't you think of someone else besides yourself for a change?"

Pru was thinking of *everyone* else, she thought. This all seemed terribly dangerous, but the idea of Cat being here and fixing everything and being the big hero was completely out of the question. "Yeah, well, I'm not going to speak to her." Pru flipped her ponytail over her shoulder.

"You don't have to speak to her." Franny was on her way back down the stairs to the phone. "Just listen."

16
Cha Cha Steps
lightly
and carries a big
JINX

Cat didn't like how she felt after the recital. Mr. Staccato had always been kind to her. She was, after all, his best student, and to be spoken to so harshly really hurt. She was also suffering from a lack of sleep, for her branch of the tree had been tossed around all night long in the storm. But there was something else—something that she couldn't put her finger on—that was very, very wrong. Cat couldn't tell anymore if it was the ESP giving her messages or what, but she wasn't surprised at all to hear from Franny—she knew something terrible had happened.

"Mr. Staccato's dead! You've gotta come over to Ivy's right away!" Franny held her breath for fear of what Cat would say.

"It's just like the *I Ching* predicted," Cat muttered.

"You've gotta come to Ivy's right away, Cat," Franny repeated. "And bring your You Ching!"

"*I Ching,*" Cat said impatiently.

"Bring that, too!" said Franny.

"Pru's there, isn't she?" Cat said.

"Hey—you really *are* good at ESP. . . ."

With the way Cat was feeling, the last place she wanted to be right now was at Ivy's creepy house, but if Pru was there, Cat couldn't chicken out. "I'll be right over."

Soon all four girls from Gumm Street were gathered around the shoes in Ivy's bedroom.

"Cool, you've got the shoes from Mr. S's case!" Cat said as soon as she saw them, momentarily forgetting her extreme unease.

True to her word, Pru had not spoken. She flounced over to the window seat and plunked herself down, sulkily ignoring Cat. Franny just rolled her eyes while Ivy explained everything, ending with Pru's copy of *The Wonderful Wizard of Oz*.

The longer Cat listened, the more uncomfortable she grew. The old man she had unwittingly conjured had flown in a *balloon* with the initials O.Z. on it—just like the wizard from the book! It had to be! Still, Pru was trying to act like the big genius know-it-all reader-expert on all this Oz stuff. Cat picked up the silver shoe and, in spite of her rising alarm, casually said, "Let me get this straight. You're saying *this* is the real shoe from Oz?"

"Yes!" barked Pru. "And Ivy had better give it back!" She folded her arms and turned away.

"Oh, come *on*!" Franny groaned.

"I'm *not* giving them back, Pru!" Ivy said.

Cat kicked off a sandal and tried to shove the silver shoe onto her foot. "Maybe if I can—get—it—on, my prince will come and take me away from all this!"

Ginger frowned, and Fred barked.

"Oh, lighten up, Fred!" Cat sniffed and took the shoe off her foot. "How about if I rub it? Maybe a

genie will come and grant me three wishes!" Cat rubbed the shoe. "I wish Pru would go jump in the la—"

All of a sudden there was a loud knock on the door.

Ivy sprang to her feet. "It's Cha Cha! Quick! Hide!" She pointed to the roof out-side the window seat.

"Oh no! I'm not going out there!" Pru shook her head vehemently.

Fred and Ginger scratched at the closet.

"Okay, in there!" Ivy opened the closet door, and Fred and Ginger raced inside.

"Why do we have to hide?" objected Cat.

"Because I don't want you getting mixed up in this." Ivy squeezed them all in. "I mean it, now go, *go!*" She shoved Pru in last and pushed the door shut.

"Leave it open a crack," Pru protested. "I don't want to suffocate. That would be Safety Tip Number One Hundred Twenty-Nine, or is it Number One Hundred Thirty? Never play in the close—"

"Oh, be quiet," Franny hissed.

With trembling legs Ivy went downstairs and opened the door.

"*So* nice to see you." Cha Cha stood, still dressed all in black, only the bathrobelike garment was gone and in its place was a black patent-leather raincoat in spite of the bright sunny skies. She still had on the lamp shade hat. The veil fluttered softly in the breeze.

Pushing Ivy aside, Cha Cha sauntered into the house.

"*An-n-n-n-d?*" she waited. "So nice to see you, too. . . ?"

"Mz-z-z-z Staccato," Ivy said, and made a face behind her back.

"I just *love* what you've *done* with the place." Cha Cha ran a gloved finger along the surface of the piano. "So . . . charming, so sort of shabby chic." She inspected her finger for traces of dust, and curled her lip. "Minus the *chic*."

"Um, I was kind of in the middle of something and all, Mzzzz Staccato, and—" Ivy ran around in front of Cha Cha to block her way up the stairs.

"I would *so* love to stay and chat, but I have a *mil-l-l-l-l-ion* things to do today, so how about that little matter we discussed earlier?"

Ivy stalled for time. "What little matter?"

Cha Cha gave her a hard look, stepped around her, and proceeded up the stairs. "You really ought to *do* something about this *railing*; someone could *hurt* themselves." She pushed on the banister and sent it crashing to the floor, narrowly missing Ivy.

Cha Cha reached the second-floor landing. "Now, if I were ruby-red slippers, where would I be?" She peeked her head into this door and that. "Come out, come out, wherever you are."

Ivy ran up behind Cha Cha and frantically elbowed past, wondering how she could have been so careless as to have left the shoes in plain sight. Dashing into her bedroom, she grabbed the shoes and held them tightly in her arms.

Cha Cha stood on the threshold, greedily eyeing them. "You know, I'm always saying that I *love* children."

Ivy backed up until her legs hit the window seat.

Cha Cha approached her one step at a time. "Guess . . . *what?*"

Ivy shook her head.

"I really don't." Cha Cha crinkled her nose like she smelled something bad. "And especially not girl children." Here she took Ivy's chin in her fingers and, raising it a little, looked into Ivy's eyes. Ivy squinted but she could not make out any features beneath the black veil. "Because they *whine*, and they carry *grudges*, and they won't *speak* to one another, and they're always whispering *secrets*."

Ivy screwed up her face and stuck out her tongue.

Cha Cha let go of Ivy's chin and clenched her teeth. She flicked her forefinger hard against Ivy's head like you would if you wanted to get a bug off your homework.

"OW!" yelled Ivy.

"Now, GIVE ME THOSE SHOES!"

"No!" shouted Ivy. "Mr. Staccato gave them to *me* and I'll never give them back! *Never!*"

"Never! Never! Never!" Cha Cha mocked in a high-pitched tone of voice. "Try this on for size, then!" Cha Cha spun

her pinky finger in a circle and said, "Come to Mummy!"

All at once there was a scratching, sniffling sound like a dog scrambling about on a slick surface trying to regain his footing. Ivy watched in complete horror as Cha Cha's shadow reared up behind her, spinning into the form of a hairy black beast with eyes and nose and a long, pink, skinny rodentlike tail. It scrambled up to Ivy with a great deal of excitement, as if it had missed her, and thumped its rat tail up and down in a sickening way that made Ivy's stomach turn over. She flattened herself against the wall to keep it from getting any closer.

"Come here, boy, come to Mummy," Cha Cha called, but it—or he—wouldn't leave Ivy. Cha Cha slipped a rolled-up newspaper from out of her raincoat and hid it behind her back.

The thing growled as Cha Cha approached, and then it lunged at her. "Ouch!" she screamed and smacked him on his snout. "BAD BOY! BAD BOY!" She swatted him several times.

The beast crouched down and snarled at her feet.

"What *is* that thing?" Ivy said, terrified.

"Don't you recognize him? He was with you for seven years." Cha Cha leaned down to pet him. "She doesn't even know her very own jinxy-winxy," Cha Cha said in baby talk, whereupon the Jinx snapped at her again. She smacked him a few more times with the newspaper.

"My Jinx?" Ivy's voice quavered, and she remembered how hopeful she had been only a day and a half ago when the Jinx was supposed to go away.

"I think she's got it!" Cha Cha warbled in a fake British accent. "Anyhoo, I'll make you a little deal: I'll take little sweetums here if you give me the shoes."

"My seven years is up . . . *Mzzzz* Staccato," Ivy said firmly. "You *can't* Jinx me and you *can't* have the shoes. They're mine!"

"I'm not sure that I heard right." Cha Cha arranged her veil. " Did you say I *can't* have them?" She put her hand to her ear.

"That's *right!*" Ivy said bravely, clutching the shoes to her chest.

"Fetch, boy!" Cha Cha commanded. But the Jinx just slithered over to a dark corner and crouched there. A low animal growl came from his throat. With a loud slurp, he licked up a long strand of slobber.

"Well, it's just like I always say." Cha Cha tossed her head. "Want anything done right, do it yourself—" With lightning speed she snaked her gloved hands out to snatch the shoes. "EYOW-W-W-W!" she screeched as a jolt of electricity sent her somersaulting backwards across the room.

Within a moment Cha Cha was back on her feet and coming at Ivy again. Ivy ran to the far corner and huddled there, still clutching the shoes to her chest. She shut her eyes and raised her right hand to protect herself.

"Rats!" Cha Cha said.

Ivy opened her eyes to see Cha Cha standing right over her, studying the mark on her upturned palm, and she immediately closed her hand and hid it in the folds of her shirt.

Composing herself, Cha Cha said, "You shouldn't have done that. It's made me very unhappy."

"What'd I do?" Ivy said, and suddenly remembered how Mr. Staccato had said, "One cannot *take* the shoes." Now she knew what would happen if someone tried.

"Hmmm," Cha Cha said, placing one hand on her hip, "I was just thinking back to how your mother was supposed to get my little Jinx friend here seven years ago."

"My mother?" Ivy said. "The Jinx was supposed to be for my mother?"

"My mother?" Cha Cha mimicked, and then scowled. "This time I won't miss!" She sat on the edge of the window seat and crossed her legs demurely. Cha Cha looked at the mirror over Ivy's dresser and snapped her fingers together like castanets. "Let's see what Pearl is up to!"

Ivy glanced over and saw her mother's reflection. Pearl was pawning her last tiara, but modeling it for old time's sake in front of . . . a mirror.

"How convenient," Cha Cha cooed. "So what do you say? Either your mother gets handsome over here"—the Jinx snarled from his corner, and Cha Cha rolled her eyes—"or you give me those shoes pronto!"

Cha Cha finally had her. Ivy figured her poor mother had endured Ivy's Jinx; she didn't need one of her own. So Ivy did the only thing she could: she handed over the shoes.

"Now, that wasn't so hard, was it? But I think you're holding out on me." Cha Cha wiggled her finger at Ivy in a mock scolding fashion. She threw the ruby red shoe over her shoulder and, holding the silver one, hissed, "Where is the other silver shoe?"

"I don't have it!" Ivy yelled.

"Temper, temper," said Cha Cha, wagging the finger again.

"I don't!" Ivy said again.

"Well, we'll just see about that." Cha Cha turned to leave. "I would advise you to keep your mouth shut about this. Not that you have any friends to tell anyway."

"I have plenty of friends," Ivy replied.

Cha Cha shook her head sadly. "*Tsk, tsk, tsk*, even your own father doesn't want to be around you, dear." She pushed the lamp shade hat firmly down on her head. "Furthermore, I had a nice long talk with your mother, and she's very concerned about your inability to keep friends. So I have no fear that you will be enlisting any whiney, whispery, dopey little girlfriends to gang up on Cha Cha."

"Just so long as my mother is okay," Ivy said defiantly.

"See for yourself!" Cha Cha said and spun her pinky finger in a circle.

Ivy looked into the mirror and saw her own reflection. Instantly it cracked, shattering into a million pieces.

"Oops!" Cha Cha said coolly. "Don't you just hate it when that happens?"

The Jinx pricked up his ears, fixed Ivy in his sights, and galloped straight at her. Gobs of drool flew off his tongue, which bounced merrily outside his mouth.

"No!" Ivy cringed, waiting for him to knock her to the ground and slobber on her, but he jumped right over her. On landing, he chased his tail around and around with such speed that he flattened out, taking up residence in her shadow once more.

THE GUMM STREET GIRLS

17

START TO STICK

(SORT OF)

*I*vy struggled to her hands and knees, the wind so knocked out of her she could barely breathe. Even so, she managed to crawl over to the closet to get away from the Jinx, but to no avail— for as you know, you can never escape your own shadow. As she sat there curled up, shaking and terrified of what was now once again a part of herself, the closet door opened.

"Breathe, breathe," Franny was saying. Slumped against her, Pru had fainted dead away.

Cat and Franny began talking all at once, while Fred and Ginger ran around them in a circle, sneezing from time to time.

"Ivy, Ivy, are you all right?"

"Did you *see* that thing?"

"Shhhh, you'll make her feel worse."

"Do you think Cha Cha knew we were here?"

"What kind of a name is Cha Cha?"

Franny fanned Pru with the Oz book.

"It's Spanish, and get that thing away from me." Pru pushed the book away and looked over at Ivy.

"Ivy, Ivy—did you see?" Franny went to her to help her up. "Cha Cha couldn't just take them! The shoes have to be given!"

Ivy knew all about it. She had done the one thing Mr. Staccato had told her not to do. She tried to get up, and crumpled back down again. She felt heavy and dull, like she had a permanent Jinx she'd never be rid of.

Now Cat knew what she had been seeing around Ivy since the very first day she'd met her, and felt guilty about all the times she had thought poorly of her. The *I Ching* had even tried to warn Cat of the danger Ivy was in, but had Cat told her? No! She'd thought *Ivy* was the danger! "I'm really sorry, Ivy," Cat finally said. There was something else, too. Cat didn't quite know how to tell them this. "I think there's a possibility that Cha Cha is the, um . . . er . . . hmmm."

"What?" Franny said.

"I'm not saying for sure—I'm just saying it might be . . . that . . . she's . . ."

"What already?" Franny's voice rose with frustration.

"The . . . Wicked . . . um . . . Witch of, like, the West," Cat finally said.

"Cha Cha?" Franny and Ivy said together.

"Oh, so you believe *Cat* when she says there's a connection to Oz!" Pru grabbed her Oz book and began to page through it furiously. "Nobody ever believes *me!*"

"Cat may be right." Franny hated to admit it.

"But Cha Cha *can't* be the Wicked Witch of the West!" Pru pointed to a page in the book. "She's dead—Dorothy killed her, remember?"

"Well, Cha Cha is *some* kind of wicked witch

then." Cat shook her head and thought about the old man she had conjured. He *had* to be the wizard from Oz—who else flew around in a green balloon with O.Z. on it? An awful feeling crept over her as she recalled what he'd said about the "b-i-i-i-i-g weather coming in from the west. Old Hurricane Cha Cha—when she hits, watch out!"

Fred and Ginger whimpered, and Ivy brought them over to the rug to sit with Franny, where they listened to Cat tell them of her conjuration.

"There's nothing about a backwards tidal wave in *The Wonderful Wizard of Oz*," Pru said impatiently from the window seat.

"There isn't?" Cat replied. "But this old guy flew down in a balloon—just like in *The Wizard of Oz*. Didn't he fly in a balloon?"

"All right." Pru rolled her eyes. "He flew in a balloon, but there was no backwards tidal wave!"

"And he said there was going to be a hurricane—Hurricane Cha Cha. As far as I'm concerned, that was a hurricane last night—and now Cha Cha is *here*," Cat said excitedly. "And he had a message for me, too!"

Franny and Ivy waited in anticipation. Pru stared out the window.

"He *said* . . ." Cat began. "It was hard to hear because of the balloon, but he *said*, Hieronymus Gumm . . . behind."

"Hieronymus Gumm's behind?" Franny said wrinkling her nose. "P.U.!"

Cat hadn't thought of it *that* way, and she started to giggle.

"Honestly!" Pru said in a huff. "That's disgusting!"

Ivy ignored this exchange and asked, "Is that it? Did he say anything else, Cat?"

"No," Cat said trying to think back. "Oh! Except he was laughing a lot, and as he flew away he wished me well, I think."

"That was nice of him," Pru snorted. "Did you wish him well back?"

The three girls looked at Pru, frowning, and were quiet for a moment, while Fred and Ginger sat like two stuffed animals.

"I know it sounds crazy, but it kind of fits," Cat said, changing the subject. "That Cha Cha's a wicked witch."

Could it really be? The girls looked from one to the other to try to measure each other's feelings.

Franny spoke first. "I say we kill her." She reached for Pru's Oz book, but Pru pulled it away from her.

"Doesn't it tell you in there to throw a bucket of water on her or something?"

"Are you crazy?" Pru wailed. "We can't *kill* her!"

The mood in the room had grown somber. Even the sun had gone in, and now it was dark outside. Pru leaned forwards and peeked out the window. It was raining. "Hey, guys, this is weird. It's not supposed to rain like this in the middle of the day."

The other three crowded around the window and looked as well.

"This isn't good," Cat said.

Franny turned to Cat. "Why don't you ask that Ching thing what we should to do?"

"What do you mean *we*?" Pru grumbled.

"The *I Ching*," Cat corrected Franny, taking the three pennies from her back pocket.

Franny and Ivy sat on the rug again, and Pru reluctantly joined them. All three watched as Cat threw the coins and wrote down the lines. They had no idea what she was doing. The house swayed in the wind, and Pru placed her hands alongside of her on the floor to steady herself, wondering all the time how she had ever let Franny talk her into this mess.

After six tosses of the coins, Cat opened the *I Ching*

to find her answer.

"What does it say?" Franny leaned over to see what Cat was reading.

"BIG T," Cat said gravely and pressed her lips together into a worried expression.

"Big T?" Franny leaned over to see for herself.

"T as in trouble," Cat clarified.

Ivy took Ginger onto her lap and pulled Fred close to her side.

"I thought the *I Ching* was an *ancient* Chinese text!" Pru grabbed the book away from Cat to see for herself. "This is your mother's cockamamie translation!" she scoffed. "Oh, this ought to be good!"

Franny snatched the book away from Pru and gave it back to Cat. "What does it mean, Cat?"

Pru stuck out her lower lip and sulked.

Cat began to read:

"Danger, danger everywhere,
underground and in the air.
Auras dark and Chakras jumbled,
face your foes and do not stumble!"

"Yeah, right," Pru said under her breath.

"Shut up, Pru," Franny said.

Cat flipped to another page. "It says here that BIG T changes into REACH OUT AND TOUCH SOMEONE. I'll read it to you.

"Drop those beads and macramé.
Get off your can right now, today!
Avoid bad karma—it's no fun.
Join hands—reach out and touch someone!"

"That's it," Cat said, and slapped the book shut.

"Your mother is completely out of her mind," Pru said.

No one answered.

Franny broke the silence. "I just got the greatest idea!"

"Oh, terrific," Pru groaned. "I hope it's better than anti-zombie spray."

"It's more like the *I Ching*'s idea," Franny said. She liked her new idea too much to let Pru discourage her. "You heard Cha Cha. She thinks that Ivy doesn't have any friends to help her. That's where we come in. She'll never suspect."

"Suspect what?" Cat asked.

"We form a secret group, like a club," Franny said.

Pru, Cat, and Ivy looked at one another and rolled their eyes. Clubs were for little kids.

"That's a terrible idea," Ivy said.

"Terrible," Pru said through pursed lips.

"Yeah, it's right up there with *cartwheel* school." Cat covered her mouth and tried not to laugh.

Franny ignored Cat. "Why is it such a terrible idea?"

Ivy placed Ginger next to her and pulled the "Carpe Diem!" T-shirt over her knees. "Because I don't want you guys involved. What if Cha Cha finds out? Who knows what she'd do?"

Rain pattered against the window.

"Yeah, Ivy's right," Pru said, and rose to leave.

Franny pulled her back down and whispered, "Cha Cha's a witch and it's up to us to get rid of her."

None of the girls said anything.

Franny forged ahead. "Look, we start by acting like we all hate each other so she doesn't suspect."

"Act?" Pru said.

"Suspect what?" Cat said.

"That we're looking for that other silver shoe—undercover, like spies, you know? It'll be so cool.

We can be just like Mata Hari!"

"Mata Whoey?" Cat said.

"Mata Hari—she was a famous spy." Franny's cheeks were flushed with excitement. "And then we get Cha Cha! That part I haven't figured out, but—"

Cat snorted, and Pru impatiently flipped her ponytail over her shoulder. Fred and Ginger sniffed, and Ivy looked worried.

"But wait! Wait!" Franny was up on her knees. She pushed her hair off her face. "Here's the *best* part!"

There was no reaction but, undaunted, Franny continued, "I even have a name for us." She motioned for them to come closer until their four heads almost touched, and then she whispered, "The Secret Order of the Gumm Street Girls." Franny waited expectantly. It was the best idea she'd ever had, she thought. "There's more—I even have a club motto!" The three stared expressionless as Franny continued enthusiastically, " 'We stick together.' Get it? Gum? Stick like gum? Since we live on Gumm Street?"

"Good grief," Pru muttered, leaning back and looking for split hairs in the end of her ponytail.

Cat rolled over onto her back, covered her eyes, and said to herself, "So lame."

"Franny, stop it." Ivy hugged her knees. "I can handle this by myself—it's not like I haven't had a Jinx before—I'm fine."

"Oh yeah, you're just great," Franny replied. "Show Cat and Pru your hand, Ivy."

"It's no big deal, Franny." Ivy took her right hand out from under her T-shirt and opened her palm for Cat and Pru to see. Fred and Ginger nudged their way in to look as well.

"It looks like some kind of an eye," Pru murmured, and backed away just in case it was contagious.

"Cool," said Cat. "Where'd you get it?"

"When I touched the shoe for the first time, I think," said Ivy.

"But you're just *fine*," Franny mocked. "So? Are you guys in?"

Cat drummed her fingers on the shag carpet, and Pru folded her arms.

"Come on, Franny," Ivy begged.

Franny talked right over her, addressing only Cat and Pru. "Ivy's got a Jinx, an eye on her hand, and a wicked witch after her, but what do you care? Pru, you're too busy reading and eating cereal all summer, and Cat's got to do cartwheels up and down Gumm Street, so of course you don't have the time. But I don't have *anything* else to do more important than helping Ivy, so whether or not you guys want to join, *I'm* having a club. Maybe I'll even be *president!*"

"Okay, okay, you don't have to get all huffy!" Cat said irritably. She had to admit that Franny had a point—a point with a dorky club attached to it, but a point. She couldn't stop thinking about the old guy in the balloon—the wizard. He had predicted the hurricane and Cha Cha. Cat had to do *some*thing, but she didn't want to do it if it meant having to hang around Pru all summer. "Just so I understand," Cat began. "We join this club and we'll be spies, right?"

"Right!" Franny said.

"It sounds kind of *dangerous*." Cat glanced at Pru. "Lots of sneaking around in the dark, right?"

"Right," said Franny.

"And jumping off fire escapes, and climbing down manholes and up flagpoles, and sliding off roofs, and hanging onto the wings of planes . . . right?"

"Right," said Franny. "Except for the planes . . . I don't think there will be any wing hanging."

"I'm in, then." Cat looked over at Pru again and smirked.

Pru's eyes were wide and her breathing was shallow. Pru knew exactly what Cat was thinking: *Chicken.*

"Pru?" Franny waited.

Pru glared at Cat. "I'm in, too," she said, and watched with relish as the smirk on Cat's face disintegrated.

Franny reached over and pressed her palm to Ivy's. "I, Franny Muggs, swear by my membership in the Secret Order of the Gumm Street Girls, to help my friend Ivy get rid of her Jinx and Cha Cha."

Fred and Ginger came forwards to offer their paws in a vote of confidence.

"Me, too," said Pru, smirking at Cat and placing her hand on Franny and Ivy's.

"Ditto," said Cat doing the same and giving Pru a dirty look.

"Here's to the Secret Order of the Gumm Street Girls!" Franny declared.

"Yeah, right." Pru pulled her hand away and hoped it wasn't too late to cross her fingers.

"All I have to say"—Cat leaned back on her arms, pushed her lower lip out, and blew her bangs up off her forehead—"is that this is a great way to start summer vacation."

Cha Cha WINS FRIENDS & INFLUENCES PEOPLE

18

*T*wo weeks passed, and soon all of Sherbet was buzzing about the glamorous new owner of #7 Gumm Street.

Have you ever noticed how we are most attracted to the worst things? We want cookies that make us fat and candy that rots our teeth; we want to stay up all night when we should rest, and we want to go out in the rain when we have a cold. To all of the folks in Sherbet (except for the Gumm Street Girls, of course), Cha Cha represented drama, glamour, excitement—all the things that usually spell trouble—and for this reason she was a spectacular hit.

To each person Cha Cha had something different to offer.

Patience Gumm, Pru's mother, lacking in any fashion sense, studied Cha Cha. In the spiral pad that had once been used to write down notes for helpful columns for *The Sherbet Scoop*, Patience recorded Cha Cha's every move: her walk, her talk, and her outfits, right down to the mysterious stranger's fishnet stockings.

Home from their travels, Babe and Angus Muggs had come back to find on their very own street a creature as exotic as the ones they usually traveled thousands of miles to see.

"She's fabulous!" Angus exclaimed.

"As fabulous as me?" Babe pouted, though she agreed with her husband. The next day she made an appointment to get some highlights.

And that's not all. Babe found that Cha Cha was a wealth of information on tonics for youth and reju-

venation, made from *potatoes*, of all things.
With Cha Cha's encouragement, she began
writing a book called *Eat Your Spuds, Change Your Life!*

Even the Lemonjellos were impressed. Cha Cha
guessed their sun signs right off the bat; contacted
Great-Grandpa Lemonjello, who sent warm regards
from "the other side"; and found the love beads that
Lenny and Lynette had lost in the mud at Woodstock.
Soon enough they were consulting Cha Cha on
every little thing and had come to think of her as
their guru.

Sherbet couldn't get enough of Cha Cha, and Cha
Cha gave them what they wanted. Why? To find the
other shoe! She gave them recipes, astrological read-
ings, beauty makeovers, counseling on love and
money. She could cure everything from warts to male
pattern baldness, and even organized a raffle to ben-
efit Sherbet Academy, to which she donated her

champagne-colored Cadillac. Much to their delight, the folks over at the Colossal Candy Bar won. They polished the chrome and champagne till the car sparkled like a gigantic piece of jewelry, placed it smack in the middle of the store, and filled it to the brim with jelly beans—creating a display that had every tongue in Sherbet wagging.

Cha Cha wormed her way into their lives, and in return they told her their hopes, their dreams, their deepest fears, everything. . . . Well, almost everything, because no one knew anything about the shoe.

"Rats!" Cha Cha said—a lot.

Ivy tried to warn her mother about Cha Cha, but Pearl was not about to listen to anything negative about her new best friend. Pearl never even recognized her own erstwhile Cadillac. "I used to have one just like!" she exclaimed when it was raffled off. In fact, none of the girls were able to convince anyone in

Sherbet that there was anything bad about Cha Cha.

Meanwhile, nobody but the four girls noticed that the weather in Sherbet had become erratic—there was a persistent wind from the west, and the daily rainbows that usually began when school let out for summer vacation had yet to show up. Nobody noticed because they had all fallen under Cha Cha's spell.

True to their promise, Franny, Pru, Cat, and Ivy told no one about their secret order, but they hadn't found out anything, either. It was Pru of all people who stumbled upon an important fact at a meeting one night in Franny's tower room two weeks after Cha Cha's arrival.

"What's your mother's maiden name?" Pru asked Ivy, when all the girls had gathered and Franny had passed out her Jelly Squirtz candy.

Ivy thought. "It was Gale."

Pru took her chewed pencil out of her mouth. "Oh my gosh." She took a deep breath and exhaled deeply. "Re-e-e-ally? Are you sure?"

"Of course I'm sure," Ivy said. "Why?"

"Because I was rereading *The Wonderful Wizard of Oz*." Pru held up her tattered copy of the book. "Dorothy's last name was—"

"Gale! I knew it!" Cat interrupted.

Pru turned her back on Cat and said to Ivy, "Dorothy's last name was Gale, so that would mean, Ivy, that your mother is possibly related to Dorothy, and—"

"And Ivy would be related to Dorothy, too!" Franny finished Pru's sentence.

Ivy caught the side of her lip with her upper teeth. "My Aunt Viola—who's dead—was named Gale, too." Ivy thought back to Aunt V's letter and was suddenly aware of her heart beating inside her chest. If Aunt V was a descendant of Dorothy, then maybe *that's* why she thought the shoes belonged to her.

"That's why Cha Cha tried to give my mother the Jinx!" Ivy exclaimed. "Cha Cha figured the silver shoes might be going to the next Gale!" She swallowed hard. "What do you think Cha Cha will do?"

"She'll probably get rid of you," Franny said matter-of-factly.

"*Franny-y-y-y!*" Pru said crossly. "You're scaring Ivy."

"Think about it." Franny said, popping a Jelly Squirtz in her mouth. "Cha Cha has the one shoe already, and Ivy is the only one who knows anything." Franny sat chewing on her candy for a moment. "If I were a wicked witch and all . . ."—Franny looked up at the ceiling—"I'd probably send you off to some dark place in Oz, to, like, get you out of the picture."

"If she does that, we're all going!" announced Cat.

"No!" Ivy protested.

"Yes, and I know *just* what we'll do," Franny said excitedly. "What we need is a plan!" With her extensive knowledge of expeditions, Franny was full of ideas. "We'll be prepared. We'll collect stuff we might need—"

"Now wait just a minute," Pru interrupted her, throwing her ponytail over her shoulder in a gesture of authority, which Cat thought was becoming an annoying habit. "None of us are going *anywhere*." She had never wanted to be a part of this crazy club in the first place, and she might as well tell them right now that she had no intention of venturing farther than her bedroom this summer. After all, she would need her rest. Pru hadn't told anyone, but in the fall she was being moved to the mysterious Bacon-Lettuce-and-Tomato at school. Nobody knew *what* they did over in Bacon-Lettuce-and-Tomato, and as much as Pru hated being stuck with Cat, the idea of moving to this weird class was worse. No, Pru was staying put. She had to rest up until the fall.

All three girls looked at Pru.

"Maybe *you're* not going anywhere," Franny said glaring at her, "but *I'm* sticking with Ivy!"

"You guys," Ivy said, trying to stop the bickering. "Who said I was even going anywhere?"

"Cat, aren't you getting any kind of vibes about this?" Franny asked.

"I hate to tell you this." It had been bothering Cat ever since the morning of the recital. "But the *I Ching* said that I was supposed to grab my backpack and leave town because heavy stuff was coming down."

"See?" said Franny.

Ginger started to howl.

"That'll do, Ginger," Ivy said, and Ginger stopped.

"I think Ivy's only option is to hide," Cat declared.

Pru anxiously began to braid and unbraid her hair.

"You can stay here with me, Ivy," Franny said brightly in an effort to break the tense mood in the room. "Come on, it'll be fun!"

Ivy raised her eyes to meet her friend's and smiled.

"But won't Pearl be frantic if Ivy is missing?" Pru said.

They were all silent for a moment, mulling over this new problem. The girls knew that Pearl would be searching for Ivy in no time flat.

"Pearl won't be frantic," Franny assured them. "I've got a great idea!"

Pru groaned.

"Step one," said Franny. "We make a list."

Here is the list Franny came up with.

1. toothbrush
2. toothpaste
3. clean underwear (4)
4. socks (4)
5. flashlight/batteries
6. chocolate bars
   raisins, nuts, etc.
7. water bottle/water
8. t-shirts (2)
9. jeans (1)
10. soap (1)
11. matches
12. rain poncho
13. vitamin C
14. comb
15. blanket

Franny gave a copy of the list to each girl. "We have to put this stuff in our own personal backpacks like the *I Ching* said to do—just in case."

"Just in case what?" Pru asked.

"Just in case Cha Cha tries to send Ivy to some dark, horrible place so that we can be ready to go with her," Franny said impatiently. "Why else—geez, Pru!"

"Quit it, Franny," Pru moaned. "I'm getting a stomachache."

"Ivy," Franny said, ignoring Pru. "You still have the ruby-red slipper that you took from Mr. Staccato's case, right?"

"Of course I do," Ivy replied.

"Step two," Franny continued. "We get rid of Cha Cha—once and for all!"

"And what's your great idea for doing that?" Cat wanted to know.

"Three words: spray paint, note, bucket."

"That's four words," Pru pointed out.

"Whatever. Cha Cha wants a silver shoe?" Franny said slyly. "We're going to give her one!"

CAT'S ESP DREAM

*E*arly Saturday morning Ivy awoke with a start to the faint beeping of her alarm. She rolled over to look at the clock: 3:35 it read. 3:35? Had she really set it that early? Ivy hit the alarm to make it stop and lay back down.

"Rise and shine!" a voice said.

Standing over Ivy's hammock was Cha Cha Staccato. "So happy to see that you have finally come to see things *my* way." She fluttered a note in Ivy's face. In the darkness, Ivy could just barely make out Franny's handwriting: "Dear Cha Cha . . ."

"Y-yes, Mzzzz Staccato," Ivy stammered, thankful that she had slept in her clothes. Ivy felt under the covers for the slipper and wrapped her fingers around it.

"I'm giving this to you, Mzzzz Staccato, just what you've always wanted, a nice"—Ivy frowned and picked off a piece of lint that had stuck to the paint—"um, sparkly *silver* shoe!"

Cha Cha's eyes glowed as she snatched it away from Ivy, but the very next moment she shook her head sadly. "Ivy, Ivy, Ivy, Ivy. First you try and steal my shoe, then you say bad things behind my back to Pearl and everyone in town, and *now* you try this pathetic attempt to trick me? The next thing you know, you'll dump a you-know-what on me like that other little brat did to my sister! Heh!" She threw the counterfeit shoe at Fred, missing him by a hair.

Ivy struggled out of her hammock. "Don't you hurt him!" she said careful to keep her voice down so as not to wake her mother.

"Hurt him?" Cha Cha zipped across the room, and in a flash she had a very unhappy-looking Fred and Ginger gripped in each hand. "You know, all my life I've been an animal lover," she said. Fred growled; she pinched him and he yelped.

Ivy was furious. "You old bag, give me back my dogs!"

Cha Cha sashayed to the window seat, looking coyly at Ivy over one shoulder. "Now, is that any way to say thanks to your Aunt Cha Cha?" Seating herself, Cha Cha crossed her legs, showing off the fishnet stockings that were the talk of all Sherbet.

"Thanks?" Ivy said as she quietly slipped her feet into her running shoes. "Thanks for what?"

"For dog sitting, silly. I'm going to take care of your little doggies while you're away at camp."

"Camp?"

"Yes, I'm sending you to an absolutely *fabulous* music camp for little geniuses like yourself—all expenses paid! Your mother will be just *thrilled* when I tell her. I bet her exact words will be 'Ah'm so pa-roud!'"

Ivy tried to grab Fred and Ginger, but Cha Cha was too quick for her, and dashed across the room. "Kids today," she said, "you give and you give and you give. . . ." Ivy could see her eyes widen beneath the veil. "I thought you'd be pleased."

"Well, I'm *not!*" Ivy lunged at her again, but Cha Cha skipped past and sprang down the stairs with Ivy in hot pursuit.

Cha Cha flung open the door of #5 Gumm, but Cat was there, ready for her. She drew the bucket backwards and heaved its contents at Cha Cha. It was a perfect shot—Cha Cha was soaking wet!

"Now look what you've gone and done!" Cha Cha screeched, dropping the two dogs. They scrambled over to Ivy.

"I'm me-e-e-e-l-l-l-l-ting!" Cha Cha screamed.

And melting she was. Cha Cha was dripping down like a lit candle in fast-forwards, until there was nothing left except some nasty brown substance and a pile of designer clothes.

Cat found a stick in the yard and gingerly picked up the dripping nylons. The only things left of Cha Cha were her fishnets . . . *fishnets* . . . *fishnets.* . . .

"Fishnets," Cat was mumbling. For a moment she didn't even know where she was. She sat up and struggled to take a deep breath. Looking around her familiar bedroom, she felt a surge of relief, but then bolted out of bed as if she'd been hit with a cattle prod.

"Ivy!" she said out loud. Cat knew that what she'd just experienced was no ordinary dream. She jumped into her clothes, grabbed Franny's stupid emergency backpack, and raced out the door to round up the others.

Cat's first stop was the wedding-cake house. She ran up the circular stairway until she reached the tower room.

"Franny, Franny, wake up!" Cat called out.

"What?" said Franny sleepily.

"Ivy's in trouble; we have to get Pru!" Cat banged on the door.

Franny stumbled out of bed and let Cat in. Then she threw on the outfit she'd kept ready all her life for just this moment: her checked shirt, water-resistant hiking shorts, and her hiking boots. The pack was in the corner ready to go. Cat tossed it to Franny. "You're going to need this," she said, and they left for Pru's.

"Pru! Pru! Wake up!" Franny knocked at Pru's window.

The light came on, and it was only the fear of waking up her parents—who absolutely, positively had to

have eight hours of sleep a night—that finally got Pru to open the door and let the two girls in.

Cat grabbed Pru's backpack while Franny got her some clothes. All the while Pru wanted to make it perfectly clear that she was only going outside to shut them both up and not to go on some wild goose chase to God only knows where, and did they both understand that?

"You're not going to talk me into doing any of these crazy things, Franny Muggs," Pru said, pulling a shirt over her head.

In minutes they were all standing on Gumm Street.

Pru finished dressing as Franny went through Pru's backpack to make sure she had everything.

"Pru, you only have one pair of socks! Now we're going to have to go back!" Franny scolded.

"Oh, please," Pru grumbled. "It's not like we're actually going anywhere—"

But Pru's words were cut short. At that moment the door to #5 Gumm Street banged open. They stopped dead and watched as first Cha Cha, holding Fred and Ginger, and then Ivy flew out of it.

"We're too late!" Cat hissed.

"Come on!" Franny called, and took off after them, Cat on her heels.

"Wait!" hollered Pru, hopping on one foot as she put the other into her pink clam diggers. "I'm coming, too!"

20

FISHNETS

With the moon to light her way, Ivy chased Cha Cha down Gumm Street and into the heart of Sherbet. Ivy never knew she could run so fast until this night, but Cha Cha was even faster, and Ivy wondered how in the world that woman ran like that in such high heels. Especially

while carrying two fat terriers. It almost looked like her feet weren't even touching the ground. They ran, and they ran, and they ran, west through the sleeping town, and Ivy was astonished to see Cha Cha heading straight toward the Colossal Candy Bar. It was 4:00 in the morning by now and way too early to be selling candy. Nevertheless, the enormous doors swung open ahead of Cha Cha and she disappeared inside.

Ivy followed. *Now I've got her*, she thought.

Ivy ran down an aisle of bins piled high with candy in brightly colored cellophane. At the very end, seated on a round stool at the bar, with not a hair out of place, was Cha Cha. She swiveled around to face Ivy.

"Looking for these?" she asked, holding up the terrified Fred and Ginger.

"Give them back!" Ivy yelled.

"Give them back, *what?*" Cha Cha sang.

"*Mzzzz* Staccato!" Ivy fumed.

"Ms. Staccato what?" Cha Cha said.

"Please give me my dogs back, *Mzzzz* Staccato." Ivy's voice shook with anger.

"You know, technically they're not really *your* dogs." Cha Cha scrunched up her nose. "But I'll just overlook that little detail—"

CRASH!

Cha Cha jumped, almost dropping Fred and Ginger and unsettling her lamp shade hat. It was Pru, Cat, and Franny, who had burst into the store and knocked over a candy display.

"Well, look who's here," Cha Cha said, regaining her composure. The front doors clanged shut.

Pru had gone completely white.

"Don't you dare faint," Franny said out of the side of her mouth.

Ginger squirmed in Cha Cha's arms. "It seems that our Ivy has her little heart set on bringing her doggies with her. Even though I so generously offered to"—Cha Cha curled her lip—"dog sit. But you know what? I'm going to be a good sport about it. You want them? Take them!" She held the dogs out to Ivy.

"Come here, Fred and Ginger." Ivy reached for them, but as soon as she did, Cha Cha snatched them away.

"Why don't you take them?" Cha Cha sniggered.

Ivy tried again and again, and each time at the last second Cha Cha yanked them just out of reach, until she seemed weak from laughter. *Click, click, click* went Cha Cha's stilettos as she headed to the middle of the store, where the champagne-colored Cadillac sat in all its glory, jam-packed to the roof with who knows how many jelly beans. Which was exactly what the sign next to it asked: GUESS HOW MANY JELLY BEANS AND WIN A COLOSSAL SUPPLY OF CANDY! Cha Cha skipped up the steps of the platform and opened the door, releasing a flood of jelly beans. "You want your mangy mutts? They're all yours!" she yelled. And with that she threw Fred and Ginger inside.

Ivy dove in after them.

"*No!* Ivy!" Pru shouted.

But it was too late. The door shut tight and locked.

Ivy pounded on the windows while Fred and Ginger howled.

"Let her go, you old cow!" Cat shouted.

Cha Cha spun around. "You know what?" She flitted down the steps off the platform. "You three are beginning to get on my nerves." Cha Cha drummed her black-gloved fingers on her hips. "Silver spray paint? Puh-leeze!" She straightened her veil. "No, I don't like the looks of you three at all! You're just like that little snot-nosed Dorothy. And honestly, if I see any more gingham or polyester, I think I may *retch!*"

Franny shifted self-consciously in her red-and-white checked cotton shirt and water-resistant shorts.

Cha Cha tilted her head and considered the three girls for a moment. "Then again," she said smoothly, and with a wave of her hand she appeared to be holding a large, round green grape between her thumb and index finger. "I think they might just *love* you where you're going."

"They?" Cat asked.

"Going?" Pru squeaked.

Franny pulled the two closer to her.

Cha Cha pushed her face an inch away from Cat's, examining it this way and that. Next Franny's, and then Pru's. "So visibly firm," she said excitedly, as if to herself, "and with no fine lines!" The girls huddled together, holding their breaths. Cha Cha grinned malevolently behind the veil. "Like a plump . . . juicy"—she squeezed it until it popped—"grape!" she crowed, and laughed as she climbed back onto the platform.

"Fishnets, fishnets," she sang to herself.

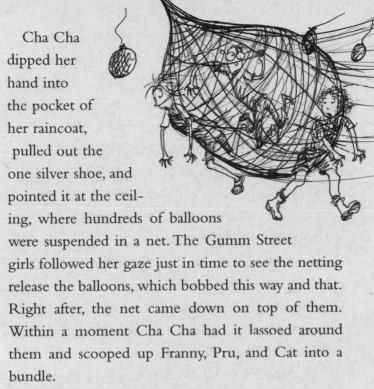

Cha Cha
dipped her
hand into
the pocket of
her raincoat,
 pulled out the
one silver shoe, and
pointed it at the ceil-
ing, where hundreds of balloons
were suspended in a net. The Gumm Street
girls followed her gaze just in time to see the netting
release the balloons, which bobbed this way and that.
Right after, the net came down on top of them.
Within a moment Cha Cha had it lassoed around
them and scooped up Franny, Pru, and Cat into a
bundle.

"I've caught my little fishies in the net," Cha Cha
warbled. "I know you're going to just *love* your new
playmates, Bling Bling and Coco!"

The bundle of girls rose up in the air,
higher and higher, until it hovered over the
Cadillac. The sunroof of the car flipped up
and the netting opened, dumping the
girls in. One by one they landed with a
jolt, the remaining jelly beans breaking

their fall. The sunroof snapped shut above them.

"Let us out!" screamed Franny. All three pounded on the windows. (Pru had passed out.)

Cha Cha turned the shoe around and around and pointed it at the car. The car's engine kicked on and the car, too, rotated around and around, and then drove down the ramp and off the platform.

"She's sending us to Oz!" Cat yelled.

"Oz?" Cha Cha sneered. "Dream on."

Cha Cha wiggled the shoe, and slowly and deliberately the big car rumbled past row after row of clear plastic candy dispensers filled with every flavor of Jelly Squirtz, jawbreaker, and gumdrop.

"Stop! Stop!" the three girls screamed, and Fred and Ginger barked, all to no avail.

"Au revoir!" Cha Cha sang out, waving the shoe at the car full of girls. "Don't forget to write!"

The giant doors glided open, and the champagne-colored Cadillac eased through them and out of the store.

"I just hate long good-byes" was the last thing they heard Cha Cha say.

21 Backwards Tidal Wave Travelers

*O*utside, the clear starry night had been replaced by nothing short of a monsoon, and inside the champagne-colored Cadillac, all was utter mayhem.

"Put it in park!" screamed Pru, who had regained consciousness. "Step on the brake! Brake!"

"I'm trying!" Franny yelled back. "There are so many jelly beans, I can't *find* the brake!"

Cat, who was between Pru and Franny, dug frantically, searching for the ignition, while jelly beans rolled off the dashboard.

Ivy leaned over from the backseat. "Pull out the keys! Open the windows! Unlock the doors!" she shouted while Fred and Ginger barked and howled.

But the car had a mind of its own. It made its way slowly around the parking lot until it reached the farthest end and stopped.

"Oh, thank God!" Pru said, and tried the handle again. The door miraculously opened. "Look, you guys!" she exclaimed.

All of a sudden the darkened dashboard lit up. The car shot forwards and turned out of the parking lot with such force that Pru's door swung open all the way—with Pru attached to it.

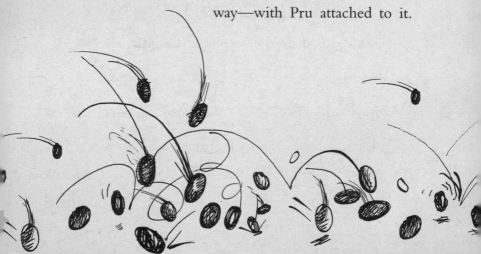

Halfway out of the car and
still clutching the door handle, Pru
looked down to see hundreds of jelly
beans raining out of the car and bouncing
off the pavement that raced beneath her.
"Help! Help!" she screamed.

Cat leaned over and, seizing the back of Pru's
T-shirt, tugged hard, reeling Pru in, and then
slammed the door shut.

"Safety Tip Number Five Hundred Sixty-One."
Cat wiped the rain off her face. "Never open the
door of a moving vehicle."

"I could have been killed!" Pru sputtered.

But the others took no notice. Frozen in their seats,
the girls sat and watched helplessly as the car raced
faster and faster straight toward the beach. They could
feel the gravel under the wheels crackle and pop and
the jarring bumps of potholes here and there. They
could hear the beating of

the rain on the roof and the *thwack, thwack, thwack* of the windshield wipers, which provided little more than a blurry view of where they were going.

"Okay, okay." Franny talked fast. "Here's what we need to do—if the car crashes into the ocean, we hold onto our backpacks like floatation devices, see?" She demonstrated by holding the pack to her chest.

"Floatation devices, my foot!" Cat shouted above the noise of the rain.

With a bang, the car hit the beach and turned again sharply, careening around on two wheels. Sand splattered against the windows, blacking them out for a moment.

Slowed by the sand, the car angrily gunned its motor and lurched forwards toward the ocean. Pru covered her face and started to cry.

"Don't cry, Pru!" Cat said. "You're making it worse—right, Ivy?" She turned around to look at Ivy.

"Oh . . . my . . . gosh," Ivy said.

"What is it?" Cat could see Ivy's eyes go wide with terror.

Cat just pointed toward the windshield. "B-backwards . . . backwards . . ."

"Backwards *what*?" Cat turned to see for herself.

"TIDAL WAVE!" Franny screamed. "Get down

into the jelly beans, guys!" She and Cat and Pru dug themselves down deep, until only their heads were sticking out.

Coming straight at them was an enormous long, black tongue of water. It curled unnaturally beneath the wheels of the champagne-colored Cadillac and licked it up, as if it were about to swallow it whole.

Ivy burrowed down toward the floor of the car, holding Fred and Ginger. She felt the weight of something close over her like a heavy quilt . . . or was it the shadow of the Jinx? Ivy shuddered as the tail of the car dipped. She drew the two dogs even closer to her and hoped the car wasn't about to slide backwards and crash onto the beach.

But the force of the wave was too strong. It washed over the car, tossing it about as if it had just been thrown into a giant washing machine. Then, like a cork, the car popped up out of the water, and the girls found that they were *on top* of the backwards tidal wave and being swept farther and farther out to sea. They braced themselves, not sure of what would happen next, literally balanced on the tip of a mountain of water. The car wobbled dangerously, high, high up in the air—so high that they could still see the twinkling lights of Sherbet growing tiny far off in the

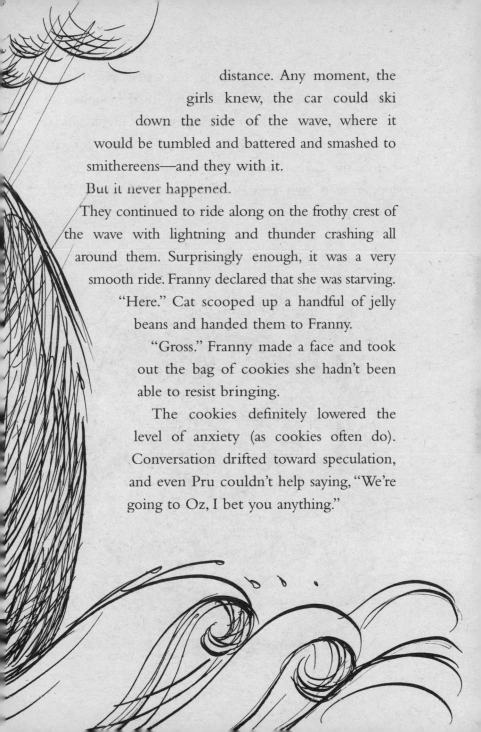

distance. Any moment, the girls knew, the car could ski down the side of the wave, where it would be tumbled and battered and smashed to smithereens—and they with it.

But it never happened.

They continued to ride along on the frothy crest of the wave with lightning and thunder crashing all around them. Surprisingly enough, it was a very smooth ride. Franny declared that she was starving.

"Here." Cat scooped up a handful of jelly beans and handed them to Franny.

"Gross." Franny made a face and took out the bag of cookies she hadn't been able to resist bringing.

The cookies definitely lowered the level of anxiety (as cookies often do). Conversation drifted toward speculation, and even Pru couldn't help saying, "We're going to Oz, I bet you anything."

And if they were *not* going to Oz, where *were* they going? the others wondered. But with the cookies gone, and having had very little sleep that night, and with the gentle rocking of the car, it wasn't long before the Gumm Street girls found they could no longer keep their eyes open and, one by one, they drifted off to sleep.

Welcome to SPOZ

The four girls awakened to find themselves in complete darkness. The car was still and quiet, and when Pru tried the door she was happy to find that it opened.

But this time, she was cautious. "Wait," she warned.

Franny opened her door as well and carefully stuck

out a toe. Satisfied to find solid ground beneath her feet, she hopped out. "It's okay," she told the others. "Come on."

Imagine for a moment that you have just stepped out of a plane and are walking down the corridor that connects the aircraft to the airport. Now imagine that the corridor is very dark except for some tiny lights like those in a movie theater on either side of the aisle. This is exactly the scene that greeted our girls when they stepped outside the champagne-colored Cadillac. The car was in a dark hangar, and a twin line of lights led away.

Holding hands, they picked their way carefully along the corridor. Fred and Ginger followed closely behind. The corridor gently turned, and they could see a pinkish glow in the distance.

"This is not at all the way I pictured Oz," Cat said as she and the others reached the threshold of what appeared to be a modern, shiny, sparkly airport.

"Maybe we can catch the next plane back to Sherbet," Franny said hopefully.

"Or the next *car*," muttered Pru.

Folks bustled about as they would in any major travel hub, but they were not dressed in business suits, khakis, or raincoats. Nor were they dressed in green outfits with pointy hats as the Munchkins had worn in the Oz movie. Instead, they were swathed from head to foot in hooded pink terry-cloth bathrobes, and on their feet they wore pink terry-cloth slippers.

"I bet they're Munchkins!" Franny said.

"Pink Munchkins?" Ivy asked in a low voice.

Like Munchkins, the people *were* all rather short, but beyond that it was difficult to tell, for their heads were hidden under their hoods, their features lost in shadow.

"Something tells me we're not in Oz," Pru said.

"Wel-come—to—Spoz," the soothing recorded voice of a woman announced.

The space the girls were in—which we will call the "galleria" (for no other word grand enough comes to mind)—was composed of marble, chrome, mirror, and other glittery, shiny materials. Perhaps because the artificial light of Spoz was so dazzling, the girls never noticed what was hiding behind a marble pillar. Its black eyes gleamed as they focused on Ivy.

The girls proceeded to the center of the galleria, where a spectacular fountain jetted out pale pink spray. High above, four condominium-sized glittering silver letters spelled out the word *SPOZ*.

"Wel-come—to—Spoz," the voice said again. "Home—of—the—Beautyliator!"

"Beautyli-*what*-er?" Cat said.

While the others were mesmerized by the fountain, Ivy had been looking all around. She felt responsible for her friends being here, and she felt as though she should assume the role of leader—or at least try. It wasn't easy. Which way should they go? There was a confusion of signs everywhere. But not for the usual things you'd expect in an airport, such as BAGGAGE CLAIM or TAXIS. These signs were for SKIN THAT'S VISIBLY FIRM!, SMOOTH AWAY FINE LINES AND WRINKLES!, DRAMATICALLY REJUVENATE!, SPIDER VEINS GONE!, SECOND CHANCE AT YOUTH!, and TRIUMPH OVER TIME!

Which way should we go? Ivy wondered. But before she could choose a direction, Pru announced, "I have to go to the bathroom."

Everybody else admitted that they did, too. As it happened, there was a bathroom a few feet ahead of them off to the left.

The four entered not the usual grim, stinky, trash-strewn, puddly, overcrowded affair where germs lurk, just itching to get a crack at you. This bathroom was immaculate—with sparkling floors, gold fixtures, fresh flowers, and scented soaps.

Normally any place with public restrooms as clean as this one would have been A-OK in Pru's book; but then again, any place that could only be reached by riding a backwards tidal wave raised her suspicions. "Don't touch anything," she said, using a tissue to turn the water faucet.

Cat brushed her teeth, Franny washed her hands, and Ivy gave Fred and Ginger a drink from little cups of water.

Franny tried some of the hand lotion and declared, "I love it here!"

Cat didn't. She had been immediately aware that these were no garden-variety Munchkins. She was on her guard, ready for anything, but so far no one had come near her or the other girls. On the contrary, the pink-robed people seemed to go out of their way to avoid the Gumm Street girls, even making large detours to get around them.

Just then, someone came out of a stall and, seeing the girls, almost tripped on her bathrobe trying to get away as quickly as possible.

"She didn't wash her hands!" Pru said, preoccupied with washing her own thoroughly—with warm, soapy water—for thirty seconds so as to prevent catching the common cold or flu virus. She was so intent on germ killing that she had not seen something.

Cat, however, *had* seen, and now her eyes were large and round. She grabbed Franny by the elbow. "Don't look, but this place is crawling with"—she paused and lowered her voice so as not to alarm the others—"witches!"

"Witches?" Franny repeated.

Cat put a finger to her lips. "The ones outside, and the face of the one that just left, were *green* . . . and she had a nose like a *gherkin*, all bumpy and gross . . . and . . . and . . ." Cat gripped Franny's elbow hard.

"Ow." Franny pulled her arm away.

"Sorry." Cat looked over at Pru, who was still at the sink rinsing off her hands. "Pru's going to *freak*."

"I'll take care of it!" Franny said.

Franny brought a paper towel over to Pru. "Is there a safety tip about not making eye contact in strange places?" Franny asked, handing her the towel.

"Franny, you *touched* it," Pru said. She took her own towel out of the dispenser and left the restroom in a huff.

Pru kept her eyes aimed straight at the ground and tried to remember the exact wording of the safety tip about avoiding eye contact in strange places with strange people. "Is it Safety Tip Number Three Hundred Seven?" Pru muttered. "No, that's right — it's Safety Tip Number Five Hundred Twelve."

Ivy kept her gaze up, though, intent on not missing any sign that could lead them to a safe place. Rounding a corner, she saw that the marbled pink floor they had been walking on came to an end. The pink-robed figures scattered as the girls reached the top of a bank of five very wide escalators that cascaded down into a dark steel canyon whose bottom they could not see. The escalators had been divided into categories: HAIR, SKIN, NAILS, TEETH. . . .

"Look," Ivy said. "There's a way out!" She pointed to a digital sign over the fifth escalator that repeated its message over and over in a scrolling tape of silvery letters: SHERBET. . . SHERBET. . . SHERBET. . .

Thank heavens, Pru thought. She hadn't been this stressed out since she'd gotten lost coming back from the girls' room in first grade.

Franny and Cat heaved a sigh of relief.

"Come on, you two." Ivy gathered up Fred and Ginger. "We're going home." She stepped onto the corrugated metal stair and the steps glided downward. Franny followed, and then Cat. Terrified of being left behind, Pru took a deep breath and did the

same, thinking of a million reasons why she shouldn't.

But she was not the last of the party to get on the escalator. At a distance, a dark hairy shape followed, never taking its eyes off Ivy.

As they descended, the girls could see that each wide escalator branched off into smaller ones, so that HAIR split up into STYLING, COLOR, REMOVAL, and REPLACEMENT. NAILS divided into PEDICURES and MANICURES. But the SHERBET escalator never changed, continuing ever downward, ever steeper and steeper. The light became dimmer as well. Finally the escalator flattened out and deposited the Gumm Street girls in front of a pink padded door.

Ivy put Fred and Ginger down. "What was that?" Out of the corner of her eye, she thought she'd glimpsed a dark, feral shape slip past the group and vanish into the shadows. She dug out her flashlight and shined it, but saw nothing. Ivy flipped it over in her hand, thinking she could use it as a weapon. Now she felt less sure about the pink padded door. Above it, the word SHERBET glittered brightly. All Ivy wanted was to get back home! She hefted up the flashlight. If there was a giant pink three-headed monster behind the door, at least she could bop it over the head and give her friends time to flee.

Thankfully, there was no giant pink three-headed monster, just a pink locker room. The walls were pink, the floors were pink, the ceiling was pink, and the lockers were pink. Four lockers all opened at the same time, revealing pink robes and slippers.

"I feel like I'm inside a bottle of Pepto-Bismol," Franny whispered.

"Wel-come—to—Spoz. Home—of—the—Beau-ty-li-a-tor!" the voice said again. "Put—on—the—robes. . . . Put—on—the—robes. . . . Put—

on—the—robes. . . ."

"I never saw an airport with robes," Ivy said. Fred and Ginger sniffed at them suspiciously.

"It *is* kind of a nice touch," said Franny. "Usually all you get is a crummy package of peanuts."

"Put—on the—robes. . . . Put—on—the—robes. . . ."

"Yeah, well, no way am I taking my clothes off." Pru hugged herself protectively.

Cat tugged at the pink padded door. "We're locked in!"

"Put—on—the—robes. . . . Put—on—the—robes. . . ."

"Make it stop!" cried Pru. "It's driving me crazy!"

"I know," Franny suggested. "We can put the robes on top of our clothes."

"Put—on—the—robes. . . . Put—on—the—robes. . . ."

"I guess it can't hurt." Ivy touched the sleeve of one. It *did* feel soft. "Maybe we'll blend in better, too." She took it out of the locker and tried it on. The robe fit perfectly, even over her clothes. Franny did the same.

"Put—on—the—robes. . . . Put—on—the—robes. . . ."

"Geez, all right already." Cat pulled one on as well.

"How do I know where this robe has been?" Pru said, holding it at arm's length.

"Put—on—the—robes. . . . Put—on—the—robes. . . ."

The others looked at Pru, waiting, and against her better judgment she gingerly slipped an arm into one sleeve. Immediately the message stopped and a door in the back of the locker room slid open, revealing an exquisite room.

There were two enormous beds covered in heavy, pink satin fabric with mounds of soft, pink pillows. Over each bed was a crystal chandelier that twinkled in the rosy light. There was even . . .

"Candy!" Franny shouted, and pushed past Ivy to the center of the room, where an enormous gift basket waited upon a sparkling coffee table. She ripped open the basket. "Look! Jelly Squirtz!" She scooped up two handfuls of the brightly colored candies for the others to see.

"There might be poison in the candy!" Pru warned, rushing inside. She slapped the candies out of Franny's hands. "Don't you have enough candy?" Pru pointed to Franny's bulging pockets: she had brought along her stash.

"You can never have enough candy," Franny muttered, popping three in her mouth at once.

Cat entered the room and looked all around, tremendously impressed.

Less impressed, Ivy, Fred, and Ginger hesitantly joined Franny.

The floor was covered in deep, squishy, pink carpeting, and the walls were outlined in fancy decorative plasterwork. There were silver mirrors with ornate frames, and pink-and-silver dressers. The pink-and-silver marbled bathroom was loaded with exotic shampoos and beauty products. There was a large-screen TV. In fact, there was everything you can imagine you'd find in the most fabulous luxury hotel suite except for . . .

"Windows," said Cat, walking around the suite like Sherlock Holmes.

Franny opened a door off the room. "There's a pool in the bathroom!"

"Windows," Cat repeated, and lifted a floor-to-ceiling pink velvet curtain only to find a blank wall. "There aren't any!"

Pru followed Franny into the bathroom to get a cold compress for her splitting headache. "I think they call that a Jacuzzi," Pru said dryly. She took a pink washcloth and held it under the faucet of the pink porcelain sink, but no water came out. "And Cat, do you know why there *aren't* any windows?" she continued in a way-too-calm voice as she walked back into the room, so that Cat turned to look at her and asked, "Why?"

"BECAUSE WE ARE COMPLETELY UNDER-GROUND!" Pru screamed.

"Underground? Do you really—" Franny started to say.

"YES!" Pru shouted. She put her hands to her forehead and brushed past Franny. Pru flopped onto one of the enormous beds and screamed, "This is a fake bed!" Pru rapped her knuckles against it, and it made a hollow knocking sound.

Franny shook her head and tossed her backpack on the other bed, and it made a loud *kerplunk!* "She's right!" Franny exclaimed, and stared at the bed.

"There's no water in the bathroom, either!" Pru wailed. "What if I have to *go*?" She was about to break into tears. Having a bathroom handy was tops on her list of safety tips: The absence of hygienic bathrooms is the number-one cause of malaria, dysentery, and dengue fever. She lay miserably on the plywood bed and covered her face with the dry washcloth. "I thought we were going back to S–Sher-her-bet!"

"Don't worry, Pru," Ivy said. "We'll get back to Sherbet. Right, Cat?" Ivy looked up to see Cat, her face ashen, standing at the foot of the bed. "Cat?"

"Um . . . Ivy?" Cat said stiffly. "I—think—you've—been—followed." Cat pointed to the dark corner right by Ivy.

He almost blended into the shadows.

Ivy leaped up and ran to the back of the room, Fred and Ginger not far behind.

"What?" Pru uncovered her face and stood up. "The Jinx!" She ran to where Franny and the two girls huddled.

"Go away!" Ivy yelled at it.

The Jinx cringed and scurried like a poisoned rat behind the bathroom door.

Cat had had many unwanted visits from mice and squirrels in her tree house, and now she tried not to think about the vast difference between a squirrel and a Jinx. "Maybe we can lock him in the bathroom!"

"I think I'm going to be sick," Pru moaned.

Cat looked around the room for something long she could use to chase the Jinx.

Suddenly there was a knock on the door.

"Hide!" Cat yelled.

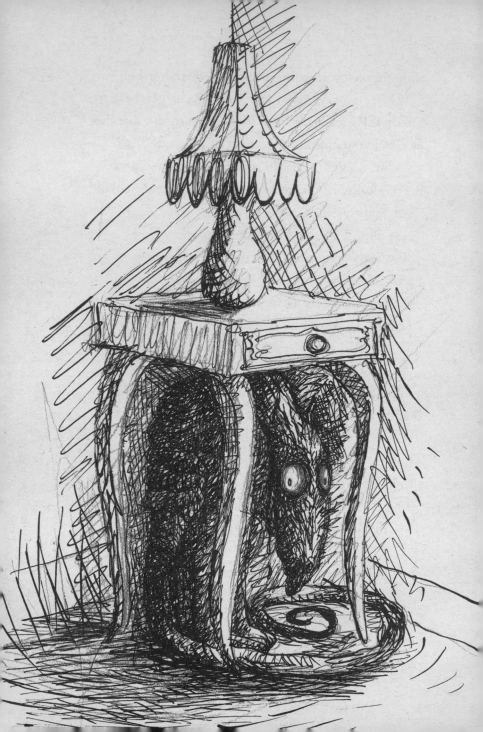

Fred and Ginger dashed around the room, nosing all the backpacks under the beds, but before the girls could jump under there as well, the door flew open.

"Aunt Cha Cha?"

Identical twins—about sixteen years old and stunning—stood in the doorway. "Where is Aunt Cha Cha?" they asked, and stared in disgust at the Gumm Street girls.

23

BLING BLING & Coco

*I*f you yourselves have an older sister or cousin or neighbor who is, say, a sophomore or junior in high school, then you know that nothing can send you running for cover faster than the disgusted gaze of one of these creatures if you dare pass within their range of vision.

Taking a few steps inside, the twins stared at the Gumm Street girls, who were all now gathered on one of the beds.

The twins were a fascinating and frightening duo all rolled up into a couple of tube tops and miniskirts. While they were quite stunning in the way that very tall, very thin, very long, straight, blond-haired girls usually are, they were also very green. From head to toe, they were a deep emerald green.

"Pathetic, Coco," said one.

"Revolting, Bling Bling," agreed the other.

Take a moment to think about the most fabulous person in your school. That person is incredibly attractive, right?

Wrong.

That person has some unattractive characteristics, too! Don't believe it? Then try an experiment. Close this book and go and find the most fabulous person in your school. Now go up to the fabulous person and say something flattering. Try: "I like your _____ (insert the appropriate: hair, sunglasses, belly button ring, tattoo). While you are doing this, try to forget that they are fabulous and look at the fabulous person—*really* look at them. If you *really* look, you will see the pointy nose, the crooked teeth, the uni-brow, the sloping forehead, the lazy eye. The real difference between the fabulous people and you or me is that they have the fabulous ability to make their unattractiveness go unnoticed!

It was the same with Coco and Bling Bling.

As green as they were, Coco and Bling Bling still had a way of inspiring instant inferiority complexes. Franny couldn't help thinking about her fat knees. Pru thought about her stupid glasses. Cat thought about her boyish figure and her big feet. Ivy thought about her chopped-off hair, the gap between her front teeth, and her ears that stuck out. And they all felt awful.

Coco curled her lip and regarded the girls as if she'd just noticed a wad of sticky stuff stuck to the sole of her designer sling-back shoe. "Pathetic *and* revolting."

A snarling sound came from behind the bathroom door.

Bling Bling was at the door in a flash and swung it shut with a bang, exposing the Jinx. "Which one of you drippy kids does glamour boy here belong to?"

Ivy raised her hand and scooched closer to the other girls.

"Hideous," Coco said. She took out her compact

to brush on some blush.

The Jinx growled, and all the fur on his back stood straight up. Bling Bling raised her handbag, ready to smack him over the head, but the Jinx was too fast. He skittered out of the corner and disappeared under a bed.

"You're lucky I don't turn you into a fur coat!" Bling Bling hissed.

The four Gumm Street girls swallowed hard.

"So where is our Aunt Cha Cha?" Coco demanded. "We saw her car!"

"I don't know," Franny said, jutting out her chin.

Coco strode over and poked Franny in the stomach with her makeup brush.

"OW!" yelled Franny.

"Didn't you ever hear of Pilates, dough girl?" Coco said with a smirk. She poked Franny again.

"OW!" Franny said, holding her stomach and trying not to cry.

"She's in Sherbet," Pru said desperately.

"She's *still* in Sherbet?" Coco narrowed her eyes. She threw the compact and makeup brush into her bag, took out a small silver cell phone, and speed-dialed a number.

Immediately a tinny *Bling! Bling! Blingy! Bling!*

Bling! came from the other twin's pocket.

"Hola?" Bling Bling said.

"Like, this is so totally *not* happening." Coco looked at the ceiling and impatiently drummed her fingers on her hip.

"Like so entirely, completely *not*," Bling Bling agreed.

"*Now* what are we supposed to do?" Coco said.

Bling Bling dipped into her handbag. She turned her back and furtively opened a tiny little box. From it she took a small pink tablet and popped it in her mouth like a breath mint.

"I *saw* that!" Coco yelled into the phone and held out her hand. "Give me one."

"It was my *last!*" Bling Bling whined.

Coco clenched her teeth. "So, did Aunt Cha Cha get the *shoes?*"

"How should I know? Ask the pea brains," Bling Bling answered with a toss of her head.

They simultaneously shut their phones with a snap.

"Did Aunt Cha Cha get the *shoes?*" demanded Coco of Franny.

"What shoes?" said Ivy.

"Oh, puh–leeze!" said Bling Bling. She bent down,

snatched Ginger by her tail, and held her upside down.

"She got one shoe," Ivy cried. "Don't hurt my dogs!"

"And where's the other shoe?" Coco grabbed Fred by his tail. Both girls began to swing the dogs, who looked at Ivy with pleading eyes.

"She's still searching for it!" Ivy said, desperately reaching for Ginger.

"Humph!" grumbled Bling Bling, and the girls let go of both dogs, who did a somersault in the air and landed on Ivy, throwing her backwards onto the bed. "Oops!" Bling Bling giggled. "She just slipped right out of my hands!" She grabbed her phone again.

Bling! Bling! Blingy! Bling! Bling! Coco flipped open the phone once more and sniffled, "Aunt Cha Cha won't come back until she has *both* shoes."

Bling Bling ran her fingertips over her dewy skin and said urgently, "Is it still visibly firm?"

Coco scowled. "Visibly firm and *no* fine lines! Did you hear me? She's—not—coming—back!" she said between clenched teeth.

"Oh, don't get your knickers in a twist. Aunt Cha Cha *won't* let us down! I can see her now," mused Bling Bling. "'Bling Bling,' she would always say, 'everything I do, I do for you and Coco—'"

"'Daughters of my dearly departed sister, cut down in her prime!'" Coco added.

"By that little snot-nosed Dorothy!" they both said.

The Gumm Street girls exchanged glances behind

the twins' backs, and Fred and Ginger raised their eyebrows.

"Um, excuse me Coco, sir—I mean, ma'am—by any chance did your mother happen to die by melting?" Franny asked, determined to know the truth.

Coco narrowed her eyes into mean little slits. "What's it to you, lard butt?"

"Oh, nothing, I was just wondering." Franny said nonchalantly.

"Yeah, well, one more word out of you, fatso, and you're going to wonder yourself right into our little Beautyliator."

"What's a Beautyliator, anyway?" Ivy asked.

"Don't make her mad," Pru whispered.

Bling Bling looked at her sister slyly and went over to a switch on the wall. Seconds later the velvet curtains parted and the wall behind them began to rise, revealing a room that looked like it belonged to a mad scientist. There were test tubes with strange multicolored fluids, and some disturbing, smoking substances bubbling out of beakers. In the middle of all this was the Beautyliator, hooked up to a high-voltage system of coiled wires and electrodes the equal of anything found in Dr. Frankenstein's laboratory.

"Would you like a demonstration?" Bling Bling said chirpily.

"That's okay," Pru said, getting up to leave. "We'll just be going now."

"That's what *you* think!" Coco yanked Pru down by her ponytail.

"Now then, it's really very simple," Bling Bling began. She held out her hand and opened her palm. There was a little black thing in it. "Take, for example, this raisin."

"Hideous!" said Coco.

"Revolting!" said Bling Bling. "Wrinkled, withered—"

"*Oo-o-o-o-old!*" they said together.

"I like raisins," Franny said.

"They're a h-healthful and n-nutritious s-s-snack," Pru said nervously, trying not to cry.

Coco gave them a dirty look and held out her hand. Inside it was a small bunch of plump green grapes.

"Oh, look! Lovely grapes. I just *adore* grapes!"

"Divine!" said Bling Bling.

"Grapes," said Coco. "So young. So juicy." She put one in her mouth. "So—"

"Green!" snickered Cat. "OW!—not that there's anything wrong with that," she quickly added, rubbing the side of her head where she'd been clobbered by Coco's handbag.

Bling Bling held the raisin between her thumb and her forefinger and said, "Don't you just wish *this* raisin could look like *that* grape?"

"Yes, but *how*?" Coco asked, her eyes wide with wonder.

"*I know!*" they both said together. "*The Beautyliator!*"

Coco went over to the machine.

"Now then." She glanced at the girls. "Pay attention! Step one: Beautyliator Extractication! I place the grapes inside the Beautyliator chamber like so." Coco opened the transparent door on the bottom part of what looked like a giant hourglass, threw the grapes inside, then kicked the door shut with the heel of her shoe. Then she went over to the blendery-looking part where the controls were and placed one long, pink nail on a big pink button. "Then I press the Beautulverizer button on the Beautyliator control panel."

Immediately the machine lit up like a Christmas tree and started to hum. Coco jumped back and gave a startled little squeal.

Seconds later the hourglass chamber flipped upside down so that the grapes were now lodged in the top part of the glass. Colored lights blinked and buzzed, and the machine vibrated dangerously.

"Watch! Watch!" Coco cried, her eyes riveted to the machine.

There was a horrible sucking sound and some bolts of lightning as the grapes were violently squizzled and squashed and beautulverized.

"I just *love* this part!" Coco clapped her hands. "See? It's turning into secret formula!"

When the last bit of it had been squished through, the egg timer flipped back around, leaving the liquid "secret formula" collected in the top portion of the ghastly device.

"Step two." Bling Bling picked up where Coco left off. "I place the hideous, wrinkled, *old* raisin in the Beautyliator chamber and press 'Beautylyize,' like thus."

The raisin started to spin, slowly at first and then

faster and faster. The lights of the Beautyliator blinked furiously, and what Bling Bling called the "specially designed Beautyliator nozzle" began to spray a mist of grape slime all over the raisin. There was a strobe light effect, some bells, a honking sound, and a sharp whistle, and then everything went completely silent.

The Gumm Street girls gathered around the machine to see with their own eyes what it had done. Sure enough, there was no longer a wrinkly raisin.

Bling Bling opened the door and snatched out— "A lovely grape!" she said. *"Ummm,"* and popped it in her mouth.

"But what if the raisin doesn't want to be a grape!" Ivy asked, her hands on her hips.

"All raisins want to be grapes, pea brain," Coco said.

"And now for the first time, we're going to try it on *people*!" said Bling Bling. Coco clapped her hands.

"You're sure going to need a lot of grapes," Franny commented.

"Actually, we're not going to need *any* grapes." Bling Bling rearranged her tube top.

Right then it hit Franny. "We're the grapes," she said softly.

"Bingo!" the twins said.

Pru started weeping. "But I don't want to *be* a grape," she wailed.

Coco screwed up her nose and squinted her eyes meanly as she dialed. When Bling Bling answered, she said, "*Unfortunately*, we have to wait till Aunt Cha Cha comes back—"

"We promised."

"But what do we do with the pea brains in the meantime?" Coco motioned her head toward the girls.

"That's easy," Bling Bling said. "They'll be our personal assistants. Which means they'll be at our beck and call. . . ."

"Indulge our every little whim. . . ." Coco said.

"Jump when we so much as move a little finger!" Bling Bling said excitedly. "Besides, I'm sick of doing all my own housework and cooking."

Coco and Bling Bling looked at each other.

"*As if!*" they said at the same time, then held on to each other, weak with laughter.

FIRST NIGHT IN THE Z

24

*B**ling Bling and Coco led the girls up*
and up and up circular marble staircases, and
private elevators, and high-speed escalators that made
their ears pop. All the while the *SPOZ* letters that
twinkled far above the fountain grew ever closer and
bigger, until the girls were near enough to see

exactly what they were. Each letter was a four-story apartment. "Aunt Cha Cha's condo is in the *S* and the *P*," Coco said, barely looking at the girls, far more interested in smoothing her hair with the palm of her hand. "*Ours* is in the *O*."

The twins' apartment was a huge place, shaped like a doughnut, boasting gold leaf on the carved ceilings and walls and illuminated by hundreds of crystal chandeliers. The Gumm Street girls were pushed and prodded with sharp objects that felt like the ends of makeup brushes through a tour of the *O*. Fred and Ginger trembled in Ivy's arms, and Pru quietly wept as they wound their way around a whimsical staircase that spiraled down to a main room. On the other side of the doughnut, they could see a series of lofts with bedrooms and baths—the main living quarters.

"It needs a bit of tidying up," Coco had told the girls.

That was an understatement. One could tell that originally much care had been taken in creating the apartment, but alas, the *O* was now less like an apartment and more like a pigsty. The gold leaf was peeling off, and the chandeliers had collected three inches of dust and cobwebs. There were piles of dirty clothes everywhere. And there were piles of dirty dishes, sometimes mixed up with the clothes. Lidless tubes and capless jars of beauty products were strewn about, oozing oily creams and lotions onto the furniture.

But before the girls had time to take in exactly what Coco and Bling Bling had in store for them, they were led down to the basement kitchen.

"You'd think they kept the crown jewels in here," Franny whispered to Ivy when she saw Coco unlatch all the chains and bolts locking the door to what Bling Bling told them was the spud room.

Pru looked over at Franny, terrified. The spud room looked like a place where something very bad could happen! It was windowless and almost pitch black—much like a crypt—and all the girls were sure that they were about to be shoved from behind and locked up in the dark forever.

But they weren't. Instead, they were given exact instructions.

"Gather them up each day," Coco said. With an evil glint in her eye, she pointed to a pile of potatoes. "Chop them up good!"

"Don't forget to cut out their *eyes!*" Bling Bling snickered from her spot outside the room.

If you know anything about witches, you will not be surprised to hear that all Bling Bling and Coco had to do was say a few magic words and *voila!* an elaborate meal instantly appeared. What was surprising, however, was that with every meal the twins absolutely, positively had to have, and seemed to get a demented pleasure from eating . . .

"French fries?" Pru blurted out.

"You got a problem with that, four eyes?" Bling Bling said, smacking Pru in the head with her handbag.

"And lock it tight when you leave, pea brains," Coco warned, bolting the door.

Thankfully, it was late; otherwise the girls would have been forced to make French fries on the spot. "And now we have to get our beauty sleep! You four will be staying in the *Z*," Bling Bling snarled. "That's the servants' quarters."

The girls heaved a sigh of relief. They would be rid of the twins, at least for the night.

It wasn't a great way for the girls to start their summer vacation. The memory of past carefree summers in Sherbet—with sunny days, rainbows, ponies, ice cream, and candy—filled Franny, Cat, and Pru's heads. Of course, Ivy's summers were mostly spent in the emergency room or sweltering in the front seat of her mom's beat-up Ford Fiesta as they moved to yet another new town to escape the Jinx. Still, Ivy had been looking forward to helping Mr. Staccato that summer. Instead, the four of them were marched out of the O through a connecting corridor and were pushed and prodded into the Z, where they were locked up for the night. Made entirely of concrete, the Z was extremely cold, and—with only one strip of dim green fluorescent lighting bolted to the ceiling—it was also extremely dark.

The girls picked their way down a jagged stairway that zigzagged forty feet below to where a row of rusty old cots sagged in about three inches of pink water. There was a constant dripping from the ceiling. If you will remember, the *SPOZ* letters were actually above a fountain, and the sound of its spray over the Z from the outside made normal conversation impossible. In short, being inside the Z was like being suspended over Niagara Falls inside a cinder block.

The girls' patience had long since disappeared. Pru's continual sobbing was like nails on a chalkboard, until Franny finally turned to her and bluntly said, "Will you just *shut up?*"

"*You* just shut up, Franny Muggs!" Pru said, splashing her way to a cot. (She did stop crying, though.) She ripped the pink robe off and threw it along with the Oz book on the soggy mattress. "I don't know how I ever got mixed up in one of your harebrained ideas! We're all going to *die!*"

"For Pete's sake!" Cat shouted above the sound of the fountain. "We're not going to die. Don't be so dramatic, Pru!"

"I'm s-sick of you, t-too!" Pru started crying again. "You a–always think you're so b–big all the t–time."

"Oh, put a sock in it!" Cat said sharply.

Ivy sat on the damp cot, holding her head. She didn't feel so good. She could feel *him* moving when she moved, sitting when she sat, turning when she turned. He was still with her, but that wasn't the worst of it, because now she could see him from time to time as well. The Jinx would dart out from under a cot only to disappear again deep into the shadows of the *Z*.

"You guys, will you stop?" Franny stood by Ivy and patted Fred and Ginger, who were shivering. "Ivy doesn't feel so hot."

"I'm all right," Ivy said, and tried to smile. But she wasn't all right. Nothing was all right, and it was all her fault. "Your talent is your *strength*," Mr. Staccato had told her. Ivy closed her eyes, and she could see him sitting in his chair by the cupboard, shaking his finger at her. "*Never* forget your unique talent."

Ivy could feel her chin and lower lip start to go all

weird and her throat tighten, but she would not allow herself to cry—it would only make it worse for the others. She would be strong. It was hard, though.

Click. Bang! Click. Bang! Click. Bang!

A row of old metal lockers lined the back wall, and Cat was going from one to the next to see if anything was inside, but all were empty. On top of them, however, was an old tarp covering something.

"Franny," Cat said. "Give me a leg up." Franny hoisted Cat so that she could reach the tarp. Pushing it aside, Cat could see several cardboard boxes. "Look out below!" she warned, and pulled the boxes down one by one, which fell and broke open only to reveal more pink bathrobes—close to a hundred, maybe.

"I never want to see another one of these again," Cat said, kicking them into a pile.

"Wait!" Franny said. "I just got an idea!"

"Of course you did," Cat muttered, and kicked at the robes again.

Franny did have an idea. She remembered how the famous explorer Sir Ernest Shackleton and his men, on their doomed expedition to the Antarctic, had washed up onto Elephant Island. There was no shelter, so they turned a boat upside down and lived underneath it for months, while they waited to be rescued. Franny had always wanted to live underneath a boat!

Franny began to turn some of the cots on their sides and placed them end to end to form a circle. She sopped up the water in the middle of the cot circle with some of the robes, and then placed cardboard from the boxes on the floor.

"You're so *weird*," Pru said from her cot.

"What are you *doing*?" Cat said irritably.

"You'll see," Franny replied. After that, she put down a padding of dozens and dozens of pink robes on the floor. She took the tarp and hung it over the tops of the cots to make a roof, so they wouldn't be dripped on.

What Franny ended up with was what you and your friends have built many times: a fort. Once inside, they were dry and surprisingly warm and snug, and even the din of the fountain was somewhat muffled. Just the same, all the girls were very subdued.

Ivy reached her hand through the springs of a cot and pushed aside a pink robe to see out. In the darkest spot of the Z, barely visible, the Jinx sat watching the tent like a sentry, tense and stoic. The foul pink water rained down upon him, over his bony forehead; it streamed past the hollows of his eyes and dripped off the beard of his long snout. Ivy let the flap of robe fall back into place. She turned back to the others and pulled Fred and Ginger close.

⋅ The girls had with them only the items they had been holding when the twins arrived in the hotel room. Ivy had her flashlight. Cat had her *I Ching*. Pru had her Oz book. Franny had her Super Colossal Bag of Assorted Candy—featuring every kind of candy imaginable—stashed away in the secret compartments of her hiking shorts. The twins had provided nothing to eat, so the girls were grateful for Franny's candy. Franny popped a Jelly Squirtz into her mouth.

"Didn't you hear Bling Bling? Franny said between chews. "They are the *daughters*—"

"Of Cha Cha's dear departed *sister*," Cat finished Franny's sentence.

Pru brooded. *Oh sure*, she thought, *everyone believes Cat, but if I had said that, they'd all be laughing.*

"It's like I thought right from the beginning," Cat said, pulling her *I Ching* out of her pocket. "Cha Cha is a wicked witch, and I'll bet anything her *dear departed* sister was the *real* Wicked Witch of the West!"

Franny remembered something else. "The twins said their mother died by—"

"Drowning!" all the others chimed in.

"More like melting!" Franny remarked, and everyone agreed.

The girls huddled under the tarp and silently watched Cat, her face looking mysterious in the glow from Ivy's flashlight. Cat threw the coins onto the carpeting of terry cloth.

"Adversity," Cat said, looking up from the book.

"Like we really need the *Ching* to tell us *that*," Pru muttered under her breath.

Franny reached for a Colossal Length Licorice Lace and chewed nervously on it. "Read it," she said.

"THE PITS," Cat began.

"Be thankful for one measly,
tofu, fat-free muffin.
Give up the fight,
And you'll get nothin'."

Cat put the coins back in her pocket. They could hear the *drip, drip, drip* of water on the tarp. "And THE PITS changes into GET IT TOGETHER, which says:

"A drop of water makes
no commotion;
Put them together and
you have an ocean!"

Unmoved, the three girls looked miserably back at Cat.

Cat shoved her *I Ching* into her pack and moved in closer. "We came here to help Ivy, right?"

"Yeah, and now look at where we are," Ivy said.

"As I see it," Cat said earnestly, "it's a good thing we're together." She brushed her hair out of her eyes.

"Cat's right," Franny said. "We're *lucky* to be together."

Pru sniffed and looked at Franny's eager face, then at Ivy, who seemed anything but "lucky," and yet . . . neither Ivy nor Franny or even Cat seemed scared. . . . .

They were so brave. How could they not be scared? Were some people just born that way? Was it like having straight teeth, or blond hair? Or was it something you practiced and worked at like the piano? Could anyone be that brave, or was it just for a select few?

Cat uncrossed her legs and, kneeling, she said to Ivy, "Give me your right hand."

Ivy slowly removed her hand from the sleeve of the robe. She held it palm down, hiding the mark. Cat grasped Ivy's hand with hers, pressing the mark of the eye to her own palm, and said, "I, Cat Lemonjello, swear on my membership in the Secret Order of the Gumm Street Girls that we will help Ivy find a way out of here."

"And we'll stick together!" Franny placed her hand over Cat's.

"We'll stick together." Pru bit her lip and placed her hand on Franny's, and Fred and Ginger each gave an affirmative sneeze.

That first night in the *Z*, the Gumm Street girls didn't know how on earth they were going to get out of the pickle they were in. But one thing they *were* sure of: They had each other.

"Who knows," Franny said before they all fell asleep. "Maybe we'll really get lucky and find some Krazy Glue to put in Bling Bling's lip gloss."

Inside the

25

Think of the worst summer vacation ever.

Here are a few I've come up with:

1. You have to go to summer school seven days

   a week, eight hours a day, or else you get left

   back—in your younger brother's class.

2. Your parents go off on a whirlwind tour of

288

all the best amusement parks in the country. You are sent to stay with some Amish relatives who give polka lessons for a living.

3. One of your siblings has just become a famous movie star, and the entire family is going to Hollywood to help out while she works on a film. Your job is to run ahead, open doors, bow, and say, "Right this way, Your Royal Highness."

Now, take these horrible scenarios and multiply them by 100,000 times and you will begin to have an idea of just how bad summer was for the Gumm Street girls.

Every morning at exactly 6:00 A.M., the green fluorescent strip high above flickered on and the door to the Z opened with a loud clang. There was only one dark moldy shower in the Z, and it delivered an icy spray, so bathing was out of the question. The best the girls could do was splash their faces with handfuls of the pink water that trickled down the side of the wall. By the end of a week, their hair was so dirty that it stuck out all over their heads at forty-five-degree angles.

Next they had to march from the Z to the O.

Their work began in the spud room, where they were to gather the potatoes so that they could make the French fries that the twins demanded with every meal.

Inside the small, vaultlike room were piles and piles of potatoes surrounding a filthy trapdoor set into the floor. Taking a few, Franny shivered and went to leave. Pru stood at the door waiting—no way was she going inside.

"Did you see that?" said Pru incredulously, and jumped back. She could have sworn she saw a little hand peek out from the trapdoor and deliver a potato as fast as lightning.

"Let's just get out of here." Franny bolted up the door.

Next they had to "chop them up good" with giant meat cleavers that could whack off a finger quicker than you could say, "putrid, slick, white lard." Speaking of which, they had to deal with buckets full of the stuff, heating it up till it melted and then frying the chopped spuds. It was extremely unpleasant work, but truly unsettling when they noticed—

"It's looking at me!" Franny announced.

Franny was right. She, Ivy, Pru, and Cat all stared as a potato lay on a drain board, staring back at them

with a dozen blinking eyes.

"What should we do?" Franny said.

"Put him back," Ivy whispered. Which is what they did.

They picked him up gently and put him back in the spud room with the others in an area where they would be sure not to pick him up again.

Once they were done in the spud room, the girls made their way to the twins' room to tidy up, where they were forced to color-code endless piles of tank tops and bell-bottoms.

Lunch was another round of French-fried potato making, followed by a cleanup of the winding staircase that had completely disappeared under garlands of discarded panty hose. These they had to sort and fold, or more often clean. By evening the girls and Fred and Ginger would stagger back to the kitchen to prepare—you guessed it—more French-fried potatoes.

And if you think that a day such as the one described above was considered a bad day, you are wrong, for it was one particular day a week they came to really, truly, dread—Toenail Clipping Day. In case you didn't know, a person's toenail clippings can be used against them in the form of a curse if they fall into the wrong hands. It was no secret that the twins had quite a few folks who would have loved to send them one of these curses, if only they could get a nail. So, once a week, on a rotating basis, one of the Gumm Street girls had to clip the toenails of Bling Bling and Coco and then—almost worse—had to place the bits in a big jar filled almost to the brim with old toenail clippings.

The girls never got a day off. Ever. Worse, as the days went by, Coco and Bling Bling's mood became more and more foul as their hair became less and less lustrous, their skin became less taut, and their bodies became less lean. Before long, the evil duo were sporting lamp shade hats just like their aunt, and by August there was no denying it: Coco and Bling Bling no longer had visibly

Before

firm skin, and they had many, many fine lines. They were aging, and *fast*.

The Gumm Street girls didn't dare say anything. Franny, Pru, Cat, Ivy, Fred, and Ginger tried to heed the advice of the *I Ching* and remain positive and not forget their mission, which was to find a way out of there and get rid of Cha Cha. With that in mind, they kept their heads down and their mouths shut, and they worked.

What did the girls get for all their pains?

Leftovers (they didn't touch the French fries) from the twins' plates at night, and the chance to start the whole process again each morning, because Coco and Bling Bling had managed overnight to transform the O back into its former stinking, filthy, pigsty self.

What if they refused to do all that work, you might ask?

They were threatened, that's what. Threatened to be sent to a place so deep, a place so dark, a place so damp and so cold that it was deeper, darker, damper, and colder than any place other than the grave.

A place called Spudz.

Escape from SPOZ

The Gumm Street girls had now been inside the O and the Z all summer. Whenever they had the chance, they gazed longingly out the twins' huge picture window that looked down onto the grand galleria below and thought of escape. They talked about it every night, but how? They were locked in the letters, and there was no way out.

"What we need," Franny had told her friends many times, "is a window of opportunity. Like on Mount Everest, they have to wait for the weather conditions to be perfect to climb to the top, and there are only about ten days in the whole entire year when they are!"

So the girls waited, and waited and waited, and at the end of August they were still trapped in Spoz.

Franny was out of ideas, Cat wasn't getting any ESP sendings, and Ivy had begun sleepwalking. Franny always woke up and led her back to the fort, but Ivy was afraid. In her dreams she seemed unable to resist the shadowy form of the Jinx, who summoned her to the dark door of the Z every night.

Spoz had been especially hard on Pru. She had more to worry about than she'd ever had in her whole life, but there was one worry above all that nagged at her thoughts. The worst had happened. Pru realized that she had become *extremely* unpopular. She knew this because whenever she made a suggestion, there was epic eye rolling and face making. She was ignored, taken with a grain of salt. She couldn't understand—why didn't anyone like her?

Pru was contemplating this one day in the *O* while

she was putting away the twins' push-up bras. She had laundered them all by hand. She had to—they had green stains under the arms and a smell that could melt the enamel right off your teeth.

The unmistakable sound of flip-flops down the hall roused Pru from her thoughts. Not wanting to get her ponytail twisted until her eyes stretched into slits, Pru dove for cover under the bed, wiggling past the shoes, smelly socks, dirty clothes, and moldy old French-fried potatoes that had collected there.

Bling! Bling! Blingy! Bling! Bling!

"It is *not,*" Coco was saying sharply as she entered the room. "No, I'm telling you it's *not.*" She went over to the full-length mirror and, standing with her back to it, she grimaced and looked over her shoulder, at her rear end. "If yours is, then so is mine, and I'm telling you I'm looking at it right now. It's just a teeny-tiny little thing."

Pru snuck a look from her hiding place. Coco snapped her gum and, turning from the mirror, tore off the lamp shade hat, revealing that her once creamy (if green) complexion was now etched with deep lines and wrinkles. Coco frantically began searching through drawers, and the contrast between the pink hot pants and a frilly top she wore and her haggard face was truly bizarre. Pru covered her eyes.

"Well, *you're* the one who got in a snit and sent Dr. Iznotz to Spudz." Coco pulled the entire drawer out and dumped it upside down. "And now we don't have our vitamins," she whined, and picked through a tangle of tops and shorts. Coco threw up her hands and flopped on the bed. The bedsprings bopped Pru in the head, and she tried not to sneeze from the cloud of dust that rose from the disturbance.

"I know what Iznotz said—I've only heard it, like, a million times." The bed creaked as Coco rolled over and sat on the edge. She turned the pillows over and then went through the drawers on the night table.

"Iznotz is an idiot. You don't have a big butt, all right?" Coco said distractedly. "I *know*. . . . I *know*. . . . You're *so* right . . . *sooooooo* right . . . totally . . . totally . . . if anybody has a big butt, it's Aunt Cha Cha." She chewed her gum. "Mm-hmmm . . . mm-hmmm . . . you are sooooo right, she has *totally* thick ankles, too." Getting up, she began rifling through her handbags.

"What would *I* do?" A handbag dangled off each arm as she spoke. "Take those brats and see if that stupid Beautyliator really works. That's what *I* would do!" She threw down the bags and, getting on all

fours, scanned the carpeting from right to left.

"I kno-o-o-o-w-w-w . . . I kno-o-o-o-w-w-w . . .
if she could just get both *shoes*! Then Aunt Cha Cha
could get lots and lots of brats to use in the
Beautyliator and we could all be cute as buttons

forever!" Coco exclaimed.

Pru gasped and quickly clamped her hands over her mouth. Coco reached under the bed, patting the floor, and Pru scrunched herself as far back as she could, her heart beating wildly in her chest. What on earth was Coco looking for?

And then she found it.

Her green fingers stopped and curled around a small pink tablet.

"I am *not* holding out on you, sweetie," Coco said slyly.

At that exact moment Pru—who had always been terribly allergic to dust—did the one thing she absolutely, positively should not do: she sneezed.

Coco's horrible face immediately appeared under the bed right at eye level with the unfortunate Pru.

"OH . . . MY . . . GOD!" Coco screamed, and dropped the phone.

Pru could hear Bling Bling's voice on the other end. "Coco? Sweetie?"

Coco dragged Pru from under the bed, almost pulling her arm out of its socket in the process.

"What are you doing under my bed?" Coco shook Pru until her teeth rattled.

"I-I-I-I don't k-know." Pru's voice trembled with terror.

"You don't *know*? YOU DON'T *KNOW*?" Coco screeched in Pru's face, and all Pru could do was shake her head no.

"Well, maybe some time in the Beautyliator will help you figure it out, four eyes!" Coco pushed Pru toward the door, and Pru went flying backwards and nearly fell before catching herself. Pru tried to rearrange her glasses, which had fallen off one ear, but her hands were shaking too much. Coco rushed toward her. "And your *other* dopey little friends are next!"

"Wait! Wait!" Pru screamed.

"I *can't* wait!" Coco grabbed Pru's arm and shook it. "I *need to dramatically rejuvenate . . . now!*"

Pru said something next that *no one*—especially Pru—would have ever expected. And if you think it was a safety tip, then you are wrong, because what Pru said was . . .

"*I'll* go! *I'll* go to Dr. Iznotz! *I'll* go and get your v-v-v-v-vitamins!"

Coco stopped. "You'll get me my *vitamins?*" she purred, and stroked the little pink tablet in her hand. "In Spudz?"

"Yes! Yes!" Pru cried. "Just don't put me and my

friends in the Beautyliator!"

Coco threw her head back and laughed in the same way that her aunt did. She tossed back her long, stringy hair, which was now a grayish yellow color. Looking every bit the wicked witch, she snarled, "The entrance to Spudz is in the spud room, through the trapdoor. You have until this time tomorrow to bring me my vitamins, *my pretty*—I mean, pea brain." Coco leaned down and put her face an inch from Pru's. "Or else . . . it's showtime!" She grinned maliciously, and the smell of her breath, of rotten eggs and Pine Sol, made Pru's eyes sting.

"Where in Spudz is Dr. I-Iznotz?" Pru asked.

"I have absolutely no idea," Coco said coolly, and then added, "You know, you're starting to look a little pale, darling. Maybe *you* should start taking some vitamins." She popped the little pink pill in her mouth and, with a giggle, turned and left.

All afternoon Pru argued with herself. *I can't go. You have to go. But I can't.* Every time she thought she couldn't go, she reminded herself that if it was Cat or Franny or Ivy, they would go. *Maybe they'll like me better if I go and feel horrible if I die.* That made Pru feel better right away, and she resigned herself to her fate. But first she had to tell the other girls about what had happened.

"Coco and Bling Bling are planning on putting us all in the Beautyliator," Pru announced that night to her friends as soon as they were inside their fort. "Unless I go to Spudz tomorrow to get their vitamins from Dr. Iznotz!"

"Vitamins?" Franny said. "Dr. Izwhat's?"

"Iznotz," Pru corrected. "He said they had big butts, so Bling Bling sent him to Spudz! I think the vitamins were, like, keeping them young," Pru said. "And that's not all. If Cha Cha gets the other shoe, she's going to snatch other kids to put in the Beautyliator to keep herself and the twins young *forever!*"

All the girls started to talk at once, and Fred and Ginger began barking.

"Wait a minute, everybody!" Cat shouted. "Didn't you hear what Pru said? If Cha Cha gets the other shoe, it won't be just us—she'll be snatching up other kids and throwing them in the Beautyliator, too! We *have* to find that other shoe before Cha Cha does!"

"Here's the thing, though," Pru said. "Even if we get the other shoe, we can't use it against Cha Cha." Pru reached for her Oz book and leafed through it.

"Here!" She read out loud:

"... *for as long as she*
—"that's the Wicked Witch of the West," Pru explained—
"had one of the shoes she owned half the power of their charm, and Dorothy could not use it against her, even had she known how to do so."

"We have to get *both* shoes!" Franny exclaimed, and everyone agreed.

"Yeah, but first we have to escape from Spoz," Ivy said.

"Yeah, but first I have to go to Spudz." Pru went to flip her ponytail over her shoulder and then decided not to and hugged her knees instead. "Or else ... be turned into secret formula."

"How do you even get to Spudz?"

"The entrance is in the spud room." Pru gulped. "Under the trapdoor."

"Are you going to go?" Cat asked. She didn't really believe Pru would.

"Yes. I'm going to go." Pru tried to sound brave, wondering if anyone her age had ever been so scared that she died of a heart attack.

"Do you want me to go for you?" Ivy said quietly, and the two dogs shook their heads no. It was the last thing she wanted to do as well, but she felt responsible.

"No, I'll go." Pru nodded her head and even tried to smile. She knew this was what a courageous girl like Cat would do, and she knew she had to as well. "I'll go," she repeated. This time there was no eye rolling or face making. Pru had not been ignored, or taken with a grain of salt.

That night before they went to sleep, Franny squeezed Pru's hand. "Be careful," she whispered.

"I will," Pru answered. She rolled over and thought that was the nicest thing anyone had said to her in a long, long time. Maybe she hadn't been born brave like the other girls, but with a little more practice, who knew?

THEN THERE WERE TWO

"Ivy and Franny are missing!" Pru cried, waking suddenly in the middle of the night. She shook Cat. "Quick! Get up!"

Fred and Ginger went and looked outside the fort for any sign of the missing girls.

"It's probably just Ivy sleepwalking again, and

Franny's gone after her," Cat said groggily, but she reached for her *I Ching*.

"Either that or they've both gone off to Spudz in my place!" Pru said, putting on her clothes. "Come on!"

Cat got dressed and shoved the book into her back pocket. Then the two of them raced up the steps after Fred and Ginger. When they reached the top, they saw the door hanging off its hinges as if it had been smashed open. "I don't like this," Cat said.

Down the hall of the *O* they went, frantically searching for their comrades.

"Wake up, you miserable twerps!" they heard Bling Bling bellow, and skidding around a corner, Cat and Pru ran right into the terrible twins.

Bling Bling's phone rang.

"I thought they were like best friends," Coco said, shaking her head sadly. "I'm *juuuust* devastated!"

"Why, sis?" Bling Bling asked, her eyes wide with concern.

"Two of them ran off without telling the others!"

"*No!*" Bling Bling said in mock surprise.

"*Yes!*" exclaimed Coco.

"Where to?"

"Spudz," said Coco, twirling a strand of her hair on one finger.

"Spudz? But no one has *ever* escaped from Spudz!"

"I know. I guess they'll be down there for the rest of their lives," said Coco, dabbing a fake tear from her eye. "But let's look at the bright side."

"Yes, let's."

"That leaves one for me." Coco pointed at herself. "And one for you!" She pointed to her sister.

"Me first!" Bling Bling jumped up and down.

"No, *me!*" insisted Coco, and shut her little silver phone with a snap before Bling Bling could object.

"You *always* go first!" Bling Bling cried, and went off to pout.

"Goody goody gumdrops!" squealed Coco as she pushed Pru and Cat toward the high-speed elevator. Fred and Ginger raced along at their heels. Down, down, down, several escalators and winding stairways later they stood in the elegant hotel suite with the chandeliers and the deep-pile carpeting. Pru hoped their backpacks were still under the beds where Fred and Ginger had hidden them. Her eyes welled up as she remembered how mad Franny had been when Pru had forgotten her extra socks. It all seemed so long ago. Where were Franny and Ivy now? Pru felt a lump in her throat.

Growing up with ten brothers had made Cat tough. She stood like a warrior, hands on her hips, eyes blazing, hot with anger—these twins had done something to Franny and Ivy, and they were going to pay! But Cat was smart and remembered what Franny had said about waiting for a "window of op portunity."

Standing next to the Beautyliator, Coco opened the door and swung her finger back and forth between Pru and Cat. "Eenie meenie minie moe, catch a pea brain by the toe! My—auntie—told—me—to—pick—the—very—best—one—and—you—are—*it!*" Coco's finger pointed straight at Pru.

Fred gasped, and Ginger got so upset that she piddled on the deep pile carpeting.

"EEEEEEEWWWWWWW!" Coco cried. "ICKY! ICK! ICK!"

As if on cue, Fred dashed over to the Beautyliator and, just as nice as you please, lifted his leg on it.

Coco screamed and, grabbing a pink towel (of which there were many), bent down to clean up the offense.

This was just the window of opportunity that Cat had been waiting for. Before Coco knew what hit her, Cat pushed her head first into the awful contraption and locked her up good and tight.

Frozen with terror, Pru watched as Cat struggled with the controls. Good at sensing windows of opportunity but bad at figuring out appliances, Cat was at a loss.

"B-b-b-b-b-b-b-b-b." *Beautulverizer button*, Pru was trying to say, but was having a hard time with the word because she was squeamish about liquefying people—even unsavory people.

But Pru knew something, too. She knew her friends Franny and Ivy were missing and that Coco, who wanted her vitamins from Spudz, was responsible. Surprising even herself, the next thing Pru knew she had lunged for the big pink button and pushed it.

What happened after that was very awful indeed—at least very awful for Coco—but very good for Cat and Pru. As soon as Pru pushed the button, the monstrous machine hummed to life.

Beep . . . boop . . . Ding! Ding! Ding! In a rage, Coco pounded the sturdy Plexiglas, and the kind of words that spewed from her lime-green lips have been the cause for many a mouth to be washed out with soap. There was a bolt of lightning and then another. The hourglass chamber began to flip over just as it had in the demonstration, and Coco howled. Cat and Pru watched in horror, thinking that it could have been them inside, as Coco screamed, "You miserable pea br—A-A-A-r-a-l-l-l-l-l-l . . . !" But her words were beautulverized along with the rest of her, which was squeezed and squizzled, guzzled and sipped. The Beautyliator pressed her and pinched her, it shriveled her and squished her as she was sucked through the Beautyliator extracticator until drip by drip Coco dribbled out the other side, transformed into a thick pea-green solution. *Secret formula.*

"Now for step two!" Cat grinned at Pru, and took Coco's cell phone from her dropped purse. "Hurry!" Cat grabbed Pru's sleeve and pulled her into the bathroom. Along with Fred and Ginger, they hid behind the shower curtain as she dialed.

They were just in time. A second later Bling Bling strolled into the hotel room. *Bling! Bling! Blingy! Bling! Bling!* her cell phone rang.

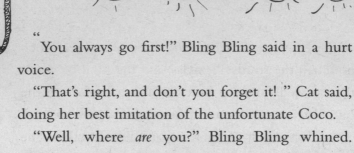

"You always go first!" Bling Bling said in a hurt voice.

"That's right, and don't you forget it!" Cat said, doing her best imitation of the unfortunate Coco.

"Well, where *are* you?" Bling Bling whined. "You've got the other pea brain, don't you?"

Cat rubbed her shirt against the phone, to disguise her voice. "Yeah, I have one pea brain and the other is already secret formula!"

"What? You sound funny!" Bling Bling strained to hear. "You're breaking up. Have you gone in yet?"

Cat continued making the static sound with her shirt. "No. I have a few eensy-weensy things to do. But you have to wait for me, sis. I—get—to—go—first."

From behind the shower curtain, Cat and Pru could practically see a lightbulb go on over Bling Bling's head.

"Suuuuure . . . I'll wait," Bling Bling cooed. "Toodles," she said, and snapped shut her phone. Bling Bling giggled and said, "Wait, my eye! She

always gets to go first!" She pushed the big pink button and hop-skipped her way into the chamber to be beautylyized.

Within the hourglass chamber, Bling Bling began to spin, slowly at first and then faster and faster. The lights of the Beautyliator blinked furiously, and the "specially designed Beautyliator nozzle" began to spray its mist. There was the strobe light effect, some bells, a honking sound, and a sharp whistle, and then all went completely silent.

In the meantime, Cat and Pru ran out of the bathroom. Cat reached under the bed and was relieved to find the backpacks still there. She tossed Pru hers and grabbed her own as well as Franny's and Ivy's and sprinted toward the door just as Bling Bling emerged from the Beautyliator.

"NO-O-O-O-O!" Bling Bling screeched. "You pea brains are supposed to be *secret formula*!" She leaped out of the chamber and went to the mirror.

As you know, the "secret formula" was essence of Coco, who was

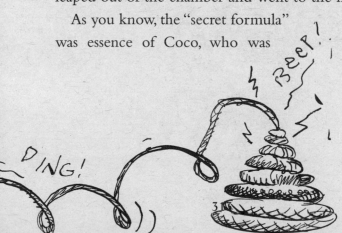

DING!

Beer!

3

extremely rotten and ugly. That is what was sprayed onto Bling Bling, and now Bling Bling, who was *already* rotten and ugly, was even *more* rotten and ugly. In fact, she was downright hideous through and through . . . and . . . she was still green.

"YOU'LL WISH YOU *WERE* BEAUTYLY-IZED WHEN I GET THROUGH WITH YOU TWO!" she screamed, but that was all Cat and Pru heard, because they were already out the door.

Both girls were good runners, and it was a blessing that Franny wasn't with them, for they zoomed up, up, up, back into the *O.* Cat stuffed Fred and Ginger into two of the backpacks, Pru carried the other two, and they hightailed it to the spud room. They heaved up the trapdoor and slid down the ladder and into the dark, down so far that it seemed they'd never reach the light again.

You are probably thinking that Ivy and Franny went down to Spudz so that Pru wouldn't have to go herself.

Well, not exactly.

As each Gumm Street girl dropped off to sleep that night, Ivy willed herself to stay awake. In the dead of night, she took her flashlight and slipped outside the fort.

There he was, darting just out of sight.

The Jinx had remained elusive since he'd become visible in Spoz, favoring shadowy places where he could not be seen. Still, Ivy knew he was always there, and night after night he had come to her in her dreams, beckoning. Now she knew why, and she knew she had to follow him.

Ivy aimed her flashlight up the crooked steps to illuminate her way. Puddles of pink water shimmered on the steps, and mold glistened on the walls. She followed the hypnotic blurred shape of the Jinx, which appeared one moment only to dissolve the next, like a drop of ink in brackish water. He was leading her to the door of the Z. The door would be open. . . . *It will be*, she just knew it.

On the landing, however, Ivy could see that the door was *not* open. She tried the handle, putting all her weight behind it, and gave it some good pushes. She pounded against the cold, slippery surface. She beat against the infuriatingly solid metal. "Open!" Ivy yelled at it. "Open!" she repeated. "Open . . . open. . . ."

"Open your eyes." Ivy woke to find herself standing on the landing inside the Z in the middle of the night trying to open the door that was always locked tight until morning. *I'm sleepwalking again*, she realized. In the darkness, confused and disoriented, she tried to piece together what she'd been dreaming. She wished that she *were* brave enough to go to Spudz for Pru, but the truth of the matter was that a trip to the post office on a sunny day in Sherbet would be a dicey undertaking, let alone going off to Spudz by herself. Was Ivy afraid? Yes, more afraid than she'd ever been in her entire life. In a matter of weeks, maybe days, she and her friends would be beautylyized. Ivy couldn't stop thinking about what Mr. Staccato had told her. Where was the strength that he said she possessed? *Mr. Staccato was wrong*, Ivy thought bitterly, and an overwhelming feeling of hopelessness washed over her.

And then there before her, partially hidden by a cover of darkness, stood the Jinx. Ivy pinched herself hard. She *was* awake.

He held his head low and averted his eyes as he inched closer.

"Look at me, you miserable beast!" Ivy yelled. In the noise of the fountains flowing over the *Z*, her voice barely registered. The Jinx came closer still.

If he is finally going to kill me, Ivy thought, *he is at least going to have to look me in the eye first!*

"Look—at—me!" she demanded, and shined the flashlight in his face.

The Jinx slowly lifted his head for her to see him.

His long, skeletal face was terribly disfigured. Teeth protruded from places where there should have been flesh, and he drooled constantly, his tongue always working to lap it up.

Ivy gasped and turned away from his ugliness. She covered her face. "Leave me alone!" she cried. Ivy waited for the worst, but it did not come. Slowly, she dared to turn back and peek through her fingers.

He stood gazing at her sadly, and Ivy found herself unable to look away from his jet-black red-rimmed eyes. Her hands gradually fell from her face, her fear replaced with a feeling as familiar as her own shadow—as if she had looked into those eyes many, many times.

But a second later the Jinx's fur started to ripple like that of a giant

cat, and Ivy watched with terror as he gathered himself up the way a tiger would before it pounces. He
leaped at her. She hit the ground as the Jinx slammed
into the door, knocking it right off its hinges and into
the O.

Getting up, Ivy tried to scramble back down the
stairs to her friends, but the Jinx was too fast. He
slithered around behind her and chased her into the
O. She ran for her life, and maybe because her Jinx
was so close, every unlucky thing that *could* happen
did. Carpeting slipped out from under her feet. Vases
tipped over. Chair legs stubbed her toes and made her
stumble. Pictures fell off walls. Ivy raced blindly
through the O in the dark, desperate to get
away from the Jinx, whose hot breath
sounded louder and louder as he
gained on her. Doors slammed
shut in her face, and furniture
slid unavoidably into her

path, blocking routes. Without being aware of it, Ivy found herself forced into a dead end right in front of the door to the spud room.

She stopped.

All was quiet except for her heart, which was hammering against her ribs. With shaking fingers, Ivy unlocked the bolts and latches as fast as she could. She opened the door and stepped inside, quickly closing it behind her. She was sure she had managed to outrun the Jinx. Sinking to the floor, she moved a few potatoes to sit more comfortably and tried to catch her breath. Ivy put her ear to the door. Faintly she heard *Bling! Bling! Blingy! Bling! Bling!*

"Like, hellooooo?" She could hear Coco's voice from her room two flights up.

"What's going on down there?" came Bling Bling's voice.

Ivy wiped her forehead with her sleeve. As she did, she turned her face and saw two blazing red eyes appear suddenly from behind a pile of potatoes. In a panic, Ivy flung herself at the trapdoor and yanked it open. She quickly lowered herself down into the cool darkness and with her foot felt the rung of a ladder, slamming the door shut behind her.

But it was no use. The trapdoor banged back open,

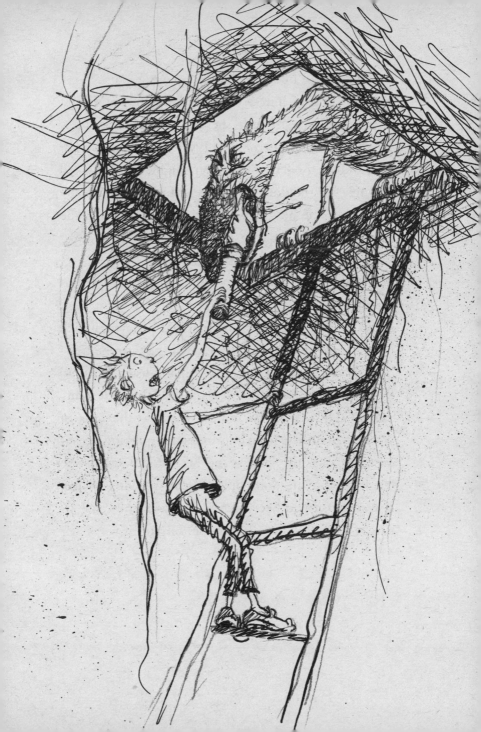

the Jinx's head filling the entire opening.

Ivy swung at him with her flashlight, but he bit onto it with a strength she couldn't believe. They wrestled for a moment, but Ivy had gravity on her side, and she pulled with all her might. The beast fell through the trapdoor and careened past her into the darkness. Clutching the ladder, Ivy listened for the sickening sound of him landing below, but it never came.

Just then the trapdoor swung shut again with a boom.

"OW!" Ivy screamed, and grabbed her arm, which had suddenly begun to hurt. Crawling up to the trapdoor, Ivy pressed her ear against it and listened, afraid that Coco or Bling Bling was on the other side waiting for her. But all Ivy could hear was the tons of water that rushed from the fountain, spraying ceaselessly up, over the letters, and back down again. She tried to push the door open, but it wouldn't budge. It was as if it had been locked—or as if someone, or maybe *two* someones—were standing on it.

*I*t was as dark as the inside of a hat.

Ivy couldn't go back up, and she was afraid

to go down. Moreover, she had hurt her arm some-

how. It was terribly painful, and there was the unmis-

takable warm sticky feeling of blood. She heaved her

shoulder again at the trapdoor, but it wouldn't budge.

All right, Ivy thought, resigning herself to taking Pru's place in Spudz after all. *I'm going down.*

The ladder seemed never ending, descending rung by rung into the abyss past roots and vines that brushed at her face and tugged at her clothes. She looked down over her shoulder, but it was impossible to see through the gloom. The only hint of light was a weak, yolky glow in the distance. Just as Ivy was about to give up hope of ever getting to the end, her foot reached for yet another rung and instead found soggy ground.

Ivy stood in deep twilight, in a large, muddy field full of rocks, a well-worn path in front of her and a mountain behind her. Roots hung in tendrils from a muddy sky, and earth rained down in clumps from above. She looked to see if there were signs of a dead Jinx lying around, but there was nothing—she didn't know if that was good or bad. Completely exhausted, Ivy sat down on a half-buried boulder and considered her situation.

On the good side: she was still alive; she still had her flashlight (she had managed to hold onto it in her tug-of-war with the Jinx); she had the name of a doctor who might tend to her arm, and she had discovered a few cough drops deep in the bottom of one pocket.

On the bad side: she didn't know if the Jinx was gone, or simply waiting to pounce; she was exhausted, hungry, and thirsty; her arm hurt; she was separated from her friends and alone in a place she did not like the looks of. Seeing a doctor from Spudz did not exactly inspire confidence, either. But one thing was certain. She would have to go to him—Dr. Iznotz—get the vitamins, and try to find a way back to her friends.

She was so tired, though.

Ivy took out a cough drop, picked the lint off it, and ate it. When that was gone, she ate another. She was about to eat another, but decided that they were making her nauseous. Just then the rock that she was sitting on got up from the ground with a sucking sound like the lid coming off of a new jar of peanut butter. Its many eyes blinked open, and Ivy could now see that it hadn't been a rock at all, but a potato—a much larger version of the lively ones she and her friends had seen in Spoz.

"I beg your pardon," Ivy said, immediately getting off it.

She figured that if it could stand there and glare at her, it could more than likely hear. Ivy was starting to get the awful feeling that it might even be measuring her for just the right size stew pot when a dark shape appeared. A shape with a long tail, which could have passed for an enormous rat, but Ivy knew better.

"I hope you're *satisfied*!" she shouted at the Jinx.

At that moment Ivy noticed that the entire field was filled, not with rocks, but with lots of grumbling potatoes, which were popping out of the ground at an alarming rate. They were all sizes—some even as big as a Volkswagen! Ivy took a few steps back and bumped into one. "Excuse me!" she said.

It glowered at her.

The Jinx wove his way in and out of the potatoes, favoring one leg. Ivy soon saw that she wasn't the only one who was afraid of the Jinx. One by one as the Jinx neared them, the angry potatoes simmered down and quickly sank back into the mud. At last, the potatoes all hiding again, the Jinx crouched in a nearby shadowy place and began licking a jagged gash on his foreleg.

Ivy rubbed her throbbing arm and pulled back her sleeve. The bleeding had stopped, but the pain was starting to move up to her shoulder, and the nauseous feeling she'd had earlier had gotten worse. She had to get to Dr. Iznotz right away to get those vitamins for the twins, and hopefully he could give her something for her arm.

Ivy set off. In the murky distance was the amber glow of lights she had seen from the ladder. It appeared to be a town.

The field ended and the path widened and serpentined in and around mounds of mud. Despite the lights, there seemed to be little or no movement, as if everyone was fast asleep. It wasn't long before Ivy realized that the "town" was really only a series of caves and pits, some quite grand and others no more than simple holes in the ground. Each cave or pit had a signpost in front of it, and the lights she had seen turned out only to be strung up haphazardly between the posts.

She passed a pit called Grubz Coffin, and then a cave named Slugz Dimple. To her left, pointing into a deep ravine, was a sign that said TO DOWNWARD SPIRALZ. Passing the sign to Rockz Bottom, Ivy touched her arm. It was hot. She touched her forehead, and it was hot, too. Rounding a corner, she saw what looked like an igloo made out of mud. 0 ARMZ PITZ, DR. IZNOTZ, read the sign over the door. She drew a deep breath. *At least he's a doctor*, she thought, and made her way toward it.

Gathering her courage and holding her aching arm, Ivy knocked on the door. She knocked several more times. Ivy was just about to give up when she heard some shuffling and a deep sigh from behind the door.

"Dr. Iznotz?" Ivy called out.

With a squishy pop—it seemed to be sealed with mud—the door opened.

Standing before her was a potato about the size of a pickle barrel. Long white roots sprung from the top of his head and curled down to the earthen floor like hair. Looking out through the tangle of roots were a startling number of eyes, so that Ivy had no idea which ones to talk to and just settled on the ones closest to the area where eyes generally were supposed to be.

DR. ARMPITZ

DR. IZNOTZ

Specializing in Vitaminz for diseesez of ze Skinz, Pimplez, Boilz, Rashez, Winkleez and fine linez

Ivy thought she'd better start off by taking care of Pru's errand for the twins. "Is this where you get the vitamins?" she asked.

"No, it'zz *not*," the doctor said.

"But it says right here it *is*," Ivy pointed to the sign. DR. IZNOTZ SPECIALIZING IN VITAMINZ FOR DISEESEZ OF ZE SKINZ, PIMPLEZ, BOILZ, RASHEZ, WRIN-KLEZ, AND FINE LINEZ.

"Well, it'zz *not*. Furthermore, mzzzz, itzzz ze middle of z'night." All the doctor's eyes blinked at Ivy in a very indignant way.

"It is?" Ivy said, surprised. It didn't even seem like it could be lunchtime yet.

"Yes, it izzz," the doctor insisted. "Itzzz *alwayzzz* ze middle of z'night." His many eyes looked suspiciously at Ivy. "Moreover," he added, "If you muzzzzt know, I have had *very* bad experiensezzz with and do not treat ze witchezzzz."

"You think I'm a witch?" Ivy said incredulously. "I'm not a witch!"

"Open your mouth and zay a-h-h-h-h-h," the doctor said urgently, and peered into Ivy's mouth. He sniffed loudly.

"H-m-m-m-m . . ." he said. "I could have sworn I smelled—" He sniffed and sniffed and sniffed. *"Aha!"*

330

he sputtered, and backed away. "It'zz juzt what I thought!"

"What?" Ivy backed away as well.

"You *stink* of ze potatoes-z-z-z!" Dr. Iznotz hissed. "Only ze witchez *stinkzz* of ze potatozz!"

"But I'm not a witch!" Ivy cried.

Unconvinced, the doctor proceeded to close the door.

"Wait!" Ivy said, and put her foot in the way. Her head was pounding and her teeth were chattering, yet she was drenched with sweat. She presented her swollen arm to him and said, "Do you have anything for this?" She could see shelves filled with bottles of pills and lotions behind the doctor.

Suddenly a low growl came from right behind Ivy, and Dr. Iznotz's roots twitched and shook. She spun around in time to see the tip of a tail slither around the side of a pile of mud.

The doctor had seen it, too, and now hurried off to some other part of his pit. Was the doctor afraid? Had the Jinx actually scared him into helping her? This was a shocking thought. And it had been the same with the potatoes in the field—they had suddenly retreated when the Jinx appeared.

Off to the side, the Jinx held up one paw and

331

panted hard. His head hung low and gobs of saliva dripped from his mouth, and Ivy wondered if she was so ill that her mind was playing tricks on her, because she felt a deep pang of sorrow for him.

Noticing Ivy's stare, the Jinx quickly turned his head, hiding his face, and limped to a darker spot.

The doctor appeared once again in the doorway. None of his eyes would quite meet hers as he handed her a small vial, with instructions to dilute in two gallons of water and apply liberally. "Itzzz a *brand*-new concoction," he said with a starchy smile. "Make sure you apply *liberal-l-l-l-l-y-y-y-y*." All his eyes suddenly narrowed in his potato head. "Good evening then, mzzzz." This time he made sure to bang the door shut before she could stop him.

"But . . . but Dr. Iznotz?" Ivy inspected the vial of medicine: DR. IZNOTZ'S WONDERFUL WOUND VANISHER.

There was no answer. But she knew she couldn't leave without asking one more question. "Do you know where I could find a silver shoe, by any chance?"

Again there was silence.

Ivy called as loudly as she could, "Dr. Izno—"

"Azzzk Mazzzz," he said through the door.

"Maz?" Ivy shouted. "Where is Maz?"

The doctor cracked open the door and slapped a CLOZZZZED sign on it with such force that Ivy jumped back. "Wormzzz Pock!" he yelled, and slammed the door again.

WORMZ POCK

30

*I*t was not going to be easy to find Wormz Pock. Ivy's vision was becoming so fuzzy with pain that she could barely see the directions on the vial of medicine. Ivy fought off a rising panic. *Does it really say two gallons of water? Where am I going to get two gallons of water?* Every step was an effort now, too. She couldn't close her fingers anymore, they were so swollen.

Ivy stopped and glanced back. The Jinx was following with difficulty. She could just barely see him out there in the darkness, stopping every now and then to rest his hurt leg, only to begin again seconds later, grimly determined not to let her out of his sight. And Ivy wondered again, what was this Jinx if she could feel sympathy for him?

And where was Wormz Pock? A root brushed her leg, and Ivy slapped it away. She passed Wormz Woodz, Wormz Bellyz, and then Wormz Pitz. *I must be getting closer*, she thought. It was very muddy here, and there was a walkway made out of flat rocks and stone. But mud seeped up between the stones, and it was slippery going. Ivy stumbled and fell to her hands and knees. To her complete horror, she could see that the walkway was alive with worms! They were crawling on her fingers, up her wrists, and on her ankles, and Ivy screamed and struggled to her feet, swatting them off as best she could.

"Ivy!" She heard her name being called as she slipped and slid on the muddy, wormy stones, but maybe she was hallucinating. Worms were everywhere—on her jeans, on her shirt—it was only a matter of time before they would be in her hair.

"Ivy! Ivy!" a mud-shaped blob said. "It's me!"

"Franny?" Ivy cried. "How'd you get here?"

"When I woke up and you weren't there, I knew you were sleepwalking again. And then when I saw Coco and Bling Bling standing on the trapdoor in the spud room, I figured out where you were," Franny said breathlessly. But before she could say another word, the two girls were seized from behind. "What are you doing here in ze Spudz?" asked the extremely large potato that held them. All at once everything

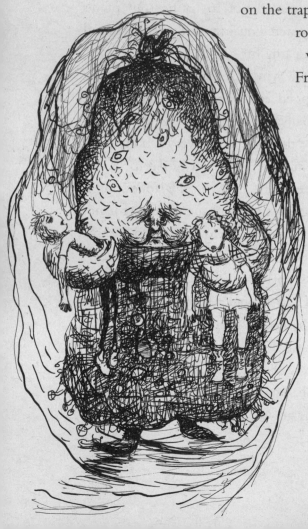

seemed very far away to Ivy. Her hearing faded, her vision narrowed to blackness, and she went limp.

"Who are you?" Franny cried.

"I am Maz, ze oldest spud in ze Spudz!"

"Please!" Franny cried. She looked over her shoulder at the six-foot-tall potato. Its burlap robe sparkled with greenish tinted marcasite and precious metals of silver, gold, and platinum that had been woven into the material. "Please, my friend is sick!"

Maz's numerous eyes could see this for herself. She looked out into the darkness where the Jinx lay in the mud, his front leg curled under him. His breathing came fast and shallow. "Z-z-z-z-z." Maz frowned and shook her head in dismay.

"Liddle sick spudzgirl out in ze wormzzy mudz"—Maz puffed as she carried the girls inside— "needz to be inside ze Wormz Pock!"

Franny was astonished to see that for a pit carved out of the earth, Wormz Pock was surprisingly clean and cozy. There were soft, thick earth-colored mats on the floor and a stone hearth with a cheerful fire burning in the corner.

Maz laid the girls down and examined Ivy's arm.

Ivy came to for a moment. She tried to sit up but was too weak. So she lay back down and, without an ounce of energy left, held out the little bottle of medicine from Dr. Iznotz and said, "I need two gallons of water, please."

Examining the bottle of DR. IZNOTZ'S WONDERFUL WOUND VANISHER, Maz grumbled, and chunks of crystal and opals that hung from her robe vibrated, making click-clacking sounds. "Thizz won't be doing you any zinky good at all!"

"But my arm," Ivy groaned.

"Thizz isn't ze *wound* vanisher, spudnik. Thizz iz ze *witch* vanishing potion!" She showed Ivy where Dr. Iznotz had put a new label over the old.

"Let me see that," Franny said, and took the vial.

Ivy lay back down on Maz's soft rugs, closed her eyes, and said, "He thought I was a witch."

"Ze Dr. Iznotz iz ze very mizzer Spud." Maz placed a pillow under Ivy's head. "Of courzze—now if you are wanting ze winzzy witch doctor, you've come to ze right plazzze!"

Maz poured some dubious brown mixture into a clay bowl and gently placed Ivy's arm in it to soak. "Ze liddle spudz arm needz Maz medicine right away."

Too sick to argue, Ivy submitted. She was handed a similar-looking muddy hot liquid to drink. Franny drank some, too. It tasted just like hot chocolate. Soon both Ivy and Franny could feel warmth spreading throughout their limbs, and that was the last thing that either one of them remembered for a long time.

Once they were asleep, Maz took a large, steaming bowl and tiptoed across the room. She opened the door and walked around the side of Wormz Pock, where crumpled up in the mud was what looked like a discarded, dirty, old fur rug.

"Mr. Jinxzz," she whispered. She lay the bowl down next to where the Jinx had collapsed and, carefully uncurling his injured leg, poured some of the mixture over the wound. She took some in her cupped hand to wet his lips. He opened his eyes for a moment. "Now you come on and drinkz zis right up, you hear me?" She wiped her hands on her robe and stood back to watch, going inside and softly closing the door only after he had begun to drink.

Ivy awoke many hours later having no idea at first of where she was. A very contented Franny was seated on the other side of the room at a large, heavy-looking rectangular rock that served as a table, its top worn smooth from years of scrubbing. Franny was eating from a bowl, with Maz fussing over her.

Ivy stretched. She hadn't felt this good in months. She smiled as she watched Maz cluck around Franny like a mother hen, and then Ivy remembered her arm and was amazed to see that it was almost completely healed.

Seeing that Ivy was awake, Franny said, "Maz knows everything, Ivy. She even knows about the shoes!"

"You do?" said Ivy. She got out of bed, went over to the table, and noticed that she and Franny were both wearing burlap tunics made from the same materials as Maz's robes. They were very soft, and the first clean clothes they'd had on for weeks.

"Maz dozant know every liddle spud in the mud," Maz said, huffing and puffing as she busied herself fixing Ivy some breakfast. "But she dozz know something about ze zoomy shoezz." Maz inspected Ivy's arm. She felt Ivy's forehead with her gnarly hand and, satisfied that Ivy was feeling better, set a bowl and a mug down in front of her. "Now zznuggle down and jizzy eatzz while itzz still warm," she told Ivy.

At the table was a seat that had been carved out of the earth. It was covered with a cloth of the same soft material. Ivy finished her breakfast, which appeared at first to be a bowl of plain old lumpy oatmeal, but tasted like blueberry pancakes and syrup all mixed together. Some folded blankets were set off to one side. Ivy wrapped herself in one to ward off the dampness and the chill and sat back with her knees drawn up comfortably, sipping from her mug. It was filled with the same hot drink as the night before. It looked like mud, but as before tasted like hot chocolate. This time, though, Ivy was sure she could taste whipped cream on top.

Maz settled herself heavily into an old rocker that was before the fire. She closed her eyes, and the girls thought she might have gone to sleep, but then she started to speak. "So you want to know about ze zoomy shoezzzz?" All her eyes twinkled merrily in the firelight.

The girls nodded their heads eagerly, and over the course of that morning and throughout the rest of the day, during which they had many hot cups of the delicious drink that Maz continually brewed over her fire, Franny and Ivy listened to the story that Maz had to tell.

31 MAZ'S STORY

"Now, you both knowzzz who ze Dorothy wazzz?" Maz spoke very slowly in a low voice.

"You mean Dorothy from Oz?" Franny asked.

"Thatzz who I mean, liddle spudz," Maz said.

"Dorothy got ze shoezzz after she killed the mizzer

Wicked Witch of ze Westez, and she didn't even have any idea ze zoomy powerzz zat wazz in zem! Well sir, finally, after she'd been all over creation looking for a wayzzz to get home, she findzzz out she could have got home all ze while by whizzz-clickin' zem shoezzz togezer. Zzzzz," Maz hummed, putting another pile of roots on the fire so it popped and crackled. "On her way home, Dorothy zoozled over ze Deadly Desert—thatzz the only wayzz outta Oz—and ze shoez, what do zay do? Zay fell off her glimzzy feetzzz in flight! Many yearz pazzzzz, and eventually don't you know ze shoezzz got up to walk zer way home. But only one shoe made it back. It walked right to za front door of ze old wizzzzard."

"The Wizard of Oz," Ivy said quietly, and thought about Mr. Staccato's story of the old man with the shoe. Franny caught Ivy's eye, and both girls knew they were thinking the same thing: Was the old man from Mr. Staccato's story the Wizard from Oz? Was he the very same old man that Cat had seen—no, had conjured? Despite the blanket and the hot chocolatey drink, Ivy could feel goose bumps rise on her arms.

"Zatz right, my little spud, ze Wizard of Oz!" Maz was saying. "By zen he waz a very, very wrinkzzy ol' wizzzzard and slowin' down—like old Maz herzzzelf!" Maz chuckled. Her entire body shook, and the tiny stones woven into the throw she had over her lap glittered in the firelight.

"Well, you knows folkzzzz—zey ninzy cannot get along. I just sayzz livezz and let livezzz. Stop and smell ze earthwormzz, so to speak. . . ." Maz clicked her tongue and shook her head. She leaned forwards in her chair. With a large wooden spoon she ladled some more of the drink into the girls' mugs and then her own. Settling herself again, she blew on it, took a sip, and then went on with her story.

"Oz was ahwayzzzz a hard place to get to. Ze Dorothy, blezz her muzzy soul, got blown zer by ze tornado, and za old wizzzzard flew zer in za balloon. But zer was another fellow named ze Nome King, and he wanted to get to Oz in ze worzt way, but he couldn't on account of ze Deadly Desert and all, cozzz if you step one little glimzzy footzzz on it, it will turn deadly on youzzz! So thizz Nome King, he thought he wazzz going to be real smart, and he dug underneatzzz it! He dug, and dug, and dug. Well sir, when ze ruler of Oz—Princezzz Ozma—got wind of thizz, she was madder zan a spud in ze sun, and she asked her friend

Glinda, who wazzz
ze winzzy good witch,
to make Oz invizzzybul."

"Could she *do* that?" Ivy asked.

"Honey spudz, Glinda could do anyzing! And Glinda wazz not only good, she wazzz ze winzzy good judge of character, too. Zer was zis ozzer mizzer witch known azzz Cha Cha."

"Cha Cha!" Franny and Ivy said. "We know her!"

"And her nieces!" Ivy added.

"Ze Coco and ze Bling Bling! Oh, I feel sorry fer you two zen, 'cause zey are mizzer bad applezz, and Glinda knew it. Now all ze riffraff of Oz—Cha Cha and her nieces—waz allzzzz related to za mizzer Witch of ze Westsez. Ze Cha Cha wazz her sister, and ze Coco and ze Bling Bling were her daughterzz."

Franny and Ivy exchanged looks as if to confirm what they'd suspected all along.

"Z-z-z-z-z-z," Maz hummed and nodded slowly. "Zayz allz zzzo buzzzy making ze mischief, zey didn't pay any mind to what wazzz going on. And one day zey woke to find zat Oz had dizappeared, kaput!" Maz snapped her fingers. "You can imagine ze zinky rukus zey made at first! OHHH baby! Zey was mad! But eventually zey cooled down, and zat liddle mizzer Cha Cha, she got thinking, and I heard tell zat black heart of herzz was set on gettin' back ze zoomy shoezzzz that belonged to her sister, za mizzer Witch of ze Westez. Now ze old wizzzzard had one of zem, like I told you, and he knew ze winzy powerzz in it." Maz stopped here for a moment and looked from one girl to the other. "I heard tell," she whispered, "zat ze shoezz choozz."

"Choose what?" Franny asked.

"Some say they choozzz whozzzz footz they want to be on!" Maz's eyes blinked all at once. "Zay travel . . . some say they can even travel through ze *time* to be with ze footzz they want!"

Ivy pulled her blanket tighter around her and recalled that Mr. Staccato hadn't been able to explain where he'd been for fifty-eight years. Had the shoe taken him forwards through time so that it could be together again with its mate?

"Ze old wizzzzard knew ze mizzer powerzz az well, if ze shoezz getz on ze wrong footzz. . . ." Maz said solemnly. "Zinky, zinky bad. So he went whiz crackin' to ze Sherbet thinkin' zat ze zoomy shoe he didn't have might jizz be walkin' to ze footzz of Dorothy's relationzz."

"My Aunt V!" Ivy interrupted, and Franny nodded

her head up and down.

"Z-z-z-z-z, Aunt V!" Maz looked troubled and studied Ivy as she stirred up the fire with a long stick. "Izz she ze relative of yourzzz?"

Ivy nodded, and for the rest of the afternoon she and Franny told Maz all about Sherbet and how Ivy's Aunt V had died and left Ivy and her mother #5 Gumm Street. Ivy told her Mr. Staccato's story and how he had left the shoes to Ivy.

"Mr. Staccato said one of the ruby-red shoes that he got in Hollywood was different from the others— it was silver!" Ivy exclaimed.

Franny had an idea. "Maybe when the shoes became separated in the desert, one of them got confused and instead of going to the wizard *in* Oz it went to Hollywood to the movie *The Wizard* of *Oz*!"

Ivy thought about how she might have laughed at such an explanation a few months ago. But a few months ago she wasn't sitting in a pit conversing with a gigantic potato, and she didn't have an indelible eye imprinted on the palm of her hand, either. "And I got this!" Ivy held it out for Maz to see. "Do you know what it means, Maz?"

"Z-z-z-z-z." Maz examined Ivy's palm for a long time, looking at it this way and that. "Very wrinkzzy old, very rare mark," Maz said, pointing to the image of the eye. "Iz a Prophet'z Mark!"

Franny leaned forwards to look at Ivy's hand again. "What's a Prophet's Mark?" she said, looking back at Maz. "Is it like ESP?"

"Izzz a protection given by ze splenjezztical prophetzz." Maz sat back in her rocker and re-arranged the throw over her lap. There was a patter of earth falling on the roof of the pit, and the girls were glad to be safely inside.

"A protection from what?" Ivy said, almost afraid to ask.

"From ze witchezzzzzz!" Maz's eyes lit up and the fire blazed, shooting blue sparks into the chimney. "Ze Dorothy had one on her forehead!"

"She did?" Fanny was surprised.

"Z-z-z-z-z," Maz said. "Ze splenjezztical Prophet'z Markz are *very* few—iz ze sign zat you are under ze watchful eyezz of ze winzzy prophetzz."

"That sounds good," Franny said, although she wasn't entirely sure.

"Izz good . . . and not zo good." Maz ran her hand gently over Ivy's hair. "Spudzgirl with ze Prophet'z Mark cannot stay in ze fizzy safe pitz for long. Spudzgirl haz ze life of struggle with mizzer peoplezz, so izz good and bad for ze marked spudzgirl."

"But Maz," Franny cried. "The mark wasn't any protection from Cha Cha!"

"That's right," Ivy said, and told Maz about how Cha Cha had come to Sherbet and how Ivy had to give the one silver shoe to her.

Maz rocked slowly in the chair, all her eyes focused on Ivy. "Ze Prophet'z Mark izz some protection but not all—ze Cha Cha cannot *kill* ze liddle spudzgirl with ze Prophet'z Mark."

"She may not be able to kill her," Franny chimed in, "but Cha Cha sent Ivy and me and Pru and Cat to Spoz, and we've been *slaves* to Bling Bling and Coco all summer!"

"Ze Spudz are in ze *same* boat," Maz said sadly. "Ze Cha Cha iz very very mizzer witch. She haz enchanted thizz world that liezz beneath ze Spoz just for ze pleasure it givzz her of enslaving ze Spudz to harvest their own people . . . to be eaten by ze witchezzz of Spoz!"

"So *that's* why the spuds didn't like us," Franny said. "They thought we were spud-eating witches!"

Both girls felt slightly sick to their stomachs at the thought and were glad they hadn't eaten any of the spuds themselves.

Maz opened her mouth and then closed it again in a frown, "I muzzt tell you more about ze Cha Cha! Thizz iz not ze first time ze Cha Cha went to Sherbet." Maz folded her great arms across her chest. "After ze Oz became invizzzybul, she found out where ze wizzzard had gone, and 'cause she still had dark mizzer magic left—she dug undeeground juzzzt like ze Nome King, and she built Spoz right undee where zem relationzzzz of ze Dorothy'z were, thinkin' someday zoz zoomy shoezzz might be turnin' up. All ze mizzer witchezz from Oz came with her, and ze Cha Cha wazz juzzzt like an old spider waitin', an waitin', weavin' nazzzzzty mizzer web!"

"Wait!" Franny exclaimed. "You mean Spoz is right underneath Sherbet?"

Franny and Ivy exchanged worried looks.

Maz nodded and continued, "Ze Cha Cha flew in on ze spinnzy hurricane to Sherbet. She went right to Aunt V's house and told her about ze zoomy shoezz and that 'cause she was related to ze liddle Dorothy, ze shoezz belonged to her. When ze ol' wizzzard died before ze new owner—"

"Mr. Staccato," Ivy said. "He had one of the shoes—"

"And the old man had the other!" said Franny. "Then he must have been the wizard!"

"Z-z-z-z-z," Maz said. "When ze Mr. Staccato arrived at ze dead wizzzard's, ze Cha Cha and ze Aunt V were waiting for him."

Ivy and Franny sat bolt upright, astonished.

"If Aunt V was related to Dorothy, why wouldn't Mr. Staccato give her the pair?" Franny asked.

"I'm not zo sure. . . ." Maz rubbed her chin with her long, white rootlike fingers, her eyes gazing gently at Ivy. "Not just *anyone* can fill ze shoezz. Maybe ze Aunt V was ze mizzer foot for ze zoomy shoezz . . . and . . ."—Maz reminded the girls—"ze Aunt V could not *take* ze shoezz from ze owner. Zey have to be *given*."

"Maybe your Aunt V tried to get the shoes and Mr. Staccato wouldn't give them to her," Franny said.

Ivy pulled her blanket tighter around her shoulders.

Maz took another sip from her mug. "Ze Cha Cha promizzed ze Aunt V she would help her. They never did get ze shoezz, and Cha Cha came back to Spoz with ze Aunt V."

All that could be heard was the squeak of the rocker, because Ivy and Franny were speechless.

"But Maz"—Franny had been thinking about this—"Aunt V died in *Sherbet*!"

"Ze Cha Cha sent ze Aunt V back on blowzzy blizzard," Maz whispered. "Ze witchezz travel on ze big weather."

Ivy shivered and thought about Aunt V's letter. *I'm not really dead*, Aunt V had written, and Ivy could see now that Aunt V had a more sinister reason for wanting everyone to think she was dead besides "back taxes." Perhaps to get Ivy or her mother to give Aunt V the shoes and disappear without anyone suspecting she had them! Ivy absently rubbed her finger against the mark of the eye. "Do you think Aunt V gave me the Jinx? I looked in a mirror, Maz, and it broke— over seven years ago—and ever since then"—Ivy's words tumbled out—"I've had a Jinx!"

"I know," Maz answered simply.

"Who did you see in ze mirror just before ze Jinx came to you?" Maz asked.

"Cha Cha," Ivy said and then hesitantly added, "and for a second . . . I thought I saw my father. . . ."

"Your father!" Maz said sadly.

"I'm not sure. . . ." Ivy bit her lip and looked at Maz questioningly. "But I know I saw Cha Cha."

"Zen it was ze Cha Cha who gave you your Jinx."

"Maz . . . how do I get rid of him?"

Maz sat back in her chair and rocked slowly. "Maz haz seen many Jinxez, liddle spud, but she haz never seen ze Jinx like you have. You have ze deep connection."

"What do you mean?" Ivy's voice betrayed her rising alarm.

Maz stared into the fire. "Tangly, tangly rootzz," she whispered. "Winzzy rootzz cling, deep rootzz, strong rootzz." For the first time, Ivy and Franny both had the idea that she might be keeping something from them. "Your Jinx will never leave you," Maz said solemnly.

"How can you say that?" Ivy cried. "You're wrong!"

"Maz izz *alwayzz* right!" she said, all her eyes flashing. "Your Jinx dozz not like being a Jinx," she whispered sadly.

Stunned, Franny and Ivy didn't say a word. The fire had burned down low, and Maz looked weary. The girls knew her story was finished for this day, but Ivy needed to learn one more thing.

"Maz," Ivy said, "I need to find that other shoe before Cha Cha does!"

Maz shook her head. "Well, I don' know about

where ze zoomy shoe izz now." Maz held a long finger up. "I can tell you one zing: you muzzt leave Wormz Pock to find ze shoe, and zer iz only one way out of ze Spudz."

"How?" Ivy said.

"Through ze Ooze, and liddle spudzz, izzz not ze place you want to be going to." Maz looked at both girls and there was fear on her kind, old, lumpy face. She whispered, "Ooze izzz ze zemetary."

"Cemetery?" Franny said.

"Where all ze dead izzzz buried!" Smoke from the dying embers of the fire curled into strange shapes. "Izzz chock full of ze ghostezzzz, and ze zzzzombiezzz—"

"Zombies?" Franny shivered. "I *hate* zombies!"

"Izzzzz spookety, and zerz hundredzzzz of tunnels and pathzzzz through ze Ooze zat you can get lozzt in forever. I heard zer iz one way out—if you make it zat far—take ze winzzy high road and juzzt head upwardzzz, liddle spudz."

Maz sighed and, with much effort, pushed her great body out of the chair. "Alwayzzz take ze winzzy high road."

AN UNEASY JOURNEY UP POTATO MOUNTAIN

32

*L*ike *Franny and Ivy before them, Pru* and Cat had gone through the trapdoor in Spoz and ended up in the mud field in Spudz.

The girls stood before the well-worn path, certain that Franny and Ivy had gone in that direction. Before they could embark on a search for their friends, however, Pru and Cat were startled when first one, then another potato popped from its muddy bed. They'd seen the potatoes in Spoz roll over for no apparent reason and stare at them in a very disturbing way, but the behavior of these fellows in Spudz was something new.

The ground rose up beneath Ginger, who found herself balanced atop a large spud. Sprouting from its sides were spidery roots that served as hands and fingers, which it used to attempt to knock her off. Ginger gasped and jumped and ran, not down the well-worn path that Ivy had taken, but straight up the side of the mountain behind them. Fred dashed after her, and the girls had no choice but to follow, a field full of grumbling, mud-caked potatoes lumbering after them like hibernating bears that have been awoken before spring.

They had speed on their side and lost the unfriendly spuds quickly, Ginger and Fred leading the

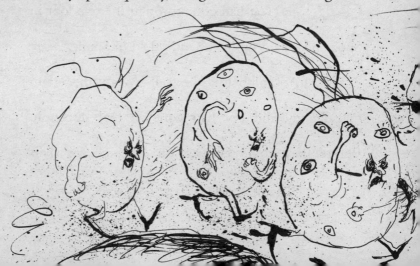

way up the steep terrain. Pru wished they'd taken the path back in the field, but Ginger and Fred seemed to know where they were going.

If you want to know what Pru and Cat's journey was like, then picture yourself hiking up a mountain made of rocks: big rocks, little rocks, medium-sized rocks. Then, in your mind, replace the rocks on the mountain with potatoes—thousands of potatoes, millions of potatoes, trillions of potatoes. So many that they stretch upward forming one big potato mountain.

Thankfully, these potatoes had been harvested and were less alive than the ones back in the field and more like the spuds they had come to know in Spoz. It was very tough going, though. Pru and Cat had their own backpacks to carry as well as Franny's and Ivy's, and with the potatoes shifting under their feet from time to time, the girls were continually tripping. Pru and Cat never lost the feeling of being watched, either.

Just put one foot in front of the other, Pru told herself after falling for the thousandth time. She and Cat had to keep going, if not for themselves, than at least for Franny and Ivy.

Cat lagged behind because for once she didn't have the heart to lead. Fred and Ginger seemed so sure about where to go, but to Cat it seemed as if Franny and Ivy were probably still far below. They should never have climbed this stupid potato mountain! Or should they have? Cat just wasn't sure. In fact, she wasn't sure of anything anymore, least of all herself, and it made her feel very out of sorts.

Many hours later they sat miserably eating their meager dinner. They had strung their ponchos over some large potatoes and dug out a little hollow to protect themselves from the steady rain of dirt that fell from above. They had almost no water left, and in another day or two they would be out of raisins, nuts, and chocolate bars.

Cat had been moody and quiet ever since they'd stepped off the ladder into Spudz, and it was making Pru even more nervous than normal. Hunched over her *I Ching* book, Cat tossed the pennies and momentarily brightened at what the book had to say: THE BEGINNING OF THE END.

"Look," Cat recited:

*"In Earth Shoes and Birkies
up the mountain you came . . .*

"Yeah, but what does that part say?" Pru said, trying to read the rest over Cat's shoulder.

"Nothing, Pru. Don't be so negative," Cat said angrily, snapping the book shut.

But Pru had seen that it said:

*"On the other side you see
nothing's the same!"*

That doesn't sound so good, Pru thought.

She looked over at Cat, who stared into space not talking, and Pru wondered if Cat was mad at her, because whenever someone stopped talking, Pru always thought that meant they were mad at her.

Cat didn't have the energy to say anything

as they sat. *Pru probably thinks I'm mad at her*, Cat thought. It made Cat mad at Pru for thinking that Cat was mad at her. Cat looked out of the corner of her eye at Pru. Pru quickly looked away, busying herself with straightening the contents of her backpack. It irritated Cat even more that Pru would look away from her. But way off, and very faintly, there was a surprised and disappointed part of Cat's self that stood sadly shaking her head at the horrible way that Cat was acting. Cat knew Pru was anxious and that she should try to calm her down. "Say something nice, make Pru feel comfortable, she is after all *trying*, and you are acting like a baby," this part of herself was saying.

Cat's eyes fell on the tube of toothpaste that Pru was about to put in her backpack. "We can always eat toothpaste if we run out of food," Cat said, trying to be optimistic, and hoping it would make Pru feel better.

"Are you crazy?" Pru said. "This stuff is full of chemicals! The *American Journal of Medical Doctors* recently reported—"

Cat smacked her hand to her forehead, her attempt to be nice instantly evaporating, and said, "Why don't you just shut up?"

"*You* shut up!" Pru said. "And while we're at it, if

you know so much about ESP, why don't you just *conjure* the *old man*—the wizard." Pru made little quotation marks with her fingers when she said "wizard." "Why don't you just get him back here again to help us find Franny and Ivy?"

Pru's words stunned Cat to such an extent that if she hadn't been sitting down, she might just have tumbled off the mountain. For a moment she was speechless. Pru had an excellent point; why didn't Cat conjure up some help from the wizard now? The simple answer to this question was that Cat *had* tried—all summer in fact—and had failed. Now Pru had guessed what Cat suspected, that maybe Cat hadn't conjured anything, maybe she didn't even have ESP.

Cat folded her arms and glared at Pru, trying to come up with just the right thing that would really get her. "You know why everybody in school says you're a big baby?" Cat let Pru stew before delivering the answer. "Because you *are* one!"

Tears immediately sprang to Pru's eyes. "Well then, maybe it's a good thing I won't be in your class next year!"

"You won't?" Cat said with a smirk on her face. She thought about how cool it would be if Pru got moved to Liverwurst. "Where will you be, Pru?"

"Bacon-Lettuce-and-Tomato, that's where! I've been moved, but I didn't tell anyone because it didn't seem appropriate, what with Ivy's troubles and all." Pru turned her back on Cat and flopped down to go to sleep.

Fred and Ginger had been uneasily watching this exchange. Their heads snapped from one girl to the other the way sports fans' will at a tennis match.

Ginger frowned at Cat. "Did you ever?"

"Never!" huffed Fred, and both dogs curled up together as far away from the girls as possible.

Bacon-Lettuce-and-Tomato? Cat mulled this over as she too lay down. No one *ever* gets put in there! Even though Cat couldn't stand being in the same class with Pru, the thought of Pru moving into mysterious BLT bugged her. Cat lay awake for a long time before sleep would come, thinking about Bacon-Lettuce-and-Tomato and wondering why in the world she hadn't been put in there as well.

*I*n many ways it was difficult for Franny

and Ivy to leave Maz. Wormz Pock was com-

fortable and safe. But then again, how were their fel-

low Gumm Street girls, Pru and Cat, and the dogs,

Fred and Ginger? Probably anything but comfortable

and safe. Maybe they had even been beautylyized!

"Maybe we should just go back to Spoz," Ivy suggested.

Ivy and Franny had gone over it a hundred times since they'd arrived at Maz's.

"If we do go back, the twins will do something horrible to us," Franny had said, biting her nails.

"We can't be very far from Sherbet," Ivy said, trying to convince herself as well as Franny. "You heard Maz."

The girls finally agreed. They had to go through Ooze and hope to find their way to Sherbet, where they would warn the town about Cha Cha, get help, find the other shoe, and come back to rescue their friends.

So the girls decided they were ready to go. Maz stuck her head out the door and sniffed. "Spudz are mud gluzzing about!"

Maz helped them into cloaks she'd made out of the burlap type material. The garments covered them from their heads to just above their ankles. Maz fussed over the girls, pulling the hoods up and tying the belts securely around their waists. "Mind you keep ze hoodzzz up!" She shook a long, rootlike finger at them. "Ze Spudz are not mizzer people, but zay will mistake you for ze witchezz! Zay cannot go zap snatching liddle Spudzgirlzz, so long azz ze hoodzzz are up!"

She took each girl in her giant arms and gave her a long hug. Franny breathed in Maz's warm baked potato aroma, and Maz patted Franny's back comfortingly. She then instructed them both, "Once you are in ze Ooze, spudkins, don't stray off ze zigzy path! Ze Ooze sucks up anything off ze path—especially liddle spudzgirlzz." She handed them each a bundle containing food and drink. Maz stood at her door and watched them start down the path. Franny and Ivy turned and waved and then rounded the corner out of her sight.

"Do you think we'll ever see Maz again?" Franny asked wistfully. It had been nice having someone care for her, she thought, even if that someone was an enormous potato.

Ivy was preoccupied and didn't answer. The Jinx was out there. She could see him looking at her from the shadows, and Ivy wondered what Maz had meant when she said, "Your Jinx doesn't like being a Jinx." She had also said, "He'll never leave you." If only Maz could for once be wrong!

"The Spudz need to stop being eaten, don't you think?" Franny was saying. "Wouldn't it be cool if we could come back and set them free?"

"If we ever get out of here *to* come back!" Ivy said, examining her ankles to see if any of the worms were crawling on her legs yet. The cloak from Maz seemed to be good at repelling them, but she was going to keep checking anyway.

Franny and Ivy walked as quickly as they dared, so as not to call attention to themselves, for the folks in these parts did not move at a very lively pace. The farther along they went, the less populated it became, and there were not as many caves, pits, pocks, nooks, or caverns. Gradually the worms diminished, too, and the miles of stony walkway that had been set down on top of the mud became less well tended. Hours later it was nothing more than roots lashed together, calling to Franny's mind makeshift life rafts that could have been built by shipwrecked survivors as a means of escape from some desert island.

Finally, after many miles, Franny and Ivy stood before a pair of massive wrought-iron gates composed of irregular twists and sharp spears. A sickening green light glowed from two heavy lanterns that swooped up on long, spiky arms. Four letters atop the gates that had been hammered out in iron spelled the word OOZE. Extending from both sides of the gate was a

fence that stretched as far as the eye could see. It seemed like the sort of place that, once entered, didn't allow one to turn back.

The girls stood for a moment wondering how they would even get inside, for the place seemed forbidding and hostile. *Maybe we should just go back*, they each thought. But slowly the gates creaked open, and they knew there was no other option but to step inside. The gates closed behind the girls with a loud clank that echoed in their ears. Franny and Ivy were now locked in Ooze.

"Zombies," Franny said in a low voice. She hated zombies—you were so defenseless against them! You could put a stake through the heart of a vampire, you could stall for time until daylight with a werewolf, but zombies, now they were another story.

"They're slow," Ivy assured Franny.

This made Franny feel a little better, and she thought that in this respect they were similar to mummies, who didn't seem so awfully speedy either. The only trouble was that Franny was slow, too. She picked up her pace.

The path now was only a thin, raised slice of muddy ground. On each side was a deep gelatinous gumbo of bubbling goo. Steam rose from pockets with a sulfurous stench, and mud dripped from above in long globs, strands of it hanging suspended, making both girls thankful for their cloaks. Here and there yellowing gravestones appeared like decaying molars that had fallen out of an elderly giant's mouth. Maz's words rang in their ears: "Alwayzzz take ze winzzy high road." Several times Ivy and Franny had to decide which branch of the path to take, among the ones that peeled off into smaller paths; each time they picked the path that rose upward. As they got farther, more and more gravestones dotted the landscape and appeared to be eerily rising in the mire rather than hopelessly sinking, as one might expect.

As she hurried to keep up, Franny tried to occupy herself with the trials of her heroes. Ernest Shackleton wouldn't be afraid. Sir Edmund Hillary wouldn't have trouble keeping up—

Oh, who am I trying to kid, Franny thought glumly. "Hey, wait up, Ivy!" she called, gulping for air.

Ivy stopped and waited. In her eagerness to get through Ooze, Ivy hadn't realized that Franny was having trouble matching her pace. As Franny approached, Ivy could now see she was completely out of breath and exhausted. Then Franny stumbled right before Ivy's eyes and almost fell off the path.

"Be careful, Franny!" Ivy shouted, grabbing her arm.

"I . . . know . . . I'm such a . . . klutz," Franny panted. "You . . . probably wish . . ." Franny stopped and leaned over with her hands on her knees, trying to catch her breath, and repeated, "You probably . . . wish you had Cat or Pru . . . here instead of me, right?" Her eyes searched her friend's face for an honest answer.

Ivy put her hand on Franny's shoulder. "I'm glad you're with me," Ivy said, and meant it. In fact, even though she had felt a little guilty thinking it, Ivy was happy Franny was the one with her. Ivy didn't know anyone as brave as Franny. Come to think of it, the only thing besides zombies that really scared her friend was the fear of being left behind. "You lead for a while," Ivy said. "I'm tired."

Franny was happy to be out in front, and Ivy was happy to make Franny happy. They climbed ever upward—if more slowly—along the ascending path. Finally, at a fork in the path, Franny stopped.

"So, where are all the ghosts and zombies?" Franny said. "Because I haven't seen any, have you?"

The names of the dead surrounded Ivy and

Franny. There were grandfathers named Boz, Baz, Beez, Coz, Caz, and Ceez. There were grandmothers named Fingzy and Fangzy, husbands and dear departed wives named Pongzy and Pingzy. There were the Phiz and the Phoz families, the McZoozzlez and the McZidzzerz. All the Danglegerkz and the Gangerklakz were there, as well as the the Ozgoodz, Ozblenkz, and the Ozdunkz. Also Zerkz, Zinkz, Zongoz, the Tiddlywonkz, and the Mummbly Kinkz as well. But so far there were no ghosts or zombies, except for Ivy's Jinx, who followed at a distance.

"No ghosts or zombies," Ivy said, shaking her head. "Only a Jinx!" She thought that he was the least of her problems as she watched the Jinx slip behind one of the hundreds of tombstones.

They started up again. It seemed as though they'd been walking for many hours, but in this perpetual darkness they had no idea. There was no sun or moon to tell them how much time had passed.

As they climbed, Ivy became aware of an annoying buzzing sound in her ears and saw a pinpoint of red that glowed off in the distance. *Perhaps it's only a mirage, like desperate people see in the desert*, Ivy thought as Franny disappeared over the rise. With shaking legs, Ivy finally reached the top and, much to her dismay,

371

discovered that all their effort had led them to a solid wall of mud. The buzzing sound was not inside her head at all, nor was the mysterious glow a mirage. Instead, a neon sign stuck out of the wall spelling out the worst two words that Ivy had ever seen: NO EXIT.

Ivy and Franny and Cat and Pru had all had such high hopes a few months ago that they would be able to take on whatever was out there—as long as they stuck together. The memory came to Ivy now of standing at the wishing well and groping for a penny. "Friends" was what she had wished for. Ivy slowly opened her right hand. The eye was still imprinted there, and she remembered their fort in the *Z* and how the girls had pressed their palms to hers and vowed to always stick together.

Franny was right. There were no ghosts down here in Ooze after all, but Ivy felt haunted just the same. The girls were separated. They had not stuck together. Ivy couldn't deny it anymore; they were doomed.

"It's . . ." Franny had her hand over her mouth. "It's . . ." Franny said again.

Ivy looked dully at where Franny was pointing.

There, sitting atop one lone gravestone, was an old

lady. Like the painting of the old lady that they'd seen on the wall in Ivy's house, this old lady wore a bright pink chiffon scarf, a beehive hairdo, and large earrings in the shape of cherries or strawberries—it was hard to tell, but Franny would know those earrings anywhere! There was only one difference. She was covered in soot and held a piece of burned toast.

"It's Aunt V!" Franny finally managed to blurt out.

Aunt V gingerly climbed off the gravestone and chirped, "Not bad for an old broad with two hip replacements." She placed one hand in the small of her back and painfully straightened up. "Well, ya know what they say? Old age ain't for sissies!"

Ivy was speechless. But she leaned over and looked closely at the inscription on the tombstone, which read IN MEMORY OF VIOLA GALE. Trying not to think of the disreputable things Maz had said about her aunt, Ivy cried, "But if you're not dead. . . ?" She pointed to the gravestone.

"Kiddo, I had it all planned. Sherbet Final Rest Home, on my way out and pretendin' to be a garden-variety Alzheimer's case. But before I had a chance to fake my own death, I had a little run-in with a toaster and a fork! Just my luck, I died!" Aunt V took a giant bite out of the charred square and tossed it over her shoulder. "Technically, I should be at the Pearly Gates, strummin' on a harp and sportin' one of those cute little nighties they wear up there, but the thing is . . . I got some unfinished business here."

Franny's face went white and she mouthed the word "zombie." Ivy's eyes grew wide while Aunt V rattled on.

"I've been runnin' all over creation lookin' for you kids—geez, my dogs are killin' me." Black crumbs stuck to her lips as she spoke. "What I really need is a new pair of *shoes*."

"Shoes?" Franny and Ivy both said.

"Yeah, I had a great little pair—seven years ago—low-heeled pumps, silver. You didn't happen to see them?"

"Maybe I did." Ivy tightened the belt on her robe and jutted out her chin. "And maybe I didn't. But if I *did*, I wouldn't give them to you!"

"I like you, kid—you got spunk!" Aunt V winked. "You and me"—she pointed a finger back and forth at

Ivy and herself—"we should work together."

"Get away from us, you . . . you zombie lady!" Franny shouted. She and Ivy backed down the path.

Aunt V came tottering down the hill after them, hiking up her stretch pants. "Wait! We could be a team!" she cried breathlessly, and then suddenly turned to scurry back. "Oh, for the love a' Pete!"

Because coming up the mountain covered in ooze—and apparently feeling much better—was the Jinx, and he was headed straight toward Aunt V, snarling and snapping.

For the first time, Ivy couldn't help being a little happy to see him, because Aunt V was really creeping her out. Franny, however, did not share this view and screamed.

"Don't forget, kiddo," Aunt V said as she reached her gravestone and climbed back on. "Winter, spring, summer, or fall—"

Franny pulled Ivy by her cloak out of the Jinx's way, at the same time his long tail curled around Ivy and tugged at her.

"All you have to do is call," Aunt V finished. "I mean, if you find my shoes!"

Ivy's arms flailed and her eyes were wild. Franny looked on helplessly as the Jinx leaped right off the path and dove into the ooze, dragging Ivy along with him.

"Ivy!" Franny cried, and lunged for her friend, but it was too late.

"I'll be there, yeah, yeah, yeah." Aunt V leaned sideways to watch Ivy and the Jinx sink into the muck.

"I'm coming, Ivy!" Franny shouted as she jumped into the air.

"Don't forget, kid—the shoes!" Aunt V called just before Franny hit the glop. "And remember . . . you've got a friend!"

A HOLE IN THE SKY

34

*F*red and Ginger and Cat and Pru reached the summit many hours later the next day, but this achievement did nothing to dispel their sagging spirits. Neither girl had spoken a word to the other since the unpleasant conversation under the ponchos at their camp.

Cat, lost in her thoughts, frowned because she had a nagging feeling that Franny and Ivy were still down below.

Pru was worried, very worried, but not about herself. She had hoped that from where she stood, maybe, just maybe, she would see Franny and Ivy below. But she could only see many ladders, like the one she and Cat had climbed down, leading up to Spoz. Now, standing on a mountain made of potatoes under a sky made of dirt, it seemed completely normal to spot a potatolike fellow scurrying up one of these ladders to deliver his basket of what they could only assume were dirt-caked spuds.

"So that's how the potatoes get into the spud room," Pru said, only dimly aware that she'd spoken out loud. Cat ignored her.

The girls sat on opposite sides of the summit. Cat took a swallow from her almost empty water bottle, while Pru picked the last of the raisins from her crumpled plastic bag. Each would have been surprised to know they were thinking exactly the same thing: *Now what do we do?*

No doubt you have heard someone say, "We felt as though we could touch the sky!" Such an expression is exclaimed generally by holidaymakers after they have ascended to some high spot—say a mountaintop or a scenic cliff. But in Cat and Pru's case, this was literally true. They really *could* have touched their sky from the top of Potato Mountain. Unfortunately, neither Cat nor Pru had the presence of mind to notice this interesting phenomenon.

Fortunately, Fred and Ginger did.

But Fred and Ginger's vocabulary was limited. They could say some words such as "Did you ever?" and "Never." They could also make throat-clearing noises, which came in handy in any number of situations, but right now they needed in the worst way to be able to say, "For heaven's sake, will you two girls please look up?" Instead, they were reduced to a pantomime of coughs, followed by looking up and standing on their hind legs and howling.

Finally Cat, her thoughts broken by the noisy dogs, got the message and looked up. Then she stood up. Then she reached up her hand. "I can almost touch the sky! Hey, give me a boost," Cat told Pru.

"Give *yourself* a boost," Pru said dryly, and looked up as well to see that there was a hole in the sky. But Pru was mad at Cat. These were practically the first civil words that Cat had spoken since they'd been in Spudz, and Pru was not about to let Cat forget it.

Pru stood up, too, and peered into the lightless hole. Perhaps it led somewhere—maybe to a tunnel

out of this
awful place! On the other hand, she reasoned,
tunnels caved in. Tunnels filled up with water.
Tunnels were dark. Pru did not like tunnels. But
being on top of a potato mountain didn't seem terribly safe either. Pru's dirty palms were starting to per-
spire. She wiped them on her pants.

"Fine!" Cat said sharply. She began to pile potatoes
on top of one another, thinking that if she could get
them high enough, she could climb up them and into
the hole. The problem was that the potatoes would
not cooperate and kept rolling off one another and
down the mountain.

Pru watched Cat and thought about all she herself
had done this summer. She had traveled in a champagne-
colored Cadillac on a backwards tidal wave to a place
where she had lived inside a fort made of pink robes,
and where she had been a slave to twins who were
witches. *Then* she had pressed the big pink button and
beautulverized one of the witches, gone through a
trapdoor, and climbed miles down a ladder into a
muddy field full of angry potatoes. And *now* she had just
scaled a mountain made out of potatoes. Pru looked at
the hole again, and at Cat who had given up and now
sat with her chin in her hands, scowling. How hard
could it be to climb into a pitch-black hole in the sky?

Much easier
than watching Cat,
as usual, be the big star—all
brave, and bold, and confident.

"I'll tell you what," Pru said with
her hands on her hips. "*You* give *me* a
boost!"

"You?" Cat said surprised. "You're
not *afraid*?"

Pru was afraid all right, but hearing the
way Cat put the emphasis on the word
"afraid" made Pru so angry that she
gritted her teeth.

"I'm not afraid," Pru said with as
much calm and composure as she
could muster. "Give me a boost,"
she repeated.

Cat shook her head
while Pru offered her
foot. Pru put
her hand

on Cat's head for balance and stepped on Cat's bent knee. Jumping up, Pru caught the rim of the hole with both arms and swung easily up inside it. She rolled away from the edge and stood up on ground that from the other side was the sky. She squinted and took in her new surroundings. The hole was the bottom end of a . . .

"A tunnel!" Pru shouted down to Cat. "It's a tunnel!"

From the blackness of the hole overhead, Cat saw two disembodied hands and arms appear.

"Pass me Fred and Ginger," Pru said.

Cat handed the two dogs up to Pru and then the backpacks.

"Give me your hands and I'll pull you up," Pru said.

The arms reappeared. Cat jumped up and grabbed hold of Pru, and—surprised at Pru's strength—Cat swung between the mountain and the sky for a second before managing to catch her knee on the rim of the hole. Pru gave a tremendous tug, and Cat was soon lying well inside the edge of the hole in the sky, covered in dirt, getting her breath back. The two girls looked down at the top of Potato Mountain, glad not to be there anymore.

"Thanks," Cat said.

"Anytime," Pru answered.

IVY GETS LUCKY 35

*A*s the ooze from Ooze closed over her head, Ivy thought she was a goner. Sucked down into what felt like a gigantic bucket of glue, she felt herself spin around and around in a corkscrewing motion, and she thought about how all her bad luck had brought her to this tragic end. But Ivy also thought about how it had brought her to Sherbet, to Franny, Pru, Cat, Fred, and Ginger. How she had met Mr. Staccato, who had told her she had a unique talent, and how he had trusted her with the mysterious shoes. All of her bad luck had led her to all these good things, and Ivy thought how right Mr. Staccato had been when he had said that things are not always what they appear, that sometimes they are the complete opposite. And then, unbelievably, her foot hit solid ground. Instinctively, she kicked against the surface and, for the first time in her life, Ivy got lucky.

To her complete astonishment, the ground gave way. Like a baby bird fighting its way out of the egg, Ivy felt her foot crack through a shell of crumbling earth, and then her whole body followed. She plopped out from Ooze, trembling and half blind, only to be assaulted by someone very strong and very wiry, and—as she wiped the ooze out of her eyes— very familiar.

"Cat!" Ivy screamed as she was being pummeled. "Stop! It's me!"

"Ivy?" Cat stopped and tried to match the voice of her friend to the blob that had just emerged from the wall of the tunnel. Fred and Ginger ran anxious circles around Ivy, sneezing and barking, until Ivy grabbed them and buried her face in their fur.

The wall crumbled further, and another blob emerged.

"Franny!" Pru cried.

They all talked at once, about being cared for by a gigantic potato, and about beautylyizing Bling Bling; about Iznotz and zombies and swimming through Ooze, about climbing up a mountain made of potatoes and about how they didn't go hungry once because Franny had made them bring—

"Our backpacks!" Franny exclaimed. She thought she'd never see them again.

Pru and Cat peeled the two girls out of their ooze-covered cloaks, and

all four of them just hugged one another and felt happier than they could have ever imagined.

As Ivy put the bundle of food and drink from Maz in her backpack, she looked around and wondered, *Where is my Jinx?* There was no sign of him anywhere, but there was no denying he had brought her back to her friends. And there was no way that could be anything but lucky!

After a moment Franny looked up and said, "Maybe we all died, because I see a white light."

Anxious to know what the light was, they began to climb. Using roots as handholds and rocks as steps, they slowly made their way up. It was not easy work, especially for Pru and Cat, who each had the added weight of a terrier in her backpack. At last Cat muscled her way to the top and heaved herself out of the tunnel.

"What's there? Cat?" Franny yelled up. "Cat? Where are we?"

Receiving no answer, Franny struggled up the last few feet and popped her head out of the hole like a

groundhog in February. Looking around, she knew exactly where they were. She heaved a sigh of relief, and she and Cat, who had been too surprised to answer Franny, helped the other two girls out of the tunnel.

In the distance was a cottage in twilight. A tarnished golden bucket lay beside it, and the ground was carpeted with coins of every kind, each one representing a wish made long ago (and one coin representing a very recent wish). The girls staggered slowly toward the phony gingerbread house for truants that had been built

years ago at the bottom of Hieronymus Gumm's wishing well.

Ivy and Franny were the first to reach the cottage. They set down their packs, and Fred and Ginger scampered inside as soon as Ivy opened the door. The girls peeked around the doorjamb, not knowing what to expect.

"So, you're in Bacon-Lettuce-and-Tomato now, huh?" Cat said as she and Pru approached the house together. Cat felt terrible about her behavior on the mountain and gave Pru a sidelong glance to see if Pru was going to hold it against her.

"I am, and I wish I weren't," Pru said candidly. "I wish I were still in Tuna-on-Rye with you."

"You do?" Cat said, surprised.

"Yeah, I do," Pru said, and meant it, and for the first time in a long time Cat smiled a real smile at Pru, and Pru gave her one back.

36

Middle C Cottage

enius entrepreneur, ahead-of-his-time visionary, merry prankster—Hieronymus Gumm was all of these. But there had also been whispered rumors that he possessed magical powers as well, and so the Gumm Street girls were more than a little nervous upon entering the gingerbread cottage.

"Don't panic!" Cat called out in a panicking voice as she and Pru entered. It was very dark.

Ivy still had her flashlight and played it around the room. The vaulted ceiling was paneled in pine, and a sleeping loft—which could be reached by way of a wooden ladder—extended out from the south wall. A braided carpet lay in the middle of the room, and there was one wooden chair set before a huge stone fireplace. Inside that was H. Gumm's infamous oven.

Next to the oven hung an eerily lifelike painting of Hieronymus Gumm himself, dressed as a harlequin, his eyes twinkling with amusement. It gave Cat the willies. She stood quietly before it and tried to figure out why the painting made her feel such an odd sense of familiarity. Sure, she'd seen his statue many times in the atrium at school, but this was different. It was as though she knew him, as though she'd spoken to him. But she couldn't quite figure it out and finally joined the other girls, who were trying to make themselves comfortable.

They found some candles, as well as some firewood. There was a little hand pump next to a basin, and they were even able to get it working. Pru objected to drinking from it at first, citing cases of dysentery caused by ingesting unclean water, but she

HIERONYMUS GUMM

gave in after the idea of using the fireplace to boil it for ten minutes was suggested.

While Cat made a fire, Franny and Ivy realized they were famished. They had not looked inside their burlap bundles from Maz until now and were delighted to see that everything was still intact. Different-colored packages tumbled out of the sacks as they dumped the contents on the rug. Soon the girls had made Maz's rich hot chocolate drink and poured it into mugs Cat found in a cabinet under the loft.

Ivy hardly even thought about the Jinx, whom she had not seen since her trip through the ooze. Was he living in her shadow once more? She had no way of knowing, but she was so relieved to be reunited with her friends that it hardly mattered. While it was true the girls weren't home yet, at least they knew where they were, and the best part was that they were all together again.

The six of them sat before the flickering fire, under the watchful eye of Hieronymus Gumm.

Pru sniffed at her cake from Maz. None of the girls knew quite what to make of the food that had come from Spudz. Each package was about as big as a deck of cards and was the consistency of fudge, but that is where the similarities ended.

Franny nibbled at a corner of hers while the others watched. "Pizza!" she announced, and with a big grin took a larger bite. "And just the way I like it—with extra cheese."

Cat tried hers. "French toast!" she said.

"Is it hot?" Ivy asked, amazed.

"Hot and crispy—with lots of maple syrup," Cat told her. "What's yours, Pru?"

"Hot dogs with mustard and relish?" she said, and tried another bite just to make sure.

Ivy unwrapped one each for Fred and Ginger and was going to taste hers when Pru stopped her.

"Wait!" Pru commanded.

All the girls held their breaths, waiting for a safety tip.

"What's your favorite food, Ivy?" Pru asked, and glanced at the others with a grin.

"Fried chicken," Ivy said without hesitation.

"Okay, go!" Pru motioned for Ivy to try her brick.

Ivy bit into hers and chewed. "Fried chicken!" she announced.

"Good old Maz!" Franny laughed. She wiped her mouth and told Cat and Pru all that she and Ivy had learned from their friend in Spudz.

Pru gave a sheepish grin. "And nobody really knows all the powers that the shoes have."

"Aside from being able to get you anywhere you want to go," Franny reminded her.

"Yeah, even another *time*. . . ." Ivy said in a low voice.

"Another time?" Cat said.

"You mean like they can time travel?" Pru asked, surprised. "Are you sure? I don't remember it saying anything about that in the book!" She reached for her backpack and grabbed her copy of *The Wonderful Wizard of Oz* and began leafing through it.

While Pru scanned her book, the other Gumm Street girls were quiet and stared at the fire, considering everything they'd just heard. Hypnotized by the flames, Cat said softly, "So underneath Sherbet is Spoz, and underneath Spoz is Spudz."

"And Maz told us that Cha Cha has enslaved the Spudz," Franny said.

"Why?" said Pru and Cat, turning away from the fire and back to Franny.

"Just for the fun of it, I think," Franny said, and Ivy agreed. "The potatoes were enchanted so that they could harvest themselves to be eaten by the witches in Spoz!"

"Gross!" Pru and Cat said.

Franny went about explaining all that Maz had told her and Ivy about Cha Cha and Aunt V and all about the splenjezztical Prophet's Mark that Ivy had on her palm.

"Wait a minute!" Pru excitedly thumbed to a page of her Oz book, "Listen to this!" She began to read:

"'No, I cannot do that,' she replied; 'but I will give you my kiss, and no one will dare injure a person who has been kissed by the Witch of the North.'

"She came close to Dorothy and kissed her gently on the forehead. Where her lips touched the girl they left a round, shining mark, as Dorothy found out soon after."

The girls all looked at Ivy's hand again. "It's round and shiny all right," Franny commented.

"But what about Aunt V?" Cat wondered aloud.

"She was sitting on a *gravestone* . . . that had her *name* on it . . . so, she's like *dead* . . . but *not* dead," Franny said, feeling jittery all over again. "In *my* book, that means *zombie!*" Franny gave a theatrical shiver. The fire inside the stove flickered from a cold draft of air. The girls wrapped themselves in the blankets from their backpacks and continued their conversation.

"Franny, remember the letter that you found on Aunt V's portrait in my house?" Ivy sat up, rousing Fred and Ginger from their slumber. They looked at her, blinking.

"Yes, the day you came to Sherbet," Franny replied.

"Aunt V wrote that she wasn't really dead. It was all a lie—Aunt V faked her death to get me and my mom to come to Sherbet and inherit her crummy old house and get the shoes from me or my mother—whoever got them—and then she and Cha Cha—"

"Could disappear and no one would look for them!" Franny chimed in. "But her plan backfired."

"How?" asked Pru.

"While she was faking her death, she accidentally died!" Ivy said.

"She said she had a run-in with a toaster and a fork," Franny added.

"Toaster and a fork?!" Pru said excitedly. "I remember my parents talking about the old lady at the Sherbet Final Rest Home who died . . . just . . . making . . . *toast!*"

"That's it!" Franny said.

"But the thing is"—Ivy gave Franny a worried look and pulled Fred and Ginger close to her—"Aunt V *still* wants the shoes. . . ."

"So how did you guys get away from her?" Cat asked.

"The Jinx came," Ivy told her, "and he pulled me into the ooze."

"And I jumped in after Ivy to save her life," Franny said proudly. "But here's the *best* part," she said, reaching into her back pocket. She held the vial from Dr.

Iznotz between her thumb and middle finger. "Witch Vanishing Potion!"

Cat scratched her head, "Now let me see. Whatever would we be needing *that* for?"

The girls laughed.

"But before we go vanishing any witches," said Pru, "I'm going to have to get some rest."

"Rest?" Franny said incredulously. "You have the rest of your life to rest—we need to find a way out of here!"

"I don't know." Ivy covered Fred and Ginger with part of her blanket. "I kind of like it here."

"Me too," Cat said. "It's like no one can get at us."

"That's how I always felt at Mr. Staccato's—safe," Ivy said softly, and the others nodded.

The girls sat lost in their own thoughts, watching the fire burn low.

"Mr. Staccato was so cool," Franny said, settled down now.

"I remember the first thing he ever taught me," Cat said. She was on her stomach with her hands crossed under her chin. " 'Miss Lemonjello,' he said, 'Middle C, this is where it all starts.' "

"Or sometimes where it all ends," Ivy said sadly, and remembered her first lesson with Mr. Staccato—

she'd had no idea then she'd have so little time with him.

Next to Ivy, Fred and Ginger sniffled.

"I just got the *best* idea!" Franny said. She was actually more tired than she had realized, and she pulled her backpack toward her to use as a pillow. "Why don't we name this place Middle C Cottage in honor of Mr. Staccato?"

Ivy looked down on the little room and thought the only thing missing was a piano.

"It's even sort of the center of things, if you think about it," Franny said. "You've got Sherbet above and Spoz below!"

"You know what?" Cat said. "That's a really good idea, Franny."

Everyone—even Pru, for a change—liked Franny's idea, and after that each dropped off to sleep in the cottage of Middle C.

37

A Secret Passage

Cat was the first one to wake up. In the half-light, she climbed downstairs and peeked outside. The ground sparkled with coins, and for a moment Cat wished they could just stay there in the cottage awhile longer. But she knew they couldn't. She called out to the others, "Wake up, you guys. We have to find a way out of here!" Cat peered inside the oven to see if there was a way to get out by going up the chimney, but the busted rope that had held the bucket dangled uselessly many feet above.

Franny sat in the one chair. "Cat?" She'd been thinking about this for a while. "So if you really conjured the wizard, why don't you—"

"No," Cat said without even waiting to hear Franny's idea.

"Why not?" Franny cried. "You can just conjure him up to help us—"

"Don't you think I've tried?" Cat said, and sat down hard on the rug.

"What was that thing again—that the wizard said to you when you conjured him, before he left?" Ivy asked, and tried not to laugh. "Hieronymus Gumm's heinie?"

"Hieronymus Gumm's *behind*." Franny wrinkled her nose.

"Actually, if I remember correctly," Pru began, "it was not Hieronymus Gumm's *behind*. It was simply, Hieronymus Gumm . . . behind."

"Hieronymus Gumm . . . behind. . . . Hieronymus Gumm . . . behind. . . ." All four girls repeated the

400

words over and over, trying to figure out what it could mean. Hieronymus Gumm . . . behind. They said it so many times that the last word started sounding like the first word. And Mr. Staccato would have been pleased, because now they were hearing it the other way around. Instead of *Hieronymus Gumm . . . behind*, it sounded like *behind . . . Hieronymus Gumm*.

They stopped. *Behind Hieronymus Gumm?*

The girls looked at the portrait on the wall and then at one another.

"Behind Hieronymus Gumm!" the girls repeated. Lifting the painting from the wall, they could see that behind it was a small door.

"Wait a minute!" Cat cried. "I just remembered—the wizard's last words were 'Wishing you well!'"

"The wishing well—Hieronymus Gumm's wishing well." Pru said. "He meant behind Hieronymus Gumm's portrait in the wishing well!"

Ivy stepped forwards and turned the doorknob. It wasn't locked. With a small push she opened it, revealing . . .

"A secret passage!" She shined her flashlight on a set of stone steps leading upward. The girls crowded around Ivy to see, and Fred and Ginger stood on the threshold, too, their tails wagging and their noses

401

twitching as they smelled the musty air.

A moment later they rushed past the girls and disappeared up the stairs.

"Hey, wait! Fred and Ginger, come back!" Ivy's voice echoed off the walls. But it was too late; both dogs had raced out of sight. Ivy chased after them, Franny right behind.

"Wait for us!" called out Cat and Pru, who ran back into the room to grab everyone's things, then dashed into the secret passage after their friends.

The steps became very steep as they climbed, and

soon they caught up with Franny, who was lagging behind as usual. The three girls held hands the rest of the way up, sometimes feeling their way along the wall when the stone steps turned here or there. "Ivy!" they called, but heard nothing in return until, ten feet from the top, they made out the figure of a girl, along with two dogs.

Fred and Ginger scratched at the wall that blocked their way, and whined.

"What is it?" Franny called. "Ivy?"

But Ivy didn't answer. She stood as still as a statue.

The three girls climbed the remaining steps.

"What is it?" said Franny, concerned.

"What's wrong?" said Pru.

"Let me see," said Cat, pushing her way to where Ivy was standing.

Cat touched her fingers to the silver lettering etched on the wall. WHAT IS MY UNIQUE TALENT? it said. Franny shone her flashlight on the curious window that was set in the wall just below the writing.

Ivy's pale face looked ghostly in the fast-fading light from the flashlight. She licked her dry lips. "Franny"—there was urgency in Ivy's voice—"what was that crazy thing that Mr. Staccato said to you just

before he . . . when he was floating over his house?"

"I'll never forget it for as long as I live," Franny whispered. "He said, 'You make a better door than a window.'"

Suddenly the strange window popped open like a door, and Pru screamed, "How'd you do that?"

"I don't know," cried Franny.

"Shhh!" Ivy warned them, and opened the door-like window wider. They took a step closer and could see what looked like the inside of a cupboard, except it had only one shelf on the left side. There was a delicate crystal glass, a decanter, a tin of biscuits, and a mug, all of them seeming to shimmer with light.

"What's that?" Cat pointed.

Below the items was something else. The halo of light betrayed its hiding place. Ivy reached into the back of the shelf, closing her hand around it. It felt cool and smooth to the touch.

"The silver—!" Pru blurted out, but was cut off as Franny clamped a hand over her mouth.

#5 GUMM Comes UNGLUED

For a few seconds there was complete silence as the Gumm Street girls' brains became used to the idea that they had the other silver slipper.

Finally Franny said, "Hide it!"

Ivy stuffed the shoe inside her jeans, just as she'd

done many weeks ago with the first silver shoe.

Facing the girls across the cabinet was another window, and the same riddle: WHAT IS MY UNIQUE TALENT?

"Are you guys ready?" Ivy asked her friends. They nodded. "You make a better door than a window."

They waited, but this time nothing happened. Ivy repeated the phrase, with no result.

"You make a better door than a window," Franny said, thinking maybe it was her voice that made it open the first time. "You make a better door than a window. . . . Why isn't it working?!" Franny kicked at the window, to no avail.

Cat covered her eyes with both hands. "Oh, great! We find the shoe, only to be trapped forever in the secret passage!"

"Wait," Pru held up an index finger and they all stopped to listen. "Always remember Safety Tip Number One!"

Everybody groaned.

Undaunted, Pru carried on. "In cases of shark bite, roof collapse, mud slide, earthquake, shipwreck, gastrointestinal disturbances far from bathrooms, or any similar emergency situations, 99.99 percent of all successful outcomes depend on doing *one* thing."

The others waited.

"Staying calm!" Pru answered proudly.

"That's it?" the others said.

Pru continued, "Einstein said that insanity is trying the same thing over and over and expecting a different outcome."

"And?" the others said.

"It seems to me that since we are now on the *inside* of the cupboard, then perhaps we should do the *opposite* of what we've done."

Fred and Ginger wagged their tails furiously.

"You make a better window than a door," Pru said softly.

The window slid upward. One by one the girls climbed out.

"I guess you're not in Bacon-Lettuce-and-Tomato for nothing," whispered Cat as she squeezed out from the tight space.

Pru smiled. She was the last one out, and the window quietly closed after her.

They were, as Ivy had guessed, in Mr. Staccato's museum room. They crouched behind the two wing-back chairs by the fireplace to consider their next move.

"Franny," said Ivy in a low voice. "Where's that

Witch Vanishing Potion?"

"Right here." Franny patted her back pocket.

"Get it ready," Ivy said.

"We're not going to kill her *now*, are we?" Pru moaned. "Can't I at least go home and take a shower first?"

Cat rolled her eyes.

They could hear some movement upstairs. "We should hurry," Ivy said. She motioned with her hand for the others to follow her into the kitchen. "We need to mix up the potion," she whispered, and bent down to get a bucket from Mr. Staccato's broom closet.

Franny measured out two gallons of water in the bucket and Ivy opened the vial and poured it in. Immediately it turned the water a sickening shade of green. Franny didn't want to look too closely, but she could have sworn she saw maggots swimming around just beneath the surface.

"This is disgusting!" Pru said as loudly as she dared.

"You can say that again," Franny replied, holding the bucket as far away as she could.

Pru was standing by the garbage and holding up a newspaper. "She doesn't even recycle!" Pru glanced at the paper for a moment. "Hey, we're in the newspaper!"

she said, and showed the others an article from the *Sherbet Scoop* entitled:

GIRLS FROM GUMM STREET PURSUE THEIR MUSICAL DREAMS!

Pru read the chirpy article for the others:

> "It must be something in the water over there on Gumm Street! Prudence Gumm, Frances Muggs, Ivy Diamond, and Cat Lemonjello have all gone off to a special music camp this summer and will remain there indefinitely. Says Cha Cha Staccato, music lover and sister of beloved departed music teacher Mr. Staccato, 'It's an exciting opportunity that—' "

" 'Any child would give her eyeteeth for!' " Cha Cha finished the sentence.

The girls froze.

"Uh-oh," said Franny, still holding her bucket of Witch Vanishing Potion.

In Cha Cha's hand was the first silver shoe. She held it up to her face like a mirror and examined her teeth for any stray smudges of lipstick. For the first time she was without her veil, and the girls could see that she was *well* past thirty-nine. Her face was overly made up, with a dark, unpleasant outline drawn all the way around her mouth, and her nostrils looked permanently flared, as if she smelled something bad. And, like her nieces, she was as green as moldy cheese. She clicked her ruby-red fingernails against the doorjamb, and the girls' nerves tingled with dread.

"You know, Ivy, dear," Cha Cha said sweetly. "I really *must* thank you."

Ivy scowled and stuck out her chin.

"And why must you thank me, Mzzzz Staccato?" Cha Cha said in a high-pitched voice, turning her head one way. Turning back, she replied in a deeper voice, "I'm glad you asked, Ivy—thanks a bunch for opening up that pesky cabinet."

"I'm not giving you the shoe," Ivy said simply.

"Oh *yes* you *are*, my pretty," Cha Cha said through clenched teeth.

"Oh no she's *not!*" Franny lunged at Cha Cha with her bucket of Witch Vanishing Potion. But the bucket was heavy, and Franny staggered under the weight.

As you can imagine, it is not so easy to kill a witch—compared to, say, a vampire or a werewolf. Even if you are lucky enough to have some Witch Vanishing Potion on you, it's still a very tricky proposition vanishing a witch. If you come away from reading this book with nothing else, for heaven's sake please know that if you are ever in the position of having to choose between a witch in your living room or a zombie, you would be well advised to choose the zombie, for they are *far* more predictable.

Cha Cha wheeled around and pointed a finger at the bucket. It levitated right out of Franny's hands and poured its contents down the sink. Then she levitated Franny, who hovered in the air for few seconds before landing on the floor right on her backside.

Fred gasped and said, "Did you ever?"

To which Ginger replied more indignantly than she ever had, "Never!"

Pru, who was standing back watching all this, ran to Franny.

"Franny, Franny, are you all right?" Pru said, kneeling beside her friend Franny.

"I think she's got enough padding to break her fall," Cha Cha said snidely.

This made Pru really angry. She knew that Franny was sensitive about her weight, and that the remark must have hurt more than the fall.

You probably think you know what happened next.

Pru rushed forwards and kicked Cha Cha? No.

She grabbed a hank of Cha Cha's bleached-blond hair and yanked as hard as she could? No.

Perhaps she punched her in the nose? Or bopped her over the head with the nearest potted plant? No and no.

Pru did none of these things. And you might be surprised to learn that for the first time, not even one safety hazard crossed her mind. Instead, she simply said, "Mzzzz Staccato, I feel it is my duty to inform you—girl to girl, if you will—that you have *totally* thick ankles."

"Thick ankles?" Cha Cha said, horrified.

"Precisely," said Pru. "And you've got a big butt."

Cha Cha rushed over to the floor-length mirror. "You mean you think I'm *fat*?" she shrieked, observing her body from every side and angle to see if there was any truth to Pru's statement.

This gave the Gumm Street girls just the window of opportunity they needed, and as one they turned and ran out the door.

"I'm *not* fat!" Cha Cha bellowed. "I'm just *big boned*!"

The four girls were halfway down the block before Cha Cha could say "Thighmaster."

Ivy rushed in through the front door of #5 Gumm. "Mom?" she called. There was no answer. Pru, Cat, Franny, Fred, and Ginger ran in behind her. "Lock the doors and close the windows!" Ivy screamed. "Then hide!"

"Where?" Pru asked. She had a point; there wasn't much in Ivy's house.

"The piano?" Cat said.

They gathered underneath it. The piano's feet were locked tightly in place, gripping the tilted floor for all their worth.

"Do you think she'll look for us here?" Franny said, pushing her hair out of her sweaty face.

"Is the Pope Cath—" Cat began to say.

"Yoo-hoo!" Cha Cha called from outside. "Come out, come out wherever you are!"

"Shhh, don't answer her," Ivy whispered.

"Maybe she'll just go away," Pru said hopefully.

They sat very still, hoping against hope that maybe Cha Cha *would* just go away. Five minutes passed, and then ten.

"Maybe she's really gone," Franny said, peeking up over the edge of the piano.

Then Pru said, "What's that funny smell?"

They all sniffed, and Cat remarked, "It's kind of like . . . something's—"

"BURNING!" they all screamed, and turned to see smoke billowing out of the kitchen.

"Fire!" yelled Pru. "Someone call nine-one-one!"

"I'll huff and I'll puff and I'll *blow* your house down!" Cha Cha cackled from outside the living room window.

Franny and Cat raced into the kitchen but a second later were back, coughing and holding their sleeves in front of their mouths.

"It's no use!" Franny cried. "The fire is out of control!"

"Give Cha Cha the shoe, Ivy!" Pru demanded as

416

she fussed with the lock on the wheels of the piano.

"No! I'll never do that!" Ivy yelled. She couldn't believe that after all they'd been through, Pru was still such a chicken.

But Cat had realized there was a lot more to Pru than her safety rules. She looked from the piano to Pru and from Pru to the piano. She understood. "No, Pru's right, Ivy! Give the shoe to Cha Cha—as close as you can to the house! Let us know when you do, and then run!" Ivy watched Cat grab Franny and run to help Pru over at the piano.

All at once Ivy understood, too. She and the dogs dashed to the front door.

The smoke was getting very thick. Pru, Cat, and Franny coughed as they knelt down at the piano's feet.

"Remove the locks on the rollers!" Pru shouted to Franny.

Once the locks were undone, the girls dug in their heels and held on, straining to keep the piano from sliding downhill to the other side of the room.

"Hey, Cha Cha!" Ivy called out from the doorway, pulling the shoe from under her shirt. She waved it over her head.

Cha Cha's eyes glittered at the sight of it, and her mouth went slack.

Ivy tossed the silver slipper up high against the side of the leaning house. "It's all yours!" she screamed and, scooping up Fred and Ginger, ran down the steps and away from #5 Gumm Street.

Cha Cha ran forwards, her arms outstretched, as if she were going to meet her beloved.

Franny, Pru, and Cat released the piano. It immediately shot forwards, gaining speed as it rolled down the long, sloping floor. Already dangerously off balance, the house shifted under the weight of the giant instrument. As the three girls escaped out the front door and sprinted from the flaming wreck to the street, there was a loud cracking, like a tree makes just before someone yells, "Timber!"

Cha Cha never noticed. Her sight was fixed on her darling, and she never, ever took her eyes from it, not even for one second.

She caught the shoe and slipped it on her right foot. Then she put on the other shoe so that she was wearing the pair. "At last, my beauties!" she warbled ecstatically.

"I can now have visibly firmer skin and get rid of fine lines . . . *forever*!"

The next moment, with a snap and a groan, #5 Gumm once and for all gave up its fight against gravity and fell—right on top of Cha Cha, squashing her like a well-dressed bug.

Before Pearl Diamond came skidding around the corner in her spangled sandals, or before the

Lemonjellos could get out of their downward-facing-dog yoga positions and call the fire department, or before the fire department came roaring down Gumm Street, or before Judge Gumm pulled up in his big black Mercedes sputtering about "hooligans!" or before Patience Gumm arrived, her notebook all set to scoop the story of the year, if not the decade—before any of this, Ivy braved the inferno, ran up, and slipped the shoes off Cha Cha's fishnet-stocking-clad feet. She ran back to the street, the shoes held tightly to her chest, her shadow lengthening before her because of the bright flames.

The shadow began to swirl. Suddenly the Jinx leaped from it, writhing and twisting as he flew through the air.

Ivy flung herself forwards, desperate to get away, but she was no match; the Jinx was fast and strong. He surged to her and seized hold of her shirt. She struggled against his powerful grip and thought of Mr. Staccato, who had said, "Your unique talent is your strength," but she was tired of fighting, tired of being strong, of being tenacious.

"Let me go!" Ivy cried, and kicked backwards at the Jinx. Through her screams, she thought she heard him growl, "I will *not* let you go!" He held her in a bear hug from behind and she fought hard. "I will *never* leave you!" he repeated again and again, until, exhausted, Ivy gave up and stood silent and still.

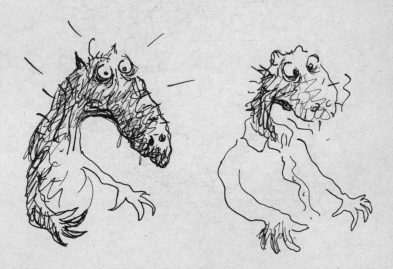

"I will never leave you, ever." He turned her to face him. "Never, ever again."

The first thing Ivy noticed was the dirty blue frayed collar on the tattered blue cotton shirt. *But Jinxes didn't wear shirts!* His hair was long and straggly, partially hiding his face, which was covered in a dark bushy beard, but she could still see his eyes. They were dark and shining, the same as those eyes had been that night in the *Z*. Ivy knew these eyes well.

Ivy began to cry, and he took her into his arms. "Daddy!" she sobbed.

Covered in soot and ash, but happy beyond words, the other three Gumm Street girls and Fred and

Ginger sat on the low curb across the street and watched Ivy in her father's arms. In Ivy's hands, the silver shoes caught the glow of the flames of #5 Gumm as it burned all the way to the ground. They twinkled and reflected the firelight, and for a split second now and again, they looked just like ruby-red slippers.

THE END OF THE END

Everything seems cool right now
and life's a bowl of granola.
But don't stop tuning into Oprah,
or discard your books on Deepak Chopra.
Yeah, it's the end of the end
and you're groovin' in the sun,
but don't put this I Ching book away,
'cause your work has just begun!

Cat closed the *I Ching* and leaned against the back of her bed. It was the last day of summer vacation and the girls had been home only a week, but to Cat the ordeal of the summer seemed more and more like a dream.

Cat was proud of herself and Franny, Ivy, and Pru, but she still felt uneasy. The first day of school was tomorrow, and there was already a chill in the air.

Cat ran her hand over the cover of the *I Ching*. "Your work has just begun." She didn't like the sound of that at all, and she immediately thought of Bling Bling. What if. . . ?

Cat reached behind her books and felt around for the

old aspirin bottle that she'd hidden. There it was. She undid the childproof cap and looked inside. Crescent-mooned in shape, some edged in bright pink and some bloodred in color, were Bling Bling's toenail clippings that Cat had stolen from the jar.

Now the trick would be to find out how to use them, because Cat was pretty sure that she and her fellow Gumm Street girls had not heard the last from Bling Bling.

Pru was a living example of the old saying that what doesn't kill you makes you stronger.

She had emerged from her trials with a great deal more confidence and a lot less fear. Yes, she did spend an entire day in her bedroom when she returned. But after that, one of the first things Pru did was go down to the beach to see a rainbow. It was more beautiful than she remembered. In fact, everything looked brighter, from the glittering towers of the Arctic Ice Cream Palace to the dazzling, undulating neon of the Colossal Candy Bar.

It was nighttime now, and Pru closed the cover on her book. She snuggled under her quilt and thought about calling Cat to see if she was getting any vibes. But Pru had a feeling that you didn't need ESP to figure out that Bling Bling and Spoz had more in store for them. Thank goodness Cha Cha at least was dead!

Picking up the *Sherbet Scoop*, Pru reread the article that her mother had written.

TRAGEDY AT #5 GUMM STREET

Ten percent of all accidents occur close to home, and last week Cha Cha Staccato was unlucky enough to become a statistic when #5 Gumm Street caught fire and fell on top of her, instantly killing the glamorous and talented woman of all trades. She'd been attempting to rescue her musical prodigies, all of whom escaped unharmed.

Ms. Staccato—as she liked to be called—lived at #7 Gumm Street, the former home of beloved, dearly departed piano teacher Mr. Staccato.

Pearl Diamond, the owner of #5 Gumm and a relative newcomer to Sherbet, lived there with her daughter, Ivy, who was featured in this very newspaper in an article along with three other girls from Gumm Street: Prudence Gumm, Frances Muggs, and Cat Lemonjello. The girls were hand-picked by Ms. Staccato to study at a prestigious music camp for geniuses. Heartbroken, the four girls are home now, their musical careers on hold. They were unavailable for comment.

Ms. Staccato was, at least, fashionable to the end. All that was recovered of her was her signature fishnet hosiery.

On a brighter note, a will was found among the personal effects of Mr. Staccato leaving his entire estate to the Diamond family, who will be moving into #7 Gumm Street shortly.

We will all miss Ms. Staccato.

Pru placed the paper on her nightstand. Tomorrow was the first day of school, and she wanted to be well rested for BLT. She knew that Albert Einstein slept nine hours a night. Clicking off her light and turning on her side, she could see Franny's lookout tower. There was Franny out for her evening's surveillance. Pru sighed and closed her eyes to go to sleep. She couldn't believe she felt this way, but it was oddly comforting knowing that her friend was right next door, on the lookout for zombies or maybe even—heaven forbid—Bling Bling.

When the Diamonds moved into Mr. Staccato's—Ivy couldn't stop thinking of it as his house—Fred and Ginger raced into the front yard and galloped up the front steps, happy to be home.

Pearl hadn't been this excited since she won the Miss Venus Constellation of Stars Pageant more than seven years ago. "I told you so, sweet pea," Pearl said all the time now. "I told you your daddy'd be comin' back to us!"

Ivy's father was happy to be home and grateful to have his family back. He said the last thing he remembered was going out for Listerine, mayonnaise, and Pop-Tarts. After that, it was all a great big blank.

Pearl reassured him that she knew just what was

wrong. *Amnesia*. It was very common. "Those people on the soap operas are gettin' it all the time!"

Ivy smiled and watched her mother and father, their arms linked around each other's waists, as they climbed the stairs. She bit her lip and absently leaned over to pet Fred and Ginger. Best not to tell her dad what had really happened. Besides, he would never believe it.

But it was true. More like a guardian angel than the Jinx Cha Cha had intended him to be, all that time it was her own father trying to *help* her! He had helped her avoid all kinds of accidents—from slipping on banana peels to pushing her out of the way of a cement mixer once. He had broken down the door to Spoz and scared off the potatoes and Dr. Iznotz in Spudz. He had taken her safely through the ooze to reunite her with her friends. He'd even got her placed her in Tuna-on-Rye. Ivy smiled to think that she could have done without *that*, but she knew her dad felt that was where she belonged.

Ivy couldn't believe her good fortune. Her father was home at last. And what a home it was. With its flower boxes and its comfortable furniture and its walls painted the colors of after-dinner mints, #7 Gumm Street was the prettiest house that she could have ever dreamed of living in.

Ivy wanted to look at everything, but first she had something very important to do—something that all the Gumm Street girls had agreed upon. She walked quickly to the museum room and, slipping the silver shoes from the brown paper bag, she put one in the case with the imitations. She and Franny had spent the afternoon disguising it with red enamel. She put a dab of black on the heel so she would always be able to tell it from the others. Ivy closed the glass door and locked it with a lock that she and Franny had found especially for the case.

Ivy listened to make sure her parents were pre-occupied upstairs. Then she knelt down in front of the cupboard by the wingback chair. Whatever powers the shoes possessed, Ivy knew that if the pair fell into the wrong hands—like Bling Bling's—it could prove disastrous. Mr. Staccato had separated them and she would continue to do the same, until she and Franny and Pru and Cat could come up with a new plan.

"You make a better door than a window," she whispered, and the door with the window in it clicked open. There were the mug, the cookie tin, and Mr. Staccato's decanter and glass. She looked at the magical silver shoe, and it sparkled back at her.

Ivy placed the shoe in the cupboard. The "shoezz choozz," Maz had said. *Had the zoomy shoezz traveled through time just to be with me?* Ivy wondered. And if she put them on, would they take her anywhere she

wanted to go—even through time . . . perhaps back to Mr. Staccato, even? The silver shoe glittered in the dark cabinet.

Pearl was calling to her from upstairs, and Ivy quickly closed the cabinet door. It clicked shut, locking itself tightly.

Ivy smiled. *Yes, their luck really had changed.*

Opening the palm of her hand, she ran a finger over the shiny round mark. The eye stared back at her. Maz had said, "Ze splenjezztical Prophet'z Markz are *very* few—iz ze sign zat you are under ze watchful eyezz of ze winzzy prophetzz." Ivy held the hand with the mark of the eye to her heart and closed her other hand over it. "Thank you, Mr. Staccato," she whispered. "There's no place like home."

At nearly midnight, Franny stood in her slicker on her lookout tower. The wind had switched around to the west as she peered through the binoculars. Scanning the vacant dirt-covered lot which was all that was left of #5 Gumm Street, Franny could see dots of rain in the puddles that were forming. She missed not being able to see Ivy right next door, but since #5 was gone Franny now had a clear view of #7. She had even come up with an emergency communications system using flashlights. One blink meant Help! Two blinks meant Okay. Three blinks meant Meeting Tomorrow!

Franny yawned and was just about to go inside, satisfied that there was nothing exciting that she was going to miss, when off in the distance she heard the faint sound of a car motoring up the hill that led to Gumm Street. *That's weird*, Franny thought, and looked through the binoculars once more.

Two beams of light appeared out of the darkness as the car chugged to the top of the hill, where it stalled and rolled slightly backwards before starting up with a forwards jerk. It did this several times before it backfired and then continued slowly weaving its way along the road. The car turned onto Gumm Street, rolled up onto the curb at #5, and sputtered to a halt. Franny realized with rising horror that it was the champagne-colored Cadillac!

She ducked down and peered through the railing.

The door creaked open and a ghostly figure awkwardly climbed out. It paused and steadied itself against the car door, ignoring the *bing . . . bing . . . bing . . .* of the car telling its driver to shut the door.

Swearing softly at the wet weather, the figure—a woman—proceeded to the center of the property and turned slowly in a complete circle.

Franny focused the glasses in closer. The woman was covered from head to toe in rain gear, which made her difficult to identify. Coming around full circle, she nodded as if pleased with herself, giggled, and said, "Yep, there's no place like home." A sudden gust of wind tugged at the woman's accordion-pleated rain bonnet, and she swore again, but managed to grab the hat before it blew off her head altogether.

"Aunt V!" Franny clamped her hands over her mouth—she'd know those earrings anywhere!

Flattened against the decking, Franny watched as Aunt V picked her way back to the car and drove away down the road, ricocheting off the curbs.

Franny slipped inside and grabbed her flashlight. She pointed its light straight at #7, hoping that Ivy was still awake. *Blink . . . blink . . . blink . . .* Meeting Tomorrow!

Franny waited. From #7, Ivy signaled *blink . . . pause . . . blink:* Okay.

Good, Franny thought. She crawled into bed and lay down. She took a deep breath, then exhaled slowly. She pulled the covers up over her shoulders and closed her eyes, hoping sleep would come soon, because Franny couldn't wait for the meeting tomorrow, after school, with the Secret Order of the Gumm Street Girls.

Dear Reader,

Now that the story is complete, I'm finally being allowed to identify myself.

Oh sure, the person who recorded my story takes the credit. That's what you can expect when you're dead. That's right. Dead. *Rest in peace?* Don't make me laugh! I'm busier now than I was when I was alive.

My entire life I was hounded by people wanting something. First I had to run *Oz*—and let me tell you, that was no picnic. Those munchkins drove me crazy with all their demands. I'd like to see one of *them* build an Emerald City—they didn't even have a halfway decent Jiffy Lube before I got there!

So I get that done and then Dorothy arrives, and you've all heard how that went—what a headache. I straightened her out, and what does she do but lose the silver shoes? I figured, Oh well, easy come easy go, but then one day one of those shoes shows up on my back porch.

The trouble with me is I'm too responsible. I should

have just kicked that shoe back to the deadly desert where it belonged and gone and worked on my golf game. But no, I couldn't leave well enough alone. I had to go to Sherbet and wait for the other shoe to show up. Then, finally, I was able to check out—but not for long.

Next thing I know, I've got some little girl on a pony conjuring me, and so long peace and quiet!

Can't *anyone* do *anything, themselves*? I mean, how hard is it to hold on to a pair of silver heels?

I've pretty much given up on the idea of enjoying my afterlife. In fact my only pleasure is in telling this story, and even that is a pain in the neck. Do you have any idea what it's like communicating from the Great Hereafter? This so-called author with the flowery, silly name (you really can't get good help these days), she's taken a lot— and I mean *a lot*—of artistic license.

Oh well. Like I said, when you're dead you have to take what you can get—even if you are a wizard.

Wishing you *well* . . .

H. GUMM
aka Oscar Zoroaster Phadrig Isaac Norman Henkel
Emmanuel Ambroise Diggs

AN AFTERWORD

(which means the story has officially ended and
you don't have to read this unless you are an Oz expert)

Dear Oz experts,

No doubt there will be those of you who will feel compelled to write a letter, send an e-mail, or fax me some bit of information regarding the accuracy of the references in this book to Oz. I beg of you not to. The story was told to me by Hieronymus Gumm (who admits to being something of a prankster), so I guess you could say he is the real author of the story. For that reason, and because he suggests Mr. Baum may have gotten a thing or two wrong, I would appreciate it if you direct all your queries to him.

Yes, I would suggest you contact him—but I have to warn you, being dead has made him very cranky and somewhat out of sorts, and he probably will not reply.

Regards,

Elise Primavera